STAR
KILLER
STAR

Also by Eyre Price

Blues Highway Blues
Rock Island Rock

STAR KILLER STAR

A CROSSROADS THRILLER

EYRE PRICE

THOMAS & MERCER

Published by Thomas & Mercer, Seattle

www.apub.com

Amazon, the Amazon logo, and Thomas & Mercer are trademarks of Amazon. com, Inc., or its affiliates.

ISBN-13: 9781477823576
ISBN-10: 1477823573

Cover design by Brian Zimmerman

Library of Congress Control Number: 2014900621

Printed in the United States of America

Like everything else I do, this is for Jaime.

I sent my Soul through the Invisible,
Some letter of that After-life to spell:
And by and by my Soul return'd to me,
And answer'd "I Myself am Heav'n and Hell:"

Heav'n but the Vision of fulfill'd Desire,
And Hell the Shadow from a Soul on fire,
Cast on the Darkness into which Ourselves,
So late emerged from, shall so soon expire.

The Rubaiyat of Omar Khayyám,
as translated by Edward FitzGerald (1889)

CHAPTER ONE

Down South London Town

Purpose and chaos.

From cradle to grave, every life is unimaginably complex. Each existence is a tapestry woven with such an intricate pattern of interlocking events that only the most cynical can deny that every individual is charged with some purpose and their steps are carefully choreographed by an unknowable Higher Power to afford them the opportunity to fulfill that objective.

And sometimes shit just happens.

Daniel Erickson was well into his forties before he was confronted by the push-me-pull-you effects of this universal paradox.

Before that, everything seemed all too ordinary: A wife. A son. A house they could only barely afford. An imperfect life that Daniel found perfectly satisfying. He thought it all gave him purpose.

Then, without warning, some shit just happened. And, in the resulting chaos, he found his *true* purpose.

Daniel Erickson's karmic grudge match all started with something as insignificant as a little boink on the side. But not his.

His wife's affair should have been no big deal in a modern age where statistically speaking far more than half of all married adults are also adulterers. Daniel probably should've taken the well-intended advice of friends and family and simply moved on. The problem with that plan was that he loved his wife more than anything, and his life without her was completely without point or purpose.

A drink or two to take the edge off his pain soon turned to chronic drunkenness, which quickly found a partner in prescription drug abuse. In no time at all, Daniel was in the front car of the Roller Coaster of Personal Destruction, waving his arms and screaming his fool head off on a 5G ride down a track that climbed and dipped and loop-the-looped right into a suicide attempt.

And then things got *really* bad.

His business as a music promoter stalled, then plummeted. He lost his connection with his teenage son, Zack. And then, when Daniel would've sworn he had nothing left to lose, his whole world went to hell.

And the funny part was that going to hell seemed to Daniel like a sort of homecoming.

At the very same country crossroads where legend claimed that blues guitarist Robert Johnson traded his soul for absolute mastery of the guitar, a man named Atibon stepped from the shadows and introduced himself to Daniel like he'd been expecting him his whole life.

The mysterious man offered a deal that couldn't be refused, not because it was too good but because Daniel's situation was too dire. So to save his son (and himself), Daniel became indentured to a contract that carried a helluva penalty if breached. And in that labor, Daniel's life found its chaotic sense of purpose.

Daniel wasn't sure exactly how many months had passed since his previous job for Atibon had reached an explosive conclusion that had left a body count of Russian gangsters, Mexican mobsters, and biker gang members spread across the campus of the Staples Center. The assignment had also cost him the friendship of the man he'd come to regard as a brother and the love of the one woman he felt was worth his travels through hell and back.

In the absence of friendship and love, Daniel's tenuous grip on his humanity began to slip, and Atibon's assignments became his only reason for getting down the road. He became a man on a mission, a walking dead man whose only interest or function was in paying off the heavy debt he owed on his soul.

And *that* is how a middle-aged music promoter from LA found his way from the darkest corner of the Mississippi Delta to the blackest back booth of a pub in London's Stratham Hill: universal chaos with a celestial purpose.

"You wouldn' think of it to look at me now," the woman said as her words drifted to the ceiling with the cigarette smoke she let slip from between her yellowed teeth. "But in my day I was quite a lovely bit of stuff, indeed." She took another drag on her fag. "Not the bleedin' bloater I am now."

An awkward silence passed as she waited for him to contradict her by insisting her loveliness hadn't faded with the years.

He would've, but he couldn't.

"Oh yes, they all wanted a go," she continued. "And I was ready to give it to them!" She let loose a bawdy hack of a laugh. "Oh, those were some days." Her eyes drifted upward and her thoughts seemed to follow.

"You said you knew something about the death of Jimi Hendrix," Daniel prompted as he checked his watch. The acquaintance of a friend of an informant he'd developed had arranged the interview with the old woman who claimed to know the truth about Hendrix's death. And while he appreciated her willingness to meet and speak, he didn't have the time or inclination to spend the evening indulging an old woman's booze-soaked reminiscences.

"About what, luv?" She seemed startled to find herself back in the present.

"Jimi Hendrix."

"Oh right," she said. "Well, of all the lads that fancied me, the one I loved back was William Gibbons. He was a good man, but on a policeman's salary he didn't see much of a future for us. Then one day he says, 'Darling Lil, would you run 'way with me?'" She took another gulp from the glass of whiskey in front of her and coughed as it burned its way down. "I said, 'Don't be daft, Will. For a year you been telling me we can't be married 'cause we don't have enough money, and now you're asking me to run off with you.'"

"And this has to do with Jimi Hendrix?" Daniel just wanted to be sure.

"Calm yourself, I'm getting to that part now." She was annoyed by his rudeness, but not so offended that she was willing to lose her audience. "Well, my William says a couple days earlier, he'd been walking his beat and just passed the Smarkand Hotel when this young bird, naked as a jay, popped out of a basement stairway screaming 'bout some men killing her boyfriend."

"The Samarkand Hotel?" Daniel corrected, hoping that confirming the detail might bolster her credibility with the skeptic in the back of his mind.

"That's what I said." The interruption scattered her thoughts like a schoolgirl's dropped textbooks, and it took her a minute to gather them all together again. "Anyway, my William rushed down to that flat and found a bunch of blokes, government goons. MI6 or sumptin' like it. An' one of 'em came up to William and told him to get himself gone.

"Well, as he turns to go, William could see the flat had been ransacked. In the back bedroom a man was being held down on a bed—a black man, you know."

Daniel thought he knew exactly. "Jimi Hendrix?"

A nod of her wrinkled chins confirmed his guess. "When the news came out, first sayin' he'd died of a heroin overdose, and then changed just as sudden to say it was wine and pills, my William knew there was somethin' queer at work, and he got it into his head he was going to get a backhander to keep his gob shut."

English provided a formidable language barrier between the two. "What?"

"He knew they'd lied 'bout him dying because of drugs and that he'd really died accidentally-on-purpose. Will thought he could get paid to keep their little secret, but I told him he was just looking for Barney Rubble."

"Excuse me?"

"Barney Rubble," she repeated.

He still didn't get it.

"Trouble," she explained impatiently. "I warned him there's just some blokes you don't go mucking about with."

"And did they pay him?" Daniel asked impatiently.

"Didn't get the chance to," she answered with a pained resignation that hadn't lessened much with time. "Two days later, he got run over by a lorry."

"And you think that was because—"

"Course it was," she rasped. "Day of his funeral, two blokes I'd never seen 'fore come right up to me. Said they was old friends

5

of his, but I'd never heard of 'em, and one gave me this look that made it clear there was a wood box wit' me name on it if I opened me mouth."

"And?"

"And?" She didn't seem to understand his confusion about responding to an unspoken threat. "I smiled as wide as I could and told them I understood." She tamped out her cigarette. "Gave me the screamin' abdabs, they did. I loved William, but I didn't want to join him just then."

"And now?" Daniel wondered out loud.

She lit another cigarette, unconcerned about the months or days it might be shaving off of her life. "Now I figure it's time to get my share."

"Of what?"

"Of whatever I can get," she crowed, like she was playing a trump card. "See, I know who talked to me at Will's funeral. I seen him later at a club I worked in—no forgetting that face—and got his name off his credit card."

Daniel pretended he was only mildly interested in the answer to the question he'd spent six months trying to answer. "What's the name?"

"Oh no," she sneered. "I could tell from the minute we met that you'd be *very* interested." She looked Daniel up and down. "And that means it's *very* valuable."

There were limits to the disinterest Daniel could reasonably pretend to have. "How much?"

She looked him up and down again. "Five thousand pounds."

The sum was more than he had to his name, but he thought that was something best kept to himself. "A hundred," he countered.

"A hundred?" The offer was an insult, but the game was still worth playing. "Three thousand pounds."

"Maybe I could go a thousand."

She'd been hoping for more, but it was still found money to trade an old secret for fresh bills. "All right," she conceded.

The sum was more than Daniel had wanted to spend, but less than it'd cost him to keep looking. "But it better be worth it."

"Oh, it is," she assured him as she held out her empty hand.

"I don't have it on me." That was true. "I'll meet you here tomorrow."

The return trip was a spanner in the works she hadn't anticipated, but one easily remedied. "Same time?"

"Fine."

Bargain struck, he slid from the booth, and she followed him.

Outside, the night was cold and dark with the promise of rain not far off. London. At any time of the year.

"I'm going this way," she announced, pointing off to her left.

Daniel was aware he had some sort of responsibility as a gentleman—or whatever it was he'd become—to ensure the old woman's safety on the often dangerous surrounding streets. He was just about to volunteer to walk with her to her final destination when something very odd and unexpected happened: his cell phone rang.

Daniel had picked up a pay-as-you-go cell at the Virgin Media store on Oxford Street as a tool for his investigation. But with the exception of the occasional "the old lady will meet you at a place called The Drunken Lion" calls, the phone never rang.

There was no one to call him. Not a soul knew where he was. And everyone he'd ever known before coming to London was convinced he was dead.

So, when the first ringtone sounded, he was startled. When he saw the 310 area code, he was genuinely alarmed. "I have to take this," he said to the old woman, and turned his back to her.

"Daniel?" The connection was broken by static and interference, but he recognized the voice immediately.

The sound of her voice hit him like a nanosecond blast of electrical pulsing, and he struggled to retain consciousness as the gritty cityscape around him began to spin. "Vicki?"

He was quick to collect himself and looked back to the old woman.

She wasn't so old that she didn't recognize the look in his eyes or the urgency in his voice. "Coo, you go along, luv. I'm a tough ol' bird." She started off in the direction she'd indicated. "But don't be late or empty-handed tomorrow."

Daniel watched her take a step or two on her way, and then turned back to the cell phone in his shaky hand. "Vicki?"

The connection made her voice sound small and warbling. "Daniel, is that you?"

He was overwhelmed by the memories that came with her call, but what pushed to the forefront of his thoughts was how she could possibly have his number. "How did you—"

And then he heard another voice, one he recognized almost as well as hers and which left his soul as cold as a stone.

The line went dead.

He was just about to press "Redial" when his attention was stolen away by the sounds of a racing car engine and squealing tires. Daniel turned instinctively toward the explosion of sound and saw the Vauxhall Insignia almost immediately as it raced out of the night's shadows with its headlamps off.

Everything suddenly went silent.

And slowed.

Daniel looked at the path of the charging auto and saw the old woman he'd just met with, crossing the street not more than twenty paces away.

The sedan accelerated.

Daniel knew what was going to happen even before the bone-crushing collision occurred. He winced in anticipation just as the speeding car struck the woman and tossed her high into the air. He braced for her impact before she'd even fallen back to the cobbled street with the sickening thud that flesh makes when it meets pavement.

The Insignia accelerated to the corner at the far end of the street, then disappeared around it with the same squeal that had announced its arrival just seconds earlier.

There is something about a tragedy that seems to draw people to it, psychically or instinctively. In a matter of moments, the previously empty street was filled with people, most of whom were confused and uncertain as to what had happened; but more than a few shouted and pointed frantically to the bloodied, old body lying in the middle of the street.

Daniel was the first to her side. She'd landed in the most contorted of positions, with both legs bent back and an arm twisted above her head. A pool of blood had already begun to form at the back of her head, thick and the darkest of reds.

"Someone call an ambulance!" he shouted to no one in particular, casting a look back over his shoulder to the crowd of curious onlookers that was gathering around him.

"An ambulance is on the way," he told her, though they both knew it wouldn't matter.

She looked up at him, not with any pain or even self-pity, but with fierce determination. She struggled to speak, but it was clear that even that exertion was taking a toll on her. A trickle of blood began to run from her mouth, and she struggled to find a voice to share her secret. Her feet began to twitch.

"Stay with me." He paused, realizing (and regretting) that he'd already forgotten her name. He took her hand. "It's going to be all right." It was the right thing to say, but still a lie.

She smiled in appreciation and tried, one last time, to speak. She could only manage a single word, and it was no more than a whisper, "William—"

He leaned closer. "What's that?"

She never answered.

CHAPTER TWO

Better Off Dead

Five thousand miles from London, Vicki Bean was watching the afternoon sun begin its slow descent into another one of those Angelino sunsets that seem more a CGI effect staged by Industrial Light & Magic than anything that could occur naturally. A thousand shades of orange and red and peach and violet smeared across a backdrop of sky until they bled into the waters of the Pacific at the far horizon.

She hated the goddamn sunsets.

Beneath the warm hues and vibrant colors that inspire all those oohs and aahs from the T-shirt-wearing tourists, there was nothing but a sickeningly thick layer of pollution. All those postcard photo ops were nothing more than light filtered through the smothering blanket of particulate and sediment that covers the valley. It wasn't beautiful at all, just a photochemical reaction of gaseous fumes and exhaust with the relentless SoCal sun. The perfect metaphor for Los Angeles itself.

What Vicki Bean really hated most about those sunsets was that every breathtaking vista, spread across the sky like a Gauguin canvas, was just another reminder that she was all alone beneath it. They were views meant to be shared with a special someone, and her love was gone now. There had been other lovers, but lovers are different from *love*, and hers was gone. Gone forever.

And those goddamn sunsets wouldn't let her forget it.

She strummed the Gibson Hummingbird in her lap, but nothing came from the loose chord progression she played except a dull headache that dampened any hope she held for lyrical inspiration. That inescapable sense of loss should have been good for a song at least, but the empty hole Daniel had left in her life had sucked all of the music out of her world, and all it left her was low.

She despised her self-pitying melancholy and resented the creative disability it had caused. Even more than that, she hated how powerless she felt to control it.

Without fully realizing what she was doing, she counted the folds in the curtains she wished she'd drawn against the afternoon. Thirty-one. Thirty-two. Thirty-three. Thirty-three divided by eleven was three. Three was a good number. She let loose a long, tired sigh.

She felt trapped, but it was a *very* gilded cage. Bohemian Grove Records had rented the apartment just off Burton Way especially for her as a writing retreat. The high-dollar space featured every luxury that any outlandish celebrity might consider a necessity: an ultramodern interior design with everything, from carpet to couches to ceiling, devoid of color. The only contrast for the eye came in the drapes, which were black as pitch at midnight.

A white room with black curtains. She couldn't get the song out of her head and surrendered to its influence, playing the opening bars as if they were her own.

"I don't hear a single."

The unexpected voice behind her startled Vicki so badly that she almost dropped her guitar as she shot to her feet and turned to face the intruder. It wasn't the first time he'd come to her like this, but there was always something about his visits that she found unnerving. And stimulating.

In his cashmere suit and his hand-sewn, kid leather slippers, Haden Koschei looked for all the world like the once and future king of the thousands of other money-minded Angelinos who turn art into big business.

Still, from their very first meeting, Vicki had sensed something sinister lurking just beneath his well-tended surface, like alligator eyes glowing on the onyx surface of the bayou on a moonless midnight.

"What you were playing there," he explained with a gesture toward the guitar she now held by the neck, "didn't sound like anything we could build a single around."

She wasn't sure if the old man was joking about the classic opening or simply didn't recognize her rendition of the Cream masterpiece, so quickly shook off the critique. "What are you doing here?"

"You know exactly what I came for," he said plainly. "But before we get to that, I wanted to check on your progress. You go into the studio next week," he informed her, as if that were explanation enough for his unannounced appearance.

"I know." She didn't need (or want) the reminder.

He stepped back from their conversation and began to wander around the apartment, admiring the room as if he'd designed, built, and decorated the place himself. "I trust you're enjoying the accommodations."

"It's a very special place." Despite regarding the posh digs as a very comfortable cage, there was genuine gratitude in her voice.

He nodded his agreement and smiled slyly. "You have no idea."

Given their discussion of modern home design, "I didn't hear you come in" was as close to protesting her benefactor's invasion as she felt she could get away with and as close to playing coy as she wanted to get. She picked at the calluses on her left hand, and then scraped at the cuticles on both.

"No?" Her alarm only prompted a smile. "I find it serves me best to keep people wondering where I am, worrying about where I might be next." The words slipped from his tongue as a joke, but the menace in the comment was clear enough.

"Should I be worried?"

"Worry is just one of the prices to be paid for success," he told her flatly. "If this isn't what you want"—he held his hands up to indicate he meant *everything*—"then it should be easy for you to walk away and leave it all behind."

She stared at him silently.

"Exactly," he said, confident he'd made his point. "So it would be only natural to worry about losing all of this when we both know it's the answer to a prayer you've been reciting in vain since you were a very little girl and fell upon music as your ticket out." He sneered like his mouth held a secret. "How *is* your stepfather?"

The reference to secrets she kept closeted away was more of an intrusion than his unexpected appearance. "My what?"

"The good reverend," he said knowingly, and then quickly shifted gears before she could collect her shock-scattered thoughts. "I've come to check up on your progress. You're a week away from the studio, and I want to ensure you'll justify the investment."

"The process is moving a little slowly," she confessed. She counted the stripes on his tie. Fourteen.

"*SMiLE* and *Chinese Democracy* were slow moving processes." His steely blue eyes looked right through her. "What I want from you is a guarantee."

"I have ten songs that are really strong," she lied, knowing there was hope only for two or three, and they were more sketches than anything she was ready to record. She pulled nervously at her jagged cuticles.

"You're going to need more than that," he said sternly, treating her fabrication as if it were truth, but making it clear that he knew better. "Much more than that. And *all* of them really strong. There's no room for mediocrity at this stage of the game."

"I'm doing the best I can." The guitar had six strings and twenty frets. Six times twenty was one hundred twenty.

He shook off the excuse. "'The best I can do' is a lie losers tell themselves as they're playing bars and coffee houses and fire halls. I'm not preparing you to play bat mitzvahs and weddings," he sneered. "Up here, you either succeed or you fail. How hard you *try* has nothing to do with it."

"I understand." And she did.

The hard lines in his face softened, and his voice took on an almost paternal note of caring: "If you're having trouble getting started, I can get you whatever *inspiration* you need."

"What do you mean?"

He reached into the left pocket of his suit jacket and produced an amber pill bottle. "Why don't you start by taking two?"

She stared at the bottle he handed her, then looked back up at him. "I don't want—"

"Believe me, I've lived a long, long life, and I can tell you with absolute certainty that, in this regard, there are only two kinds of people: Those who've never had drugs. And those who want drugs." He looked her up and down, slowly and methodically, like a CAT scan. "We both know you're not someone who's never had drugs."

15

She looked blankly at the bottle in her hand, racking her troubled brain for a reason to avoid the solace-in-a-capsule she was now craving.

"Two will make you feel better," he assured her.

She went to the kitchen and did as she was told, washing the two white pills down with a swig of Diet Coke.

"Better?" he asked, when she returned to the living room.

She took a seat on the couch and folded her bare feet beneath her, nervously playing with her toes. "Maybe in a bit."

He smiled like he knew she was right. "So, what *is* keeping you from writing?"

She didn't feel the need or desire to answer.

His grin told her she didn't need to. "I can't believe it," he said in mock shock, as if he'd discovered another of her dirty little secrets. "I bring you to LA. Give you this beautiful apartment. A car. A collection of guitars. I assemble a backup band. Book studios and shows. I give you my *personal* attention. I do everything for you, and you're just letting it all go to waste because you're pining away like a little girl who got left at the middle school dance."

Eight months earlier, when the unexpected offer from Bohemian Grove Records had brought the fulfillment of a life's wishes at a time of depthless sorrow, Vicki had answered Koschei's questions about her personal life as vaguely as possible. Slipped between repeated "I don't wanna talk about its," she'd laid out the thumbnail sketch of a love story gone wrong.

There was a man. There was a love, a legendary love. There was complacency, one too many misunderstandings, and a separation. And then, before either of them had the opportunity to realize and atone for their mistakes, the possibility of reconciliation had been snuffed out by the cruel, absolute finality in Death's stone-cold touch.

"I'm mourning." She corrected him as defiantly as she dared.

"Mourning whom? Our dear, departed Mr. Erickson?" Koschei said the name like he'd eaten it whole and retched it back up again.

Months had passed since Vicki had heard the name spoken aloud, and it hurt her heart to hear it sound like that. "Don't."

It wasn't until a heartbeat later that Vicki realized the thin, old man had made another casual reference to some intimate secret she'd never shared with him. "I never told you his name."

Koschei smiled as if he were about to tell her something she should've already known. "Did you really think that I would have made my investment if I didn't know everything there was to know about you?" His cold stare dared her to contest the point. *"Everything."*

With unwavering certainty, he told her, "I know you, Vicki Bean. Not just your musical career, such as it is. I know where you've been and what you've done there. I remember everything you've tried so hard to forget, and I hold a firm grasp on all that you've spent your life trying to outrun. I'm everything you fear. And love. And love to fear."

Vicki was silent, frightened because in her soul she knew everything he'd said was true.

"Call him." Koschei pulled a cell phone from the pocket of his suit coat—a Vegas magician producing a deck of trick cards—and offered it to her like a dare.

She was horrified by the suggestion. "What?"

"Call him."

"I *can't* call him." The levee she'd erected to contain her emotional deluge began to buckle.

"And why's that?" He grinned like he already knew.

"He's dead," she exploded.

"Is that what he told you?"

"Told me?" She compressed her outrage into mere indignity.

"Well, what do you say we get Lazarus on the line?" Koschei pushed a button on the phone, and the speaker pulsed with its ringing.

"Who are you calling?" Her question was a bluff meant to disguise her fear.

"*Him.*" The line rang once. "Isn't he what all this is about?"

"I don't understand." Her world spun around her, but she was not at its center.

He smiled wickedly and held the cell phone out to her. His gloating eyes glistened with the certainty that she wouldn't be strong enough to meet his challenge.

And for no other reason than that, she took the phone and put it to her ear. "Daniel?"

In the months that had passed since she'd watched the news networks' coverage of a riot at a rock concert in Los Angeles, she'd become convinced that Daniel had died in its violent wake. *What other conclusion was she to come to in his absence?*

In the aching void that he'd left behind, Vicki had prayed for nothing more than the opportunity to talk to him one last time. She'd prayed and prayed, but never really believed her grief-borne petition might actually be granted.

"Vicki?" She wasn't prepared to hear his voice, and the sound of it made the whole world drop out from beneath her. "Vicki?"

"Daniel, is that you?"

Her voice was a desperate plea for connection, but before either one of them could say another word, Koschei snatched the phone away. "She's here with me," he hissed into the phone, and then ended the call. "There," he snapped. "Consider yourself inspired."

For a moment she sat on the couch, dazed and confused, and then her suspended sense returned with a jolt, like she'd been roused from a Kublai Khanesque dream. "What the hell? Inspired?"

"Your writing," he explained, as though it were that simple. "That's all that should matter to you now. And *hate* writes hits. There's never been a decent love song that was written by someone actually in love." He scoffed at the very idea, then paused to consider the best example. "Fleetwood Mac's *Rumours* is a lovely thing from start to finish, and forty million units have moved to date. But every track was penned by someone who was getting torn out of love, run over by love, dragged down the street and left in a ditch by love."

Vicki's thoughts were still back on the phone with a walking dead man. "What are you talking about?"

"Your Mr. Erickson used you, lied to you, and left you thinking he was dead." He listed the offenses like an indictment. "That's not love."

"He didn't . . ." Vicki wanted to object to the charges and the verdict, but found she couldn't. She picked harder at her nails. "He loved me."

"Love," he scoffed with a snort and a chuckle. "In the music business, love is all the shit from the slaughterhouse floor that we stuff into hot dogs. We make that lie into pop songs to sell to fools, from naive preteens who still think heartache is romantic, to the frumpy hausfrau mothers they're all destined to become: bitter, bulbous balls of remorse, overstuffed with love's unfulfilled promises."

She sat still, stunned and silent.

"Take Taylor Swift," he continued. "She's made a wonderful career out of nothing more than her insatiable need to couple up with the biggest douchebag on the block. Bitch. Moan. Complain. Key change. Bridge. Chorus. People love her heartache because, in their sad, little lives, it reminds them of their own. Now you've got your own pain you can use to connect."

Daniel's ghost, his voice still ringing in her ear, prevented her from cobbling together a coherent thought. "Connect to what?"

"Pain is the mother's milk the unwashed masses want to suckle. Offer them *your* pain." He got up from the couch and went to the window to look out over the city. "Look at them all down there, people as far as the eye can see, and every one living a shitty, little meaningless existence. So, when they're standing in the grocery checkout line with their basket overflowing with chemically processed death nuggets and corn syrup-saturated shit, they look over at the tabloids and see poor Taylor's had her heart broken all over again, and they *connect* with her because their hearts are broken too. The inescapable shittiness of life is the only thing the crappy people have in common with the beautiful people. And that connection makes them feel better about themselves. It's like you're performing a public service." He sneered, "For a profit."

"It's about more than money." Her voice trembled, but she recognized that whatever was in the pills she'd swallowed was beginning to have its way with her.

"Nothing in business is about more than money, that's why they call it business. And the music business is for people who are single-mindedly fixed on success and who don't give a shit about anything else—including music. And especially love."

She didn't have a response she could put into words.

He didn't wait for her to find one. "So, if you want to call your fugitive ex-boyfriend and beg him for a reason why he left you thinking he was dead, then here's my phone." He tossed her the cell and she caught it. "But when you're done with that call, you get together whatever you came here with and get out. I'm not wasting any more time or money on someone who's not as devoted to their own success as I am."

Vicki looked at the phone he was tempting her with, and then up to the eyes he was scolding her with. She opened her mouth, but nothing came out.

There was something in the confrontation, something in the way he stood above her and talked down to her that she found exciting. The blood in her veins began to boil and bubble with a bad intent she knew she couldn't control. She hoped her building lust was just a chemical reaction to the pills and nothing deeper within her reacting to him, but she knew she was wrong.

He walked back to her, snatched the phone, and took a seat next to her on the couch. Much closer than he'd been sitting before. "We both know this is your last chance. If all this doesn't work out for you"—he made a point of looking around the room he'd provided to her— "everything that I've given you . . . Do you want to lose it? Give it up for love?"

Vicki picked and scraped at her nails and cuticles till her flesh was raw, and then continued on until they bled. "No."

"Then what are you prepared to give for what I'm offering?"

She looked into his lifeless eyes, and they drew her in. "Everything."

He took her bleeding fingers and led them to his crotch.

She did not resist.

CHAPTER THREE

Back with Me

For most travelers, the room nearest the elevator is the least desirable location in a hotel, but for Daniel Erickson it was the accommodation of choice. He'd long ago given up on ever again getting a good night's sleep, and the groaning cables in the elevator shaft alerted him to every movement in the hotel. The dinging bells and the mechanical thud of opening doors might be a nuisance to tourists, but to him they were an early warning system that alerted him to every new—and possibly life-threatening—presence.

Bang. Ding. Thud.

Those sounds pulled Daniel from a restless half sleep that had been haunted by the nightmarish image of the old woman bouncing off the speeding sedan's hood and the echo of a voice from half a world away. The old woman fell in slow motion, her contorted body colliding with the cruel, cold pavement and breaking against it. He rushed to her and held her broken body as she struggled to speak, but the voice that escaped through staggered breaths and gurgled blood bubbles was not her crone's cackle, but Vicki's voice, pleading with him to save her. "Daniel, please."

Bang. Ding. Thud.

He woke with a start, uncertain whether it was the nightmare or the elevator that had shaken him from sleep.

Out in the hall, the mechanical doors thunked open, and then thudded closed.

Daniel listened for footsteps. Or silence. For anything out of the ordinary.

He thought he could hear activity in the far distance. Maybe. Just the slightest sounds of footsteps on the hall carpeting. Perfectly normal. Not an intrusion, just a hotel guest returning from what little remained of the night and looking forward to sleeping it off.

Nothing to worry about. Daniel had almost convinced himself.

And then the room's doorknob jiggled.

It wasn't a loud or violent shaking. Anyone else would've slept right through it or dismissed the barely perceivable tremor as a boiler starting up or a generator cycling down. Even Daniel questioned whether he'd heard anything at all.

And then the doorknob turned.

For a split second the darkness in the room was violated by an intrusion of light as the door opened. Almost immediately the light was blotted out by a figure moving into the room, and then the room went pitch black again as the door closed with a soft click.

There were no footsteps to be heard on the carpeted floor, but Daniel could still sense movement as the intruder stepped into the room and edged around the bed. The chair in the corner creaked as the weight of a body—a *big* body—settled down on it.

And then there was silence. Dead silence.

23

Daniel shared his makeshift bed in the closet with a Weatherby over/under he'd picked up in the back of a shop in Exeter. Great Britain is not the Wild West. There are strict handgun laws in the United Kingdom and severe penalties for those who break them. It is, however, an island of people who love birds and small mammals—on plates. Throughout the island, shotguns are remarkably easy to purchase. He held the weapon at the ready and waited, until he realized there was no point in continuing his possum game with an intruder who was well aware of his presence. And position.

"You're still wearing that damn Sean John cologne." Daniel called out, calm and steady. "I smelled you coming all the way down the hall."

A familiar laugh. "When'd you start sleeping in the damn closet?"

"I can't remember a time when I didn't." Daniel's answer sounded sad and tired. Even to himself.

"Well, it seems to be workin'. You still alive." The chair creaked as the man adjusted himself to find a more comfortable position. "And word out there is that there's more than a few who've tried their best to do something about that."

Denial crossed Daniel's mind for a split second, but just as quickly he realized the futility of dodging what was a stone-cold fact. "I only did what I had to. It's not like I set out to—"

"Hey, none of us 'set out to,' but they all dead just the same." That same familiar laugh. "Good. You know who they was? Who sent 'em?"

It was impossible to tell whether the inquiry was genuine or a clever test to gauge how much Daniel knew about his situation. "I'm closing in on them."

"I'll bet you are." The deep voice trailed off into a chuckle. "Well, get your ass up off the closet floor." The light on the desk by the chair clicked on. "If I'd come to kill you, you'd be dead by now."

There was a time in Daniel's life, which he could still vaguely remember, when such threatening words would've iced over his soul like spring sleet on a Minnesota two-lane. But now—after everything—he only heard them as a challenge. "One of us would be."

"Yeah." Another chuckle. "One of us."

Daniel got up from the floor and nudged open the closet door he'd left just slightly ajar with the shotgun's barrel. The light in the room stung his eyes, but it was still good to see his only friend.

Moog Turner rose to his feet, every bit as big as Daniel remembered him. "Been a time."

"Little while," Daniel conceded.

The pair had first met when Daniel was a to-do item on the oversize contract killer's hit list. But despite Moog's unparalleled skills as an ender-of-lives, Daniel had proven to be one ticket that was impossible for him to punch.

In the end, it was easier for the two of them to give into whatever force it was that had drawn them together. In the years that followed, their friendship had been road tested for more miles than either of them could count, and they'd shared the sort of bond that can only be forged in the hottest of fires, those that are fanned by the constant struggle of life and the looming certainty of death.

But even ties of blood (shed and spilled) can be shattered.

There were misunderstandings between the two men. There were things each left unsaid and secrets they should've shared with one another. It was no one's fault. Or maybe both of them

25

were to blame. And it was something they each could've lived with, until Moog's mentor—the closest thing he'd ever known to a father—wound up dead on a parking garage floor by the big man's own hand. That act had proven to be a hurdle the pair couldn't clear so easily.

In the wake of that loss, there was no easy way for the two to greet one another. A handshake would have seemed foolishly superficial for two men who had faced death—and dealt it—as often as they had. An embrace might have been more appropriate, but there were too many razor-sharp shards of broken memories between them to allow them to get that close. In the end, they settled on an exchange of awkward nods that silently conveyed the myriad of emotions for which they could not find a voice.

Daniel took a seat on the edge of the bed and carefully set his shotgun beside him, next to the decoy of pillows he'd made beneath the sheets. "What brings you here?"

Moog sat back down in the chair. "You."

"Is that right?"

"You ever know me to joke around when it come to business?"

"So, this is *business*?" Daniel was well aware what that distinction meant.

Moog noticed a pen on the desk and casually picked it up. "You can always tell the quality of a hotel by the kind of pen they put out." He put it down. "You really should stay in a better class of place."

"One closet's just as good as the next."

"I suppose." That point wasn't as important to the big man as the other. "And, yeah, business brought me."

Daniel wondered if the hired gun had made a career change. "And just what business is that?"

"You." Moog's eyes fixed on Daniel. "I come lookin' for you."

The pair had been through hell and back, but Daniel still cast a quick eye toward the shotgun beside him. "And now that you've found me?"

"I need to bring you back." It wasn't a threat, just a statement of purpose.

It gave Daniel pause nevertheless. "Back? Back where?"

"Back to the States."

"Can't do it." The matter was simple, and Daniel shook his head to end any further discussion. "I've got things I've got to take care of here."

Moog leaned forward in his chair. "You don't understand."

"I understand I need to make good on a debt I owe."

"How 'bout the debt you owe me." The look in his eyes raised the question why the big man had ever needed a gun to kill a man. "He's got my daughter."

"Who has her?"

"Koschei." The way Moog spoke the name was a less-than-subtle accusation that the underlying responsibility for the situation was Daniel's. "Your friend from LA."

"He's not my friend." That was the first item Daniel wanted to set straight. He thought about the call from Vicki—and Koschei's unexpected guest appearance.

The coincidence of Moog showing up on the very same night Daniel had received the call from Vicki (and Koschei) was curious enough, but what troubled him most about the big man's story was that anyone—including Haden Koschei—could've come anywhere near Moog's girl and not wound up scattered across the Southwest in bite-size pieces. "What do you mean Koschei *took* your daughter?"

Moog shifted in his chair, more uncomfortable with the question than with his seat. "Well, he didn't exactly *take* her." He made the admission reluctantly. And sheepishly. "More like he lured her. But he's got her. That's what matters."

Daniel didn't bother to hide his skepticism. "I see."

"You don't see nothing." Moog's angry outburst quickly subsided into something that looked a lot like fear. "Sonofabitch got my little girl."

Daniel had never seen that look on his old friend's face, but it didn't elicit the expected response. "Got her how? In his posh recording studios?"

"He got Vicki too." Moog dropped the reference like they were playing Texas hold 'em and her name was an unexpected ace that guaranteed him the pot.

Before the phone call earlier in the evening, her name might've led Daniel to fold, but he'd heard what he'd heard. "I know. She's where she wants to be."

"Forget *wants*. She belongs with you."

"Then that's her misfortune."

Moog was confused by Daniel's cold reaction. "What the hell happened to you?"

"You have to ask?"

"That's right." Moog was quick to correct himself. "I *know* what you been through. What *we* been through. But it ain't no coincidence the sonofabitch got my daughter and your—"

"I'm sure it's all part of a plan." Daniel thought again to the call he'd received.

Moog slid back in his chair like there was reason to be relieved. "That's what I'm saying."

"But people make choices in this life. Your daughter. Vicki. And they have the right to make bad ones. Even dangerous ones."

"That how you playin' this one?" The big man slouched back further in the chair, but this time it was a posture of defeat. "And Koschei?"

"Can't hurt anyone who doesn't let him."

"Well, fuck you then." Moog bent forward, leaning his arms on his knees and interlocking his fingers. "'Cause I still need you to get my daughter back. And you owe me."

"I got greater debts right now." Daniel's eyes fell to the floor, moved quickly to the shotgun beside him on the bed, and then back to Moog. "And you don't need me to get your daughter back. If she was in any kind of real danger, there'd be dozens of bodies in bags right now, and she'd be back in her bedroom texting her friends about how mean her daddy was."

Moog nodded like he understood, though he clearly didn't. "And Vicki?"

Daniel replayed the call in his head and tried to convince himself it didn't mean what he knew it meant. He couldn't do it. "If she's with Koschei, then I suppose that's where she wants to be."

"You know that's not true."

"I know she does what she wants. She always has. And I know if she wanted me to come riding in on a white charger to rescue her"—for a split second he wondered if the call had been a cry for help, and then forced himself to dismiss the thought—"she would have called me by herself."

The big man sat back in the chair, and it groaned under his shifting weight. Whatever preparations he'd made for the awkward encounter of seeing Daniel after so long hadn't included his old friend just simply refusing his request. "So that's it?"

"You're welcome to stay the night," Daniel offered as he got to his feet. "I don't use the bed anyway."

"And tomorrow?"

"I keep right on doing what I'm doing. And if you're really worried about what's going on in LA, then hop a flight back there and put Koschei on a slab in your own inimitable way."

"Ain't that simple."

"Sure it is. You want me to help you and I'm not going to. What could be simpler?"

"I never said I wanted your help." He turned his attention to the cheap pen, tapped it a time or two and tossed it back on the desk. "I said I need *you*." The words came out of the corners of the big man's snarled mouth like the growl of a junkyard dog that's just gotten a whiff of a midnight trespasser. Or really good barbeque.

"Me?"

"That's right. I need to bring *you* back. That's the deal *I* made."

The words all went together, but Daniel couldn't make sense of what Moog was saying. "You sold me out?"

"To get my little girl, I made a deal to bring you back." It was business. There wasn't any guilt involved.

"Like a bounty?"

Moog seemed uncomfortable with the word but not afraid of it. "If that's what you wanna call it."

"Does it make a difference what we call it?"

"Not a one. I'm bringing you back. That's all. I was hoping it was going to be simple, but—"

"You thought I was going to turn myself over just because you made a deal with—"

"Don't matter what nobody thought," Moog was quick to point out. "I made my deal and I'm bringing you back."

"And if I resist?" Daniel cast a not-so-casual eye at the shotgun.

The big man noticed but didn't seem to care. "You tell me."

Daniel took a moment to consider his options. "All right."

Moog had dug in and he was slow to catch on to the change-up Daniel had pitched him. "All right, what?"

"I'll come with you. If you got your mind locked down on something, then that's damn sure how it's going to go down. Right? I mean, what can I do about it?"

The sudden reversal was welcome, but as confusing as Daniel's initial refusal. "For real?"

"What other choice do I have?"

"Just two." Moog chuckled. "Not much. And none."

"It's a done deal then." Daniel seemed to accept his fate with a smile and a nod. "So let's just get however much sleep is left in this night, and then in the morning—"

"I got arrangements made."

Daniel wasn't surprised. "You wouldn't be here now if you didn't already have tomorrow tucked away."

"Damn straight."

"You can bunk here." Daniel gestured toward the bed, the shotgun dangling casually from his right hand. "I've gotten used to sleeping in a hole." He pulled the closet door wide open with the shotgun barrel.

The big man got to his feet and took hold of the chair. "All that double-o-seven, secret agent, sleepin'-in-the-closet shit's fine, but you always best brace the door." Without the slightest effort, he picked up the upholstered chair and carried it over to the door. "You just put something under the doorknob, and ain't no one getting the slip on you." To demonstrate the proper chair-wedging technique, Moog turned toward the door and away from his friend.

That's when the butt of the shotgun struck him at the base of the skull and dropped him to the floor.

Daniel looked down on his friend. "Unless they're already inside."

It wasn't as easy as moving the chair, but Daniel managed to get the big man up onto the bed. He checked the base of the skull where he'd landed the blow and was thankful that it hadn't opened a wound. He slid a pillow under Moog's head and pulled the covers over him.

"I'm sorry," he said aloud, though he knew Moog couldn't hear him. "I'd help you if I could, but I've got debts, and it's a heavy price that needs repaying."

Then Daniel pulled his coat out of the closet and wrapped it around him so that no one on the street would spot the shotgun he held under his arm.

CHAPTER FOUR

A Brown-Eyed Handsome Man

South Kensington is the jewel of the Royal Borough of Kensington and Chelsea. The neighborhood is one of London's most exclusive residential enclaves, and those who call it home are the expected collection of bankers, corporate captains, and those with no talents greater than having been born into money.

Among the entertainers and capitalists and trust fund babies however, South Kensington also holds its share of unusual residents, and one of them resided at 66 Markingham Place. No one who lived along the fashionable street knew much about the family at that particular address except that the lady of the house seemed nice enough, while the gentleman seemed quite possibly the meanest man in all of Great Britain. They had absolutely no idea just how right they were.

In his day, Jackie Dredsley had been one of the most lethal men in the UK. Maybe even all of Europe.

He'd spent the better part of four decades as a coldly efficient killer, taking lives without question or concern in the service of Queen and Country. There was no government license to sanction his activities, no tricked-out sports cars or jetpacks, just the understanding that people needed to die for England's greater good, and a willingness to make it so.

That, however, had been some time ago. While he'd managed to put enough aside, here and there, to cover the expenses of living in South Kensington, the years had left him a much different, much lesser man. Age had stripped him of his lethal prowess, and retirement had left him with a gold watch, a civil pension, and a lifetime of secrets he had to keep to himself. No matter what.

The previous night had been its own little slice of hell. A trip to Stratham Hill made for a miserable evening under any circumstances. The collision had dented the Vauxhall's bonnet, and now there was the issue of replacing it. But there was more to it than just these inconveniences.

Death is death. Or, at least, it should be.

Jackie Dredsley was a professional who'd long ago lost track of the exact number of lives he'd personally snuffed short. Still, there was something about killing the old lady that had really bothered him. And was troubling him still.

Maybe killing was harder when it was done to protect his interests instead of England's. Perhaps his personal motivation had made the act too intimate for his comfort. What he worried about most was that he'd begun empathizing with his victims, and causing their deaths was harder the closer he came to the end of his own life.

He hadn't had a wink of sleep all night. He'd spent the hours as still as a corpse between the sheets, listening to his wife's shallow breathing as she slumbered. Caught between the inescapable memories of the life he'd taken and the one he cherished beside him, Jackie Dredsley was caught between heaven and hell.

"Bloody hell!" Now the neighbor's damn cat was caterwauling on the front stoop with the sun almost peeking above the horizon of rooftops, and the first waves of sleep were just beginning to wash over him.

He stomped to the front door and quickly entered the alarm code before reaching for the front doorknob. He threw open the door, intent on dispatching Mr. Kittypants with the same stealthy skill he'd used on enemies of the Crown in his prime.

Instead, he stood there flat-footed in his fuzzy slippers and stared with an almost childlike amazement at the cat's consternation. The poor thing was dangling by the tail, trying in vain to free itself from the left hand of the man who held it in midair.

A second after the door came open, the agitated cat was tossed to the old man, who juggled it a bit like a startled street performer, and then dropped it to the ground. He couldn't help but watch as it dropped to its four paws on the stoop, shot off into the bushes, and then raced down the street. By the time Dredsley could refocus his attention, he was staring down the barrel of a Weatherby shotgun.

"Good morning." Daniel Erickson wasn't smiling.

Jackie had survived his years of service by always being prepared—even when he wasn't. There was a Kimber .45 secured just inside the door. In his prime, he would've already reached for it, but something that morning—age or weariness or the sense of dread he instinctively got from the man standing with a shotgun on his doorstep— slowed his hand for just an instant. It was an instant too long.

"You can make your play." Daniel's voice was as cold as the shattered remnants of night that were giving way to a morning that was just as dark. "But we both know you can't make it in time."

For a split second, Dredsley debated the accuracy of that warning. He was pretty quick, even now. For half a second, he considered whether it even mattered any longer. In the end, his arthritic hands settled the debate, and he rubbed them bitterly, silently cursing them for their betrayal. He hated aging: everything it brought with it, everything it took.

Still, there was something Jackie Dredsley hated even more. "*He* sent you, didn't he?"

"He?" Daniel didn't understand what he thought was an allusion to Atibon, who'd offered a muddy explanation that there were forces beyond explanation that prevented him from crossing the Atlantic. "I'm my own man."

"You may think so, but you're not," the man answered with certainty. "You've got Pushkin's same dead eyes."

The reference was more troubling than puzzling, and Daniel was quick to insist: "I've never heard of any Pushkin."

"Doesn't matter, I suppose," Dredsley said, though it was clear he was unconvinced. "I'm just glad the monster didn't show up himself."

Daniel felt marginalized by the comment. "You might just find me monster enough."

"There's no monster like him."

Something about the man's words chilled Daniel to the bones, like they'd somehow scratched at a memory he'd fought to suppress a long, long time ago. A wave of unexpected terror swept over him for a second and took with it whatever pithy comeback he might have had at the ready.

"So, have you come on business then?" Dredsley recognized the momentary silence as a sign of weakness, an indication that the man with the gun suddenly wasn't so certain about his motivation. "Or did you just come for a cup of tea?"

"Tea would be nice," Daniel said, hoping he'd covered his misstep but knowing he hadn't. He gestured into the house with the shotgun.

Dredsley turned and stepped inside, leaving the door open for Daniel to follow.

"You're just wandering deeper into the spider's web," he warned as his unwelcomed visitor followed him past the living room and den, back to the home's kitchen.

"I'm no fly," Daniel said, tapping the shotgun. "I've got a stinger of my own."

"Do you suppose I'm frightened of a field gun?" Jackie said with a dismissive scoff. "I'm not a bloody pheasant. And I've faced far worse than you." The old man meant it as a warning.

Daniel took it as a challenge. "I suppose we could go upstairs and ask your wife just how serious I should be taken, but I think everyone would rather if you just trusted me on that."

Dredsley's eyes flared with anger, but that did little to conceal the fear behind them. "If you—"

"Let's not get ahead of ourselves," Daniel cautioned. "Why don't we just sit down and enjoy our cup of tea."

Dredsley evaluated his options like he'd been trained and quickly resigned himself to the inescapable conclusion that he didn't have any. His only course of action was to wait for whatever opportunity might eventually present itself. What he needed now was time. "I'm likely to drop in a bit of rat poison, you know."

Daniel took a seat on a stool and put the shotgun on the counter in front of him. "That's just how I take it."

"One lump or two then?"

"Doesn't matter."

The matter-of-fact response bothered Dredsley, and he worried that maybe his unexpected guest wouldn't have any trouble consuming arsenic if he'd had it. He busied himself with the kettle and tried to ignore the fact that for the first time in a very long time, he was completely unnerved by another man.

"She died, you know." Daniel's words were as casual as if they were talking about the last Arsenal match. "She was dead before the ambulance could even get her to the hospital."

"That was rather the point." Dredsley took down two cups. The everyday ones.

"But she didn't die quiet," Daniel bluffed. "She told me everything."

Dredsley considered the man sitting at his breakfast counter. "Evidently."

"I mean *everything*," Daniel fished.

All he caught was a smile. "I wasn't trying to keep her quiet, you stupid sod."

In that moment, Daniel couldn't conceal his confusion.

"You really don't get it, do you?" He didn't wait for Daniel's dumbfounded confirmation. "Who the hell would care about anything that old bird would have to say? I was only trying to cover my tracks, afraid she might lead you to me. And apparently I was right."

"She said you killed Jimi Hendrix." It was a lie, of course, but the only play that made sense to Daniel.

The accusation didn't have the intended effect, or any effect at all. "Then she lied to you," he said plainly. "I didn't kill him, your boss did."

And that didn't make any sense to Daniel at all. "You keep talking about my boss, but I'm telling you I'm here all on my own."

"You really don't know, do you?"

Daniel's silence confirmed Dredsley's suspicions.

"Do you have any idea what you've gotten yourself involved in with someone . . ." He hesitated, and then corrected himself. "With *something* like Feodor Pushkin?" In the silence that followed, Dredsley wondered if a full disclosure of all the shocking facts wouldn't be the catalyst he needed to spark the escape opportunity he was waiting for. "Well, let me tell you."

Daniel felt no need to correct Dredsley's insistence that he knew or had ever heard of a man—or monster—named Feodor Pushkin. That wasn't because he didn't have anything to say. He was simply more eager to hear the secrets Dredsely was too willing to spill.

"I first met your boss when I was just a lad. I was SAS for two years. Operation Claret in Kalimantan. Keeni Meeni in Aden. I racked up a body count that I guess earned me a spot in what they called the Wentworth Protocol. Official designation was that Wentworth was a black ops branch of the UDR, the Ulster Defense Regiment, but we was just a bunch of blokes who killed anyone, anywhere."

"And this Feodor Putin?" Daniel fished.

"Pushkin," Dredsley corrected. "Came to them as a Russian Cossack. Or, at least that's what he told them."

"And what did he tell you?"

"It's not what he told me, it's what I saw. And that's what's scared the hell out of me for more than forty years now."

Daniel's curiosity left him muted.

As for Dredsley, his long-held secret was out. Or, at least, it wouldn't protect him anymore. The shotgun on the counter was the only decider. If he managed to get his hands on it then it wouldn't matter that he shared his tale with a dead man. And if he didn't . . . Well, that wouldn't matter either.

"Under Wentworth, they sent us out as two-man teams," he continued. "I'm not sure whether it was to support one another or to keep an eye on each other. I suppose a bit of both. I had the great misfortune of being partnered with Feodor Pushkin." He stopped to recall something that made him snicker. Or grimace. "Christ, they loved him. Middle of the Cold War and they had a Russian who would kill Russians."

"And that's what you did? Killed Russians?"

Dredsley took a sip of tea, swirled the cup, and then looked hard into the dark concoction like there was something more than leaves dancing around the whirlpool at the bottom. "We killed *everyone*."

"Including Jimi Hendrix?"

"I was a fan of his, you know." Dredsley offered his admiration like it somehow offset everything else. "Before his dossier ever came to us, I saw him at the Polytechnic when he sat in with Cream back in 1966. Clapton may have been God, but God was dead as soon as Hendrix took that stage." He shook his head as if he could still hear what he'd heard that night—and was still in awe.

"Then why kill him?"

"You have to remember, it was 1970—and it sounds like horseshit—but the whole world was changing too quickly. Just ten years before that, music was just something that played in the background while you had a pint at the pub or at a dance hall while you tried to dance too close to some bird. We all listened, but no one really cared. It was just music. No one gave it any real mind. Then suddenly, almost overnight, music became"—he paused to find the word he wanted—"*everything*."

He took a sip of tea and continued. "The sixties started with everyone worrying about the bleeding Communists, and just a few years later, the real threat to our Western way of life was coming from our own homes, with a bunch of long-haired tweaks in frilly frocks with guitars and lyrics and all that.

"I'm part of a generation that grew up like our fathers, and their fathers before them. But the kids just a year or two behind us at school, Christ, they didn't look like anything we'd ever seen before. They didn't act or think like anything we'd known. And at the center of it all was music." He was engaged in his explanation, but he stopped to look off to the garden beyond the kitchen window as if he couldn't quite decide whether he'd heard something outside.

"When that tosser said the Beatles were more popular than Jesus, the infuriating thing wasn't that some ponce had had the nerve to say something so outrageous, it was that we all knew he was exactly right."

"And that was a problem?"

"Change is always a problem for those that run things. Slow, gradual change gives the power people fits, but cultural revolution is a goddamn crisis. There was a fire raging and they wanted it put out." The old man thought about what he'd just said and was satisfied in his response. "They wanted a fire put out, and Hendrix was a white-hot coal at the very center of it all."

"They?" Daniel was willing to take a guess. "The government?"

"'The government'?" Dredsley repeated with a snort. "The government is a service provider. They pave streets and write checks for the dole, they only do what they're told. Who do you expect? There are wealthy men in this world. Not rich men. You can knock on any door on this street and find a rich man behind it. I am talking about the truly wealthy. Wealth is where money stops being a means of exchange and becomes a tool of power."

"What does wealth have to do with killing a guitar player?"

"Wealth has to do with everything, son. The wealthy only want one thing: to stay wealthy. And the best way to ensure that is to maintain the status quo. They need to keep the base of the pyramid stable because no one is so precariously balanced as those at the very top. And in 1970, a black man who preached love and peace, banged every white girl he met, and was damn near worshipped as a god—well, he was shaking the pyramid like a bugger."

"And you?"

"Like I said, the government performs services. They haul away your trash or deliver the post. When necessary, they stabilize the pyramid. I was just a government man who did his job. At least, that's all I ever wanted to be."

"What else was there?"

"It was easy being partnered with Pushkin. He didn't say much when we were working an operation together, and when it came time to push the button on a target, he always insisted on being alone to do it." Dredsley took another sip of tea. "I was young. What did I know? Killing is still work and not much fun at that. If he wanted to do all of the work, who was I to insist on getting a bit of it?"

"And Hendrix?"

"We broke into his flat. He and some bird were going at it, but somehow he sensed we were there. Hendrix got up from the bed and came at us. His eyes were wide and wild like he was possessed." Dredsley shook his head. "Little did I know."

"Know what?"

"Hendrix was a big man, surprisingly strong. He'd had Army training. By the time we were able to restrain him, the bit he was banging had managed to slip out to the street. Feodor sent me out to retrieve her, but the next thing I knew, there was a copper standing there. I sent him on his way, but I knew the show had become compromised. And I was hurrying back to the bedroom to collect Pushkin and get the hell out of there when I saw it happen."

"You saw him kill Jimi Hendrix?"

"Kill?" He took another sip of tea but his expression made clear he wished it was something stronger. "Hell, no. No, I saw Feodor Pushkin suck out the man's soul."

Daniel's disbelief precluded words.

"When I came back, he was straddling Hendrix's chest, and the two of them were thrashing and moaning. For a minute I thought they were having a go at it. And then Pushkin made this low moan and he arched his back like he was about to come. Beneath him, Hendrix did the same. And then, I swear to you, a small blue ball of light came out of Hendrix's mouth and popped into Pushkin's."

"A ball of blue light?"

"Swear to Christ." Dredsley raised his right hand. "In a heartbeat, Pushkin has me up against the wall. Thought I was going to die there too. And I likely would've if the bird hadn't gotten more coppers and an ambulance. We slipped out just as they was coming in."

"And this partner of yours?"

"Didn't have time to kill me, I suppose. By the time we got back to our safe house, he was as calm as if nothing had happened. Or as if that sort of thing happened to him all the time." Dredsley looked back to the kitchen window. "'Cause it did."

Daniel was growing tired of stories. "What the hell are you talking about?"

"You don't believe me?" Dredsley put down his tea as forcefully as one can slam a china cup to a counter. "This is a nation that has its own church, for Christ's sake. We've gone on crusades and fought wars for hundreds of years, lost millions of souls in the course of it all. Then you're shocked and cynical when I speak of something that's not quite of this earth? *Hell* is exactly what I'm talking about. And hell happens to be your boss's hometown."

Daniel felt they'd reached a point in the conversation where he needed to correct the misunderstanding over his employment, but there was no opportunity. "My boss is—"

"I know exactly what your boss is. He told me himself that night. He's a soul eater." He braced himself against the counter and said plainly, "They're actually surprisingly common, you know. Ammit. Ježibaba. Teyollocuani. Maita. Hix. Every culture has nightmare tales of their existence."

"Fairy tales," Daniel interjected. "No one thinks they're anything . . . physical."

"Twenty-one grams," Dredsley countered. "It's the amount of weight that a human being loses at the time of death, without any scientific explanation."

"And you think that's the soul?"

"Soul? To quote one of my countrymen, 'What's in a name?' Soul. Spirit. Life force. It's just a form of energy we don't understand. And what do we do all day long but consume food. To get what? Energy."

"You're saying, instead of fish and chips, this Feodor Pushkin ate the soul of Jimi Hendrix?"

Daniel's question was meant to sound ridiculous, but that's not how Dredsley found it. "I *know* he did because I saw him do it. Because I helped him do it to others a dozen times over."

"You what?"

"After we left Hendrix's flat, we drove around for a while. Silent. And then he explained that if I was going to continue to survive, I was going to help him." He gestured back to himself. "And here I am, so obviously I did just that."

"You helped him *how*?"

"Turns out souls are just like steaks or sushi, some're better than others. There was something about Hendrix's soul, something special I guess, something that made Pushkin crazy, like he was just addicted to the stuff. He wanted more like that. And I helped him get them."

"Souls?"

"You're not listening," Dredsley scolded. "Not just souls, *special* souls."

"Like the Kobe steaks of souls?"

Again, Daniel's attempt to mock Dredsley only served to reinforce the man's point. "Exactly," he said gratefully. "He craved tender souls, tortured souls. Sweeter that way, I guess."

"So, Hendrix. And?"

"And three weeks later I watched him do the same bloody thing to Janis Joplin."

"Janis Joplin died in LA," Daniel offered, like he'd just debunked the whole story.

"Yes, well, we had *aeroplanes* back in those days," Dredsley answered dryly. "I couldn't tell you how he chose them or why, but he was his own kind of addict. And for a long while, I helped him feed his habit. I was with him in Paris, July of the following year."

"Jim Morrison?" The question was halfway between disbelief and fandom. "You killed the Lizard King?"

"No." Dredsley shook his head like that was ridiculous. "But I watched him die. I watched a lot of talented people die. It was simple enough really. Booze and pills and powders, same old medicine. That's the best way to kill them. No one ever questions a musician who has drunk and drugged himself to death. The public *expects* it almost." He said it as if it were a commonly known fact.

"Gram Parsons and Tim Buckley," he continued. "I was there when he made Mama Cass that ham sandwich, and I was there four years later to see Keith Moon die in the very same bed in the very same Mayfair flat. I know what he whispered to Nick Drake, and I heard him promise Keith Relf that the amps weren't switched on when he handed him that guitar knowing it was a goddamn live wire."

Daniel still wasn't convinced. "And all of these famous—"

"It wasn't just the famous," Dredsley was quick to correct. "People equate pop and rock with riches and fame, but I couldn't tell you how many guitar gods or songwriting geniuses I watched die in complete obscurity."

"And this just went on until—"

Dredsley had a date certain. "1981. May. Miami. I watched him take the soul of Bob Marley. That was too much for me. I walked to the beach that night and put my Walther to my head.

"I was just about to put a round in my brain when he suddenly stepped out of the darkest shadow and told me not to bother. He said that he'd found a better way to get what he wanted and that I should consider myself retired."

"What happened to him?" Daniel wondered.

Dredsley shrugged and shook his head. "He left the service, and I was so relieved to be done with it all that I never looked back." That wasn't entirely true. "Except to keep a watch over my shoulder."

"So, you don't know where I could find him today?"

"No. He's not anything I would ever go searching for. That kind of trouble will find you all on its own."

"But if I wanted to," Daniel said. "If I was looking for that kind of trouble?"

"Then I'd say you're a bigger fool than I already take you for, but I can't imagine it'd be hard to find." His head wagged sadly. "I hardly ever look at the headlines that I don't see some tragedy and wonder if he's had his hand in it."

Daniel tried to put all of the pieces together in his mind. "So, the old lady last night?"

"Just closing a book I should've closed all those years ago. I don't think any of this would bring down Parliament or Downing Street. I don't think you have enough to sink the city, but I'm still a professional, and it's always better to clean up your loose ends so that they don't send someone round to clean you up."

"Just a preemptive act?"

"Word got back to me that someone was turning over stones and asking about Hendrix's death. I was just trying to cover my tracks, because I knew it was just a matter of time before Pushkin came back to cover *his*."

Dredsley took a sip of tea and put down his cup. "So, how is it that you so conveniently managed to wind up on my doorstep? I'd removed my number plates last night, and there must be thousands of Vauxhalls in London."

"You didn't have a plate on last night," Daniel admitted. "But you've had one on for the last week you've been tailing me."

Dredsley acknowledged the oversight with raised eyebrows. "In the service I would've had a fleet of vehicles available to me."

"But now you only have the two."

"Two?"

"The Vauxhall," Daniel was quick to identify. "And the Mercedes."

Dredsley shook his head. "I only have the Vauxhall. I thought for a moment about nicking a car, but I'm an old man, and it seemed like too much bother. That's the problem with age. You end up cutting corners to accommodate it." He took another sip of tea. "You must have another friend." He thought on that. "Curious."

Dredsley put his empty cup down. "I've finished my tea. And I've no more stories to tell. So, you best get to whatever it is that Feodor's *really* sent you here after." He braced himself against the counter.

"You still think I'm here because of this Feodor Pushkin guy?"

"I know one of his men when I look him in his dead eyes." Dredsley wasn't interested in the denial. "Why don't you just get on with whatever it is he's sent you here to try to do."

"I gave up *trying* to do things." Daniel pulled the shotgun from the counter. "Now I just *do* them."

"Fair enough. And maybe it's right, maybe it's time. But let us, at least, step outside. This business between us doesn't have anything to do with up there." He pointed toward the second story where his family was still sleeping.

The gesture just made Daniel sad. And tired. "I told you, I came here for answers, not to kill you."

Dredsley seemed relieved for just a heartbeat or two.

But one man's intentions can't change another man's fate.

The shot shattered the glass of the kitchen window, then continued straight on its path to the old man's chest. The impact of the slug spun him around and dropped him to the floor, flat on his back.

Daniel put his shotgun to his shoulder and took cover behind the kitchen counter. He waited a second, then peered around the edge. Dredsley was lying on the tile floor, a pool of blood building around him.

Hunched over for cover, Daniel worked his way over to him. "Hey. Hang in there. You're going to be all right."

Dredsley couldn't help but spit up a little blood with his laugh. "You're a lying bastard."

"All right," Daniel conceded. "You're not going to be all right. You're going to die."

"I sure as hell am." He chuckled, then coughed up a little more blood.

Daniel looked past him and out through the shattered window. In the shadows of early dawn he caught just the slightest glimpse of a figure hopping a far hedge and dashing around the garden fence.

Dredsley grinned.

"I've done what I've done for Queen and Country. I did what I did for Pushkin. I'm not about to look back now with regret, but I've always wondered what would've happened—where we'd all be right now—if people like me hadn't fought so hard for the people who want to kill the music." He let out a last, soft puff of breath and a gurgle that stopped when he could not take another.

Daniel left the dead man on the floor and raced for the kitchen door. He ran as fast as he could across the dew-soaked lawn, hopped the far hedge, and came around the garden fence he'd seen the shooter disappear behind. It led out to an alley where Daniel caught a fleeting glimpse of a figure just as it turned to the left and ran out of sight.

Daniel sprinted the length of the alley, and then made the same turn. It put him out on the street, a place where he was certain he didn't want to be seen running with a shotgun in his hand. Still, he was getting closer to whomever had pulled the trigger on Dredsley, and he couldn't afford to slow down.

Ignoring the ache in his legs and the burning in his lungs, Daniel ran all the harder. Whoever had shot the old man was a step closer to the top of the pyramid, and he needed to chase him down.

Daniel turned a corner and spotted his prey, closer than he'd expected. The chase was taxing Daniel, but his quarry was no runner. There was just forty yards between them.

It was a twisty pursuit. Down one narrow street, and then up another. They crossed through early morning traffic, but with every stride, Daniel managed to gain a step or two on his slower-moving quarry until finally he wasn't any more than twenty feet behind him.

Daniel forced himself to pick up the pace and blocked out the pain that the extra exertion caused him. He dug down to find the strength to keep going, to find the extra steps to reach his prey. Just five feet behind.

The man made a desperate attempt to shake Daniel by turning down another alley.

Daniel made the same turn, moving too quickly to cautiously check where he was heading.

And that was when the board caught him right across the bridge of his nose.

There was an explosion of wood and blood as the impact swept him from his feet and knocked him straight back till his head struck the pavement.

He had to get up. Get up and catch the shooter.

The figure he'd been chasing appeared as a looming shadow over him. And then was joined by another. One of them pulled a pistol from a coat pocket and aimed down at Daniel, who was unable to get up. And that was the very last thing he saw before everything went black.

CHAPTER FIVE

My Generation

C D G

Guitar's most basic chords. The bedrock on which almost everything that's been played on the radio in the last fifty years is based. Hundreds of songwriters have written thousands of songs and made millions of dollars with nothing more than those three chords.

D C G

G C D

Vicki played them over and over. She strummed and picked and plucked in varying tempos and rhythms. She tried every possible combination, conscious that there was magic within them but unable to harness any of the power that remained just beyond her grasp. She added major chords and minor chords. She tried sevenths and ninths. She exhausted everything she'd ever learned or heard, but everything she played sounded flat. There was nothing magical in any of it, and she worried that the lifelessness in her music was really within her.

She knew it should be easier. The musical universe should be mathematically finite. She had ten fingers. Her guitar had six strings and twenty frets. Some socially addled adolescent at MIT should have been able to write it all out as a mathematical equation. The song was just at her fingertips, teasing her and taunting her, but she couldn't pull it to her.

The frustration she felt was only heightened by the set of eyes that stared at her, half waiting for something to happen, half judging her because nothing was.

"What?" Vicki finally exploded.

"'Scuse me?" Malaika Harris was as impatient as any teenager, but the anxieties of her age were heightened by the expectations inherent in her situation. "I been sittin' up here for over an hour watching you play the same lame-ass tune till I'm so bored I feel like my brains gonna run out my ears, and you ask me, 'What?'"

"Yeah." Vicki looked straight back at the girl. "What?"

"Mr. Koschei got expectations on me." She put her right hand to her clavicle as if she were touching something precious and delicate.

"Please." Vicki was unimpressed. "He found you in a mall food court in Kansas City."

"And told me I had *it*!" Malaika added. "Brought me to LA to become a star, not sit around listening to some Alison Morrissey wannabe."

"First off, it's Alanis Morissette," she corrected. "Second, you hopped on a bus to get away from home just like I did when I was younger than you. Just like ten thousand other girls. That doesn't make you a star, it just makes you a runaway."

"He don't want me to be no star?" Her question was a statement of outrage. "Well, then why he payin' for my voice lessons and dance lessons? Why he buying me all these threads and stones?" She swept her hand over her new clothes and jewelry.

Vicki didn't bother to look up from her guitar. "I'm guessing for the exact same reason he does it for me." Her voice was low and sad and resigned. If there was guilt or shame in the dark corners of her comment, neither of them was willing to let on.

"I don't even know why Mr. Koschei paired me with you," Malaika continued, as if that particular door didn't exist and hadn't been opened. "How the hell am I supposed to write a song with someone like you?"

"What's that supposed to mean?"

"Look at us," the girl shot back. "I'm not anything like you."

"Don't think so?"

"You're all into that guitar shit. I'm a rapper. I'm Miss Behavior. And you're . . ." Her voice faded as she hesitated to say what she was thinking.

"I'm what?" Vicki challenged.

Malaika was politely reluctant to say it out loud, but she was more concerned with being seen as backing down from the dare. "You old."

The words hit and stung like a twelve-gauge blast of rock salt. "I am not." Vicki put her guitar aside, but was tempted to swing for the little brat's head.

"You're like my mom's age."

"Then your mom must be one kick-ass chick in the prime of her life too."

"That ain't prime." Malaika got to her feet, raised her hands above her head, and then fluttered them down her body like a Vegas magician's visually distracting assistant demonstrating there were no (visible) wires on her sequin-covered form. "This is prime. I'm all pimped out."

"I've never understood that," Vicki readily admitted. "The whole *pimp* thing. There's nothing cool about a pimp. They're just monsters who use girls to bait the street for even worse monsters."

"It doesn't mean *that*. It just means cool." She pointed accusingly at Vicki's tight, faded jeans and threadbare Misfits T-shirt. "And what are you?"

"You know what the difference between me and Beyoncé, Rihanna, Nicki Minaj—all those women you follow—is?"

"About a dozen platinum albums and a couple hundred million dollars?" the girl offered snarkily.

Vicki ignored the jab. "I've been with a lot of men–a lot of men—but the difference is that *I* fucked every one of them."

"What's that supposed to mean?"

"Sex was never something I let someone do *to* me. I just don't get all of those women dressing themselves up and holding themselves out there like they're playing some role, like they're willing to be someone else's trophy. Goddamn it, be your own trophy."

Malaika didn't have anything to say.

"There was a time when a woman needed some talent to make it as a musician. Now they just Auto-Tune her voice and choreograph her like a stripper, like Miley twerking her ass off. You think Big Mama Thornton could've made it today? Billie Holiday or Bessie Smith? Music today says if a woman wants to be anything, she has to do it in someone's bed." Vicki shook her head. "You wanna get laid, good for you. But stand up, be strong, and own your pussy. Don't be someone else's prop."

"And that's what you're about?" Malaika looked straight back at her. "That what you got going with Koschei?"

The truth hung up Vicki a second too long to cover, and she started picking at the scabs of her cuticles. "Just because I'm a hypocrite doesn't mean that I'm wrong."

"That what I thought," Malaika said. Point. Game. Match. "Is there anything you're *not* wrong about?"

Vicki wasn't sure any longer. She'd been so wrong about so much. She wondered if there was anything she could be certain about. "Love."

"Love? I don't see you with no man."

Vicki sniffed defensively. "Because I don't need one."

Malaika understood completely. "That means you ain't got one."

"I love one."

"Ain't the same thing."

"No. No, it's not." Vicki picked her guitar back up. "Then let's just get back to work. Someone told me writing a love song has nothing to do with love anyway."

"Is that right?" The question was halfway between smartass and sincere.

Vicki could work with half-sincere. And she could appreciate half-smartass. "I understand why you think so, but trust me on this: being a young woman is so hard that you can't even see that right now you're a *loooong* way from your prime."

"Trust you? Why would I trust you?"

"Because I know you."

"You don't know shit about me."

"I know it looks like that," Vicki admitted. "You're black. I'm white. I like punk and you're a rapper. You're young and I'm—" She wasn't going to say it.

So Malaika said it for her. "Old."

"*Less* young," Vicki was quick to correct. "But life just doesn't have that many different chords to play. Each of us has our own song to write, but they're basically all the same chords."

"That right?"

Vicki nodded. "I know what it's like to always feel just a half step out of pace with everyone else. Maybe more than half a step."

"What are you talking about?" the girl challenged. "I was like the most popular girl at my school."

"I was too," Vicki said. "Which means we both know it's harder to explain why you feel so alone when there's so many who want a piece of you. I know what it's like when music is the only thing that makes everything all right. I know what it's like to think you're going to bring the world to its knees. And still be terrified that the world is going to grind you under its heel."

The girl remained uncharacteristically quiet.

"And as far as punk and rap go," Vicki continued, "they're really just different sides of the same coin."

"How you figure?"

"They're both the raw, primal sound of people who don't have anything but anger because they don't have anything at all. They don't require an understanding of music theory or expensive instruments and equipment. They're both the music of people who have no voice, but need to be heard. My punks are screaming about the same inequalities you're rapping about."

"Yeah, but—"

"You're eighteen years old. You can't tell me that you're not filled with songs."

"I'm filled with raps," Malaika said defiantly.

"You're filled with emotion that needs a place to go." Vicki strummed the three chords again. "And we've got a song to write. So, for once in your life, drop the front you've thrown up—"

"This ain't no front."

Vicki knew better. "You're a kid from suburban Kansas City. Saying *ain't* is a total front."

Malaika wanted to protest, but she knew she'd only lose face.

"Forget all of that other shit for just a minute and just tell me something real."

G C D

Vicki played the same chords, but this time she sang along.

Well I'm scared to be loved. More scared to be alone.
I don't want to need someone, but I'm so tired on my own.
I need your arms around me, but I'm so damn mad.
Why does love feel so good, when it hurts so goddamn bad.

Vicki kept playing, and without a word of encouragement, Malaika began to rap.

Give you my heart. You take it for a joyride.
Drive-by lover, you kill a girl from the inside.
You playin' at stayin', so, boy, go and run and hide.
Stealin' what I gave, but you can never take my pride.

Together they worked late into the night. And when they were done, they'd written a love song that had nothing to do with love.

CHAPTER SIX

Telephone Line

Gerald Feller had spent countless hours mapping out the European tour he'd planned to take with his wife after he retired from the Bureau, but he never got to take the trip. The Bureau dismissed him before he ever got the gold watch. And the wife left him, went back to Peoria, and remarried some jackass.

He had, however, made it to Europe. As a special assistant to Haden Koschei, Gerald Feller had traveled all over the world— much farther than he ever would have gotten on a government pension with a middle-aged, midwestern harpy at his side. He'd been places she never could've imagined, and seen things she never would've believed. And he'd done things she never would have thought him capable of. All sorts of things.

He pushed the memories of them—and her—from his mind and refocused on the business he had to attend to. With a deep breath, he braced himself and made the call he was afraid to make.

The line rang once. Another deep breath. It rang again. He hoped against hope that there would be no answer. It rang again. He was almost home free. A fourth ring.

And then his heart sank.

The line went live. "What news?" Distance distorted Haden Koschei's voice, but it was still just as smoothly menacing as Feller remembered it to be.

Always lead with the strongest suit. "Dredsley is dead."

"That's of no interest to me," Koschei said without a note of remorse for his fallen comrade.

"I thought you'd want that chapter closed."

"You don't have any particular talent for *thinking*, Mr. Feller. I've told you what I want you to *do*."

Gerald Feller knew better than to offer a defense or explanation.

And Koschei knew exactly what the silent pause in their conversation meant. "Am I to assume then that your assignment is not complete?"

A deep breath prefaced the explanation he couldn't help but offer. "It wasn't my fault. The two contractors I hired. They—" There was no real way to explain what had happened to them. Not without autopsy photos at least. "His friend, the big black guy came out of nowhere and—"

"I'm beginning to lose faith in you, Mr. Feller, and I'm not exactly what you'd call a man of faith."

Feller closed his eyes and pictured the cruel sneer he knew had accompanied the cold words. "I can get him for you." Feller had listened to enough motivational CDs to know he had to frame his failures as successes he hadn't achieved just yet. "I'm sure of it."

The manufactured optimism was not shared. "The only difference between *saying* something and actually *doing* it, Mr. Feller, is success."

"I could've *killed* him a hundred times by now if you'd just let me do it."

"That's not what you've been hired for, Mr. Feller. And I think you'd find that killing the man might prove to be more difficult than you would expect."

"I can kill a man." Feller said it proudly.

And he was proud. Killing was right at the top of the list of things his ex-wife never would've thought him man enough for. But one day, he'd teach her just how wrong she'd been about him. One day.

"Yes. You've proven your sloppy skills," Koschei conceded contemptuously. "But our Mr. Erickson is something completely different."

"He's just a man."

"Then you should have no future problems in bringing him to me."

"No, sir."

But there was more to the assignment than simply retrieving him. "There's only so much sand in the hourglass, Mr. Feller."

"Yes, sir."

"And yours is down to its very last grains."

"Yes, sir."

"Don't disappoint me, Mr. Feller. You can't imagine the weight of my wrath."

That was all there was to the call. It ended with the unveiled threat still hanging in the air like the mist in the London morning. Gerald Feller slipped the phone back into his pocket and stepped over the bodies of the men he'd hired, careful not to get their blood on his fine Italian shoes.

CHAPTER SEVEN

Back in the U.S.A.

The only landscape was ice. Lifeless and foreboding, it stretched in all directions to the far horizons, where it collided with a darkening sky that was cluttered with clouds.

Without direction or destination, Daniel took step after step without ever seeming to make any discernable progress on his path. Instead, each frozen footstep was only a crunchy reason to wonder whether he'd been sentenced to this otherworldly desolation as eternal punishment for having died an ignoble death or for having lived a dishonest life.

He wandered until his feet could no longer endure the pain and his legs refused to carry him. He dropped to his knees in a single motion and collapsed to the ice in another. He struggled but was too weary to get back on his feet.

His breath was labored and shallow, and for what seemed like a long while, he lay on his back doing nothing but watching the crystalline vapor that escaped from his lips drift up and disappear into the threatening storm above him. He knew he had to get up. He was aware that a lack of action was a decision to die. But it was too cold to move, and no matter how hard he searched his soul, he couldn't find the motivation within himself.

"Daniel."

Just the sound of her voice made his temperature rise. His chapped lips cracked into a smile at the sight of her standing above him, and his faith was instantly restored. Everything was going to be all right. "Vicki."

He tried to get up, but couldn't budge. He thought at first that he'd become affixed to the ice like a naive kid's tongue to a frozen flagpole, but then realized he wasn't caught. He was being held down.

Vicki stood over him. She was dressed in a white lace peignoir, which he thought was an odd fashion choice for the climate. And she'd cut her hair so that the long red mane she'd always been so proud of was now a clipped tuft on her head. But what was strangest of all was that she had one of her stiletto pumps planted firmly against his chest. "You're not going anywhere. Don't even try."

And then Koschei was there, beside her. He too seemed inappropriately dressed for the environs, in pajamas as silken and silver as his hair. "She's right, you know. There's no point in resisting her. Just give in and give up. Once and for all."

"Get your ass up!" It wasn't Vicki's sweet voice or Koschei's suave timbre, but the spoons-on-a-washboard rasp of the old bluesman he knew as Atibon. "You got work to do, son. Stop worrying 'bout the ladies and get to your feet," he ordered. "You still got a debt to pay off."

The desolate scenery spun, and the sky above Daniel swirled until he realized it was no longer sky at all, but a ceiling. And not just any ceiling, but the arched dome in the living room of the Malibu house he'd shared with his wife and son a lifetime ago. The strong, sweet smell of vomit brought back a memory he'd pushed from his head, but he knew at once that he was reliving his death-by-pills-and-Scotch suicide attempt from the long-past time when he'd first learned the cruel consequences of love's unfaithfulness.

His head reeled as his view of the ceiling was interrupted by two men leaning over him. He thought it incredible that after so much time he still recognized the faces of both of the EMTs who had attended to him that night, but there they were: shining lights in his eyes and running their blue-gloved fingers through his mouth, checking for obstructions just like they had when he'd first made their acquaintance.

Everything about the scene was frighteningly familiar. Everything except that now there was a third man there. Not an EMT, but a new player who hadn't had a role in the original production of this particular drama.

His gray beard was snarled like brambles across his black face, and his eyes were black as a moonless night and twice as deep. "You got a debt to pay, *mi key.*" The voice was as hypnotic as the almost-audible whispers in a crackling fire, and the sound filled Daniel with a burning desire to get to his feet and follow his old friend wherever he was leading. "If you quit on you, you'll be lost forever. So get your ass up and live!"

"You all right?" This voice was from a different speaker altogether, low and booming, like thunder on a summer afternoon. And this time it sounded . . . *real.* "Yeah. You gonna be all right."

Daniel shivered, not quite sure where his dream had ended and reality had resumed, although he guessed the excruciating throbbing between his ears was a good starting point. Suddenly, the imagined whistle of wintry winds and the chatter of phantom EMTs was replaced by a dull hum he knew was the drone of engines.

He tried to open his eyes and focus his sight, but both were more difficult than he'd expected. Everything around him was gray, but not distant and cloudlike as in his dream. Instead, his surroundings, his *real* surroundings, were metal and rivets, industrial and confining.

"Just lie back down, man. You gonna be all right." The voice he'd confused for thunder was Moog's, but he wasn't sure whether that was a cause for relief or alarm.

"Where am I?" His words were so weak that even Daniel could barely hear them over the engines.

"Had to fly you cargo," Moog replied, as if that answer alone should've straightened out every jumble in Daniel's head.

It didn't even come close. "I'm cold."

"They don't bother to heat these things just to keep the packages warm." Moog looked around the belly of the Boeing 757F as if he were just noticing the cargo hold. "Sorry 'bout that. No other way. Not with so many looking for you, and you in the condition you're in and all."

"Condition?" Daniel tried to get up, but couldn't.

"I had to give you a little sumpthin'—sumpthin' to get you through the trip."

"Something?" Daniel strained to express his confusion.

"Can't have you whacking me from behind every chance you get," Moog explained as he rubbed the back of his head where the welt was still raised and sore. "I had to knock your ass out to get you into this thing. And to keep you in it."

Daniel forced himself to sit up, and realized only then that he was lying in a coffin. The lid of the box was open and propped up. "What the hell?"

"Not yet," the big man joked. "This time it's just a means of transportation." He slapped the casket good-naturedly.

He had a growing awareness of his reality, but none of what returned to him made any sense to Daniel. He struggled with his most recent memory—a chase . . . and an alley . . .

"There were two guys."

"*Were* is the word." Moog smiled. "Neither one of them boys gonna be gettin' outta their boxes anytime soon."

"Damn it," Daniel snapped. "They were my best lead to finding—"

"They were your best lead to finding out what it's like to be staring up at the satin lining of one of these things for real." Moog started to close the lid. "You can think about that and thank me when I open this up for you when we get there. Now lay back." The big man's hands settled on Daniel's chest.

Daniel wouldn't go back so easily. "There's one thing."

"What's that?" Moog sounded like a parent waiting to put a recalcitrant child to bed.

"Vicki."

"What about her?"

"You think she could ever . . ." Daniel thought back to his dream. Or vision. Or whatever it had been. "Hurt me?"

Moog laughed, but in the way people sometimes react to something profoundly sad. "You left that woman all kinds of brokenhearted."

"I didn't mean to." That was the truth. "I thought what I was doing was for the best."

"Doesn't matter what you 'mean to.' Fact is that you hurt her."

Daniel knew better than to follow that any further. "I know."

"And I killed more men in more ways than I care to remember." It wasn't a confession, just another statement of facts. "But there ain't nuthin' in heaven or hell that can bring the pain like a woman been hurt." Moog gave off another sad and uncomfortable half laugh. "And Vicki's a helluva woman. I imagine she could bring down a helluva hurt." That was all the big man had to say about that, and he cut off the conversation by bringing down the coffin lid.

"Wait." Daniel tried to resist, but he wasn't in any shape to try very hard.

The satin-lined lid was shut, and there was nothing Daniel could do to change that. There'd been one last moment of light, and in it, Daniel made his peace with everything. With everything except the woman whose heart he'd broken. And who had broken his. He knew better than to bring that with him into the darkness.

CHAPTER EIGHT

Sharp Dressed Man

Most of those who believe in the existence of hell consider the path there to be a straight descent. But there are those who know for a fact that belief has little to do with evil's existence, and they are aware that there are all sorts of ways there—even some that are straight up.

Brian Dendrake rode the elevator to the penthouse suite and felt his heart sink further and further in his chest with each floor that was counted off on the video screen above the button board. It wasn't the closed space of the car or the sensation of ascent that caused his apprehension. What was troubling him was his destination.

The elevator came to a gentle stop, and a mechanized female voice announced seductively, "Penthouse." The chrome doors slid silently open.

Dendrake took a deep breath and stepped out of the car.

He wasn't the sort of man who dealt well with anxiety. That failing wasn't because of some social inadequacy or emotional disorder, but simply because he so rarely had any experience with the emotion.

The Dendrakes were a whole clan built on confidence. Three centuries earlier, a failed bootblack named Benjamin Drake had left his wife and three children in a London debtors' prison and followed the triangle trade across the Atlantic to a new life in the New World. There was little family discussion of the particulars, but somehow the man—now known as Hammond Dendrake—had used a stake in sugar, tobacco, and slaves to create an eighteenth-century empire that was still thriving in the twenty-first century.

No matter how humble (or morally reprehensible) its origins, prosperity earns respect, or at least, it engenders supplication from a great many people. Brian Dendrake was used to people courting his favor and, as a result, he was very uncomfortable leaving that perch of power for a position that was decidedly more precarious.

"To what do I owe this surprise?" Haden Koschei was aware of almost everything before it happened, including the arrival of his unannounced guest. So he asked the question and pretended to have been caught off guard only to underscore his omniscience.

Brian Dendrake didn't share Koschei's prescience, but he knew when he was being taken lightly. "We both know it's no surprise at all."

"No. No, it's not." A slight smile strained Koschei's thin lips. "But it seemed a much sweeter greeting than 'What the hell do you want?'"

"I'm not interested in sweeter."

"Then what the hell do you want?" Koschei sneered.

"I'm concerned."

"Tell me." Koschei made a gesture in the air, indicating the empty chairs in front of his desk, and his visitor took one.

Dendrake's entitled station in life had led him to any number of overindulgences, and it took him a moment to settle his more than ample frame into the Danish modern chair he'd been offered. "I'm concerned about recent developments." He unbuttoned his suit coat and carefully crossed his thick, sausage legs, but neither adjustment made him any more comfortable. "And the state of our relationship with you." It needed to be said, but he was careful to say it respectfully.

Koschei seemed unfazed. "There's nothing to be concerned about."

"That's not the message I got from London."

"And whose appraisal would matter more to you?"

"I'm not interested in appraisals. I deal in facts. And the fact is that there's a rat within the grain."

Koschei smiled on the outside. "He's just one man."

"I shouldn't need to remind you, of all people, what 'just one man' can do."

The unspoken comparison that the fat man was drawing irritated Koschei. "This man is hardly in my league."

"London tells me 'this man' may well know about Hendrix. May be able to *prove* it," Dendrake stressed. "May be able to prove your connection to the deaths of—"

"'*May*' is no reason for concern," Koschei said dismissively.

With so much riding on the "Don't Pass" bar, Dendrake was not so willing to have his concerns about the mysterious Daniel Erickson casually swept aside. "It sure as hell is when this man *may* be able to prove to the world what you've done—what we've done with you. What we're doing right now. When this man *may* be able to bring down everything that we've accomplished with Siren Song, then you better goddamn believe I'm going to be concerned." When he was finished, even he realized that his tone had slipped from his self-imposed safety zone.

Koschei tolerated the fat man's attitude because it suited his long game, but he'd reached an end to any interest in the conversation. "I'm a busy man, Brian, so why don't you bottom line me on just what exactly it is that dropped you into my den."

Dendrake's personal philosophy was that the greatest factor in success was simply knowing what one wanted. "What I'd *like* is for you to tell me that I don't need to be concerned about the future of Siren Song, not because there's no reason to be concerned, but because that reason has disappeared like he never even existed."

Koschei's patient smile strained even more. "I've told you, I'm working on it."

The fat man nodded both of his chins. "And I've come here to tell you that so am I."

For a man who prided himself on his ability to anticipate all the moves on the board prior to his opponent (or partner, if there was any difference), Koschei couldn't hide his surprise. Or his alarm. "Perhaps, I haven't made clear that *I'm* taking care of this situation in a very particular manner. In my own way. For my own reasons."

"Well, *your way* isn't working, Haden." Dendrake knew there were some people that even he could push only so far, and he took a moment to settle himself and quiet his tone. "At least, it's not working quickly enough. There was a time when we could plug every leak, but if this information gets out on the goddamn Internet, there's no telling what could happen. If people were to learn just how much power we exert over them simply by controlling the popular music they listen to . . ." It was an endgame he didn't want to contemplate. "I don't think that's something even you could survive."

"You'd be surprised what I can survive," Koschei countered.

"I simply mean, they can't ever know. And that means this Erickson fellow must disappear. Everything about him must disappear."

"Everything's fine, Brian. You're overreacting." Koschei's tone was soothing and hypnotic. But not quite convincing enough.

"Maybe so, but I'm not willing to take that chance. I'm here as a courtesy to tell you that whatever operation you've got working is now facing competition."

The old man ground his porcelain caps as his jaw clenched in politely (and barely) suppressed rage. "There's no need for that."

"Like I said, I deal in facts. And the fact of the matter is that I need to see this man dead. So, I'm exercising every resource at my disposal to make sure that gets done before this all gets any worse." Dendrake knew he was in too far to turn back now. "I'm taking this to Madam Pompadour and the Council."

"I understand," Koschei lied through his still-gritted teeth.

"I hope you do," Dendrake said with as much earnestness as a man of his station can muster. "I'm not looking to step all over your Berluti loafers, but this has to be done. Your way or my way. No matter. It just needs to be done."

Koschei thought again of his long game and nodded. "I appreciate the courtesy."

"This doesn't change things with us," Dendrake assured him. And he paused a moment, seeking assurances of his own. "Does it?"

"Of course not." Koschei lit up the biggest of fake smiles. "It's a collateral matter. I understand."

"Good."

"Fine."

Koschei rose from his chair to signal that he was ending the conversation with their exchange of pleasantries. And lies. "Would you join me for lunch?"

"Can't do it. The Lear is still on the tarmac waiting to turn me around."

Koschei was not nearly as disappointed as he pretended to be. "Then someday soon?"

"Maybe after Bohemian Grove," Dendrake offered as he struggled to his feet.

"That would be perfect."

"All right then."

The two men shook hands, though both were left wondering whether the gesture was an expression of affection between two old associates or a requisite sign of respect between two combatants before the ringing of the bell.

CHAPTER NINE

Signed, Sealed, Delivered

By the time the 757 cargo carrier had come to a bone-rattling landing on a strip at the far north of Baltimore-Washington International Airport, the dose of ketamine Moog had given Daniel to keep him sedated in his coffin-carrier had worn off almost entirely. By the time he felt the box being jostled as it was being unloaded, what little of the drug was left in his system had metabolized enough to allow him the sense to reach for the knife he carried in his back pocket.

Given the satin-lined confines of his situation, getting his hands on the blade was a struggle. Still, with a little bit of wriggling, he was able to work the weapon free and take hold of it. Careful not to drop it and lose it beneath him, Daniel slowly worked the blade open, then turned it a time or two until his hand found a sure and comfortable grip on the handle.

Daniel knew that catching the big man by surprise was his only chance. If he failed in his first attempt, he wouldn't be getting a second one. In his mind, he forced himself to walk through every step of what he'd have to do. He pictured the lid coming open, and he knew he'd have to force his way up as soon as he saw light, popping out like a lethal jack-in-the-box.

He pictured himself shooting up to his feet. He knew that he'd have seconds to find his target and that as soon as he did he would have to—

Daniel knew what he had to do, but no matter how hard he tried to force himself to think through the last step, he could not picture himself plunging the blade into his old friend. His only friend.

Still, he asked himself what choice Moog had given him. The big man had made it clear that he was desperate to retrieve his daughter from the clutches of Haden Koschei. And he'd made it equally clear that he'd already made a deal to do exactly that.

There was no choice. Moog had created the scenario that had put their lives on either end of Death's teeter-totter. It was simply a matter of survival. No choice at all.

Although he'd been running the same ten seconds over and over in his mind for a good forty minutes, Daniel was still caught off guard when his coffin finally came open. He was a second or two late in hitting the lid, but it still flew open, and he still managed to spring from the box almost exactly like he had planned.

And that's where his plan stopped dead.

With nothing between him and his friend but a six inch steel blade, Daniel froze. He knew what he had to do. And why. But he couldn't bring himself to do anything about it.

Moog himself stood stunned at the sight. "What the hell are you doing?"

"Get back!" Daniel warned, and the knife moved through the air, though nowhere near his old friend. "I swear I'll cut you!" he bluffed.

"Oh, you'll cut me." Moog didn't seem threatened at all. "You think you can cut me?"

At his best, Daniel wouldn't have been able to push the confrontation any further, but after having spent ten sedated hours in a coffin, the standoff left him dizzy and unsteady on his feet. "I'm the one with the knife, so yeah, I think I can cut you." His words were every bit as weak as he felt.

"Man, what the hell's happened to you?" Moog backed away from the blade, swatting in the air at Daniel, not in an attempt to drive him away, but as a sign of disgust.

"Happened to *me*? You're the one who doped me up and stuffed me in a coffin."

"You laid me out with the butt end of a shotgun," Moog was quick to remind him.

Daniel was quick to defend his actions. "You didn't think I was just going to let you turn me over to Koschei, did you?"

"Turn you over?" The accusation seemed to strike Moog more sharply and deeper than any knife ever could. "To Koschei? Are you kidding me? You think, after everything we've been through, you think that I would turn you over to *anyone*, much less the monster's got my little girl?"

There was deep hurt in his friend's eyes, but Daniel still saw the logic in his assumption. "It's your little girl. Of course I'd *expect* you to sell me out to save her."

"Man, you're a true one-of-a-kind asshole, you know that?"

Daniel had heard that before.

"I need you to save her," Moog explained. "But I sure as hell don't need to *betray* you to get it done."

"But you said you made a deal." Daniel's trailing voice contained a concession. Maybe even the beginning of an apology.

Moog didn't seem overly interested in either. "I did make a deal. To bring you back, not to turn you over to anyone."

"Bring me back? Bring me back to who?"

"He make a deal to bring you back to me." The voice came from out of the shadows, but Daniel didn't need to turn toward the darkness to know its true source. "He bring you back home 'cause your time has come, *mi key*."

CHAPTER TEN

Black Magic Woman

Angelina Silvano was the sort of woman who served as explanation for why someone had once thought it necessary to invent tequila. And satin sheets. And scented oils.

Her curves were so sinful and her proportions so perfectly obscene that she seemed more like a hormonally charged adolescent's notebook drawing than a flesh-and-blood woman. Still, there she was: stretched out, naked, warm, and waiting.

The distraction she created would've been irresistible to a substantial percentage of the sexually active public, but Haden Koschei's thoughts were focused on the afternoon visit from Brian Dendrake. And what that might mean to his long-term plans.

Her hair was the color of ravens' wings, so much blacker than black that it seemed to turn metallic and purple in the flickering light of the candles. She brushed some errant strands back from her face and asked him, "What's wrong?"

"Just something's come up."

"Or won't." Angelina's ruby lips puckered into a pout.

He rolled away from her. "It's a professional problem."

She scribbled something on his bare back with the tip of her finger. "Perhaps we should order up a *professional* solution." She nipped at his ear.

He swatted her away as if she were a mosquito annoying him. "I was thinking of going in another direction."

"And what direction would that be?"

"I was thinking south."

"I'm all about going south," she purred, and started that way.

He stopped her. "I was thinking south of the border."

"So was I." She started that way again.

"I was thinking about your husband."

This time she stopped herself and let out a very disappointed, "Oh."

The big buzzkill was Santo Silvano, Angelina's husband of thirteen years. While the mention of his name had killed nothing more than her mood, it was much more commonly associated with killing people. Lots of them. And in very, very bad ways.

As the head of the most ruthless drug cartel in Mexicali, Silvano was as feared by friends as he was by his enemies. And for very good reason.

He was a man of passions. And in addition to his Angelina and the power and wealth of his cartel, the things he loved most in life were cats. Big cats. Very big cats. And he'd earned (really, he'd bestowed it upon himself) the moniker El Tigre as his declaration of love for the creatures and his penchant for tossing enemies and innocents to his private collection of them.

While no other man could've looked at Angelina and *thought* of her in his bed without becoming human Meow Mix, Haden Koschei had made her his mistress without any fear of a man he controlled completely. She, in turn, had responded in kind.

"He has what I need."

"No. No, he doesn't." She rubbed his arm tenderly. "You have everything you need right here." She put Koschei's hand on her waist, but it remained there and did not migrate the way that she hoped it would.

"I need men," he calculated aloud.

"I do too." She kissed the nape of his neck, then bit him harder when he ignored her.

"I'll need a lot of them."

"I do too," she purred. "I'll give you whatever you need," she promised, still unable to get his attention. "You want to watch?"

"No." Her attempts at seduction only annoyed him. "I need men of a certain sort and he has quite a lot of them."

She gave up on the evening and settled down to the business she couldn't compete with. "And how exactly are you going to ask my husband to help you?"

"I'm not going to *ask* him, my dear. I'm going to *tell* him." He thought that part over. "Or, rather, you're going to tell him."

She was curious. "Why me?"

"Because fear—even fear of me—will only make a man do so much. But for you, my dear, I think we both know a man would do anything."

She smiled and chuckled, pleased that he'd said it aloud. "We both know what a *man* would do for me. My question is what would *you* do?"

"In time, I promise I will take you away from all of this."

"In time?" she teased.

He nodded, still focused on his plan. "In the morning, you'll call Santo and tell him that you need him to find our Mr. Erickson."

"And why would I need that?"

"You're a high priestess of Santa Muerte," he reminded her. "With that kind of connection to the infinite darkness, I would've thought you'd have sensed his presence by now."

She'd harbored suspicions about her lover's obsession with what seemed like such an ordinary man, but his cryptic comment was the only confirmation she needed. "Are you telling me he's *muertos vivientes*? One of the soulless ones?"

Koschei didn't answer, but it was the first time that she had seen fear in the old man's eyes.

"Well, we can deal with your walking dead man tomorrow," she whispered. "What about right now?"

Without a word, he rolled her over and showed her.

CHAPTER ELEVEN

Good to See You

"Well," Moog said pointedly to Atibon. "You wanted your boy brought back and here he is." He cast a resentful look at Daniel and grumbled under his breath, "Lucky I'm a professional with a guaranteed delivery or I'd put that blade in him now."

Daniel looked down self-consciously at the weapon he held limply in his hand, flipped it closed, and slipped it back in his pocket. "I don't understand."

"Son, how long I known you now?" Atibon laughed out loud. "And I don't know that you ever understand nothin'." He shook his head good-naturedly, but with more than a nod of contempt. "So, what gots you all sortsa confused now?"

Daniel wasn't sure where to begin. "You're the one who sent me to London in the first place."

"London?" Atibon screwed up his face. "Why in the hell would I send you there, boy?"

"You told me to find who killed Jimi Hendrix," Daniel reminded him defensively.

"And did ya?"

"I think so." Daniel looked accusingly at Moog. "Pushkin. A man named Feodor Pushkin."

"Never heard of him."

"Well, I could've found out more if you hadn't sent this guy to stuff me in a coffin."

"You lucky that's all I stuffed you into," Moog muttered.

Daniel ignored the comment and looked straight at the old man. "You couldn't have just called?"

"Do I look like the cell phone type?" Atibon retorted. And then, as an aside, he offered, "Those damn things is evil itself."

"So, you went with a hit man instead?"

"I went with your *friend* instead." Atibon nodded toward the big man. "He your only one, if'n you keepin' score."

It was Daniel's turn to look away.

"I went with your brother." The old man placed his weathered left hand on Moog's bookshelf of a shoulder. "And now you gotta forgive your brother, 'cause what he done, he done to hold up his end on a bargain he made with me. That's the who, what, and why of all this."

"I don't understand. You sent me off to run down what happened to Hendrix—"

"And I woulda loved nothin' better but that you got down to the very bottom of it all. But things changed, son. Your time came 'round sooner than I thought it would."

"My time? You're telling me I'm going to die."

"Ain't nearly that simple, son. When it come down to it, dyin's the easy part. It's livin' that can be harder than hell."

"And what have I been doing for the last forty-some years?"

"You been goin' through the motions, boy. Same as most folks. But now you're gonna have to make up your mind. You got a hard decision to make. And a heavy price to pay once ya make it. No matter what you end up choosin'."

Daniel nodded like he understood, but the only thing he'd gained was a sense of the odds he was facing. "Sort of a lose-lose proposition?"

"You were never going to get out of this clean. I told you that from the beginning." Atibon offered his words like alms to purchase forgiveness.

"So, now is my hour?"

"It ain't quite yet. But it comin'. And when it comes, I need ya to face it here. And when you face it, you gonna need your brother by your side."

"The brother who sandbagged me, drugged me, and shipped me around in a coffin?"

"That's the one." The old man grinned. "And he gonna need you if he gonna get his little girl back too."

"Get her back?" Daniel shot, as if that assertion were the most outrageous of them all. "She's livin' in the lap of luxury, recording with the biggest man in music."

"I woulda thought you of all people woulda figured it out by now," Atibon sneered. "The *lap of luxury* is right where Life hides the big dick of consequences."

The insensitive nature of what he'd said struck the old man an instant later, and he offered Moog a quick "No offense."

Moog shook off the comment and its apology.

"Koschei has that man's baby girl," Atibon continued. "Maybe not like the sonbitch snatched her straight up, but he's got her tight in his clutches and he's holding her, and he been twisting her like bait on a line, trying to get Mr. Moog to trade your life for hers. Instead, Moog came to me lookin' for a way to save you both."

Daniel had no response, but it was clear that the old man's point had been made.

That didn't, however, mean that Atibon was finished. "And Moog, you've got to forgive Daniel."

It was the big man's turn to complain. "Besides being a pain in my ass the whole goddamn time, he knocked me upside my head with a bird gun."

Atibon nodded. "But just like you, Daniel had a reason for what he done. He done it to pay off what he owed me, and he ran up at least a part of that debt in a bargain for your safety."

The suggestion seemed outrageous and offensive. "My safety?"

"You're a big, bad man," Atibon easily admitted. "And from time to time you get to feelin' like you're Superman. But listen up, son, this whole damn world made outta kryptonite, and it's a safe bet you woulda departed a long time ago if Daniel hadn't stepped up for you."

Moog and Daniel looked at one another but neither had a word to say.

"Ain't no one never gonna change the past. And you two ain't no exceptions. The past is what it is. And it is what it is for a reason. Ain't no accidents in this world."

"What are you talking about?" Daniel scoffed. "My whole life's been an accident. A damn train wreck."

The old man shook his head, as if Daniel's point mattered. "Everything you done—and everything and everyone that come before you in that long human chain you ain't nothin' but a link in—it's all led you to where you is right now."

Daniel looked around him. "A warehouse? In . . ." He couldn't even guess the location.

"You right where you supposed to be," Atibon advised. "But what you both need to decide is where you goin' from here. Neither one of you going to make it far without the other. I'm as sure of that as if it already happened. So, you gotta decide whether you're gonna toughen up, suck it up, and take care of business like the brothers you are. Or whether you just hack at each other till you both wind up losin' everything worth livin' for anyway."

He looked at them, but neither seemed ready to make a decision.

"But you gotta decide quick, 'cause you runnin' out of time."

Without waiting for either of them to say a word, the old man moved to a set of doors at the far end of the warehouse. "Now come on and take a little walk with me."

He opened the doors and stepped out into the bright day beyond.

CHAPTER TWELVE

The Men at the Top

There is no risk in gambling. If you own the house, that is.

Although luck and happenstance are always in play, a well-run casino will always beat the players who crowd the floors with dreams of breaking the bank. It's not that the house orchestrates each roll of the dice or every turn of the cards, but they maintain a (not always so) subtle control over enough of the other variables to guarantee their desired outcome. The world is no different.

It's not that there is any one organization with a collective interest in constantly overseeing the tiresome day-to-day antics of the hoi polloi. At the same time, it would be foolish not to expect that those with the greatest fortunes—and with the most to lose in life's fickle twists and turns—would not assemble from time to time to ensure themselves the same favorable odds as any gambling den.

There were eleven such individuals gathered around the long table. And although each of them held a net worth that would've made it a losing proposition to stop their day long enough to pick up a ten thousand dollar bill, they all kept their seats more or less patiently, checking the wasted time (and money) on wristwatches that cost more than most single-family homes.

When the door at the head of the grand ballroom opened, all eleven heads swiveled to watch their leader's entrance. It was not a scene that anyone outside of their most exclusive circle would've imagined.

She was an old woman, though none of the eleven men would've been brazen enough to have asked her just how old. "Gentlemen," she said, as the manservant in attendance pulled out her seat at the head of the table. "And lady." She nodded to recognize the only other woman in the room, a former presidential cabinet member who presently sat on the boards of ten companies among the Fortune 50.

"Madam Pompadour," they all said in unison, more or less.

"I'll get right to the point. My granddaughter has a ballet recital at four this afternoon. I do not intend to be late. So, if there's something important enough to gather the Council together today, I suggest we cut the shit and get right down to it." Her blue-gray eyes were unflinching, and no one at the table bothered trying to catch them.

"It's about the Siren Song Project," Brian Dendrake answered matter-of-factly.

"How the hell is this our problem?" the one with the cowboy hat asked from the other end of the conference table.

"It's our problem," Brian Dendrake responded defensively. "Because this is our world and everything that happens in it is our problem. Whether we like it or not."

"Well, I don't like it. Not one damn bit." The man leaned back in his leather chair and propped his cowboy boots up on the conference table that had been rendered from a single piece of redwood. "We got a sayin' back in Texas: if you got a gun, you best have a shovel too."

"I'm from Massachusetts," Dendrake explained. "I have no idea what the hell that's supposed to mean."

"The meaning couldn't be clearer. If you're gonna make a problem, you need to be ready to clean it up."

"Gentlemen," Madam Pompadour snapped. "If I wanted to watch children bicker, I would have stayed at home." She turned directly to Dendrake. "Still, it seems to me as if we've all lived up to our bargains with Mr. Koschei. I don't understand why he won't just take care of this matter."

"Mr. Koschei handles things in his own way, as I know you're all aware." Dendrake looked pointedly at each of the eleven individuals who were seated around the enormous table, and then at the old lady at its head. "If any of you have complaints you wish to bring to him directly, I invite you to do so." He stared at them all with an unspoken dare, and none of them was willing to take him up on the offer. Not even the old lady.

The Texan pulled his boots off of the table and sat up.

"The reality is that Mr. Koschei has handled the situation over the years in a manner that's been very advantageous for us." Dendrake searched for an example. "You all remember 'Ohio'?"

"Remember it?" The well-coiffed one with the perma-tan quipped. "I'd rather forget it."

"Not the state," Dendrake was quick to correct. "The song. With the tin soldiers and 'Nixon's coming.' When is the last time you heard a president criticized in a pop song?" No one could offer an example. "We're currently engaged in the longest war of our nation's history, and there's no antiwar protest songs anymore. There's no concerts to protest the wars or climate change or—"

"Ain't no goddamn such thing as climate change," the Texan asserted angrily.

"We all know it's a fact," Dendrake countered. And then added, almost as an aside, "There's a difference between not knowing it's the truth and not giving a shit that it's the truth."

The Texan just scowled.

"The point is that we are fortunate to find ourselves in a situation where music doesn't do anything more than focus people's attention on whether Ke$ha can really have sex with a ghost or who Justin Bieber's pretending to date. Music has the power to inspire people to consider the world around them, to think dangerous thoughts—to incite revolutions. We've seen it happen. But today's music? It numbs people. We can't run our businesses the way we want, or influence the government, or do any of the things we need to do if the general public is conscious and aware. Thanks to the Siren Song Project, the general public is sufficiently distracted and zombified so that we can continue our other endeavors. And we owe Haden Koschei for that."

"Pop music," the Texan chortled. "The roofie that knocks America out before we screw her."

"And it's imperative to us that the American people don't regain consciousness any time soon," Dendrake added. "Because if they wake up and find out what we've done while they were lost in a haze of Katy Perry's sparkler tits and Miley Cyrus's twerking ass—if they discover we've intentionally anesthetized them, they're going to be very, very pissed off."

"I can't imagine that anyone would be too happy to hear that we've systematically eliminated artists of influence from Otis Redding to Kurt Cobain," said the only other woman at the table.

The guy with the perfect hair was quick to agree. "And the Lord knows we can't afford that."

Dendrake seized the opportunity they'd created. "*That's* why this is our problem. And that's why we need to take care of this directly."

"What does Koschei say about this?" Madam Pompadour wondered. "If there's even a possibility that Siren Song is about to be exposed, then I would think it would be his concern, not ours."

"I've spoken with him," Dendrake assured the group. "For reasons he's not divulging to me—"

"What reasons?" the old woman demanded, as if the answer meant something more to her than just what was being discussed at the table.

Dendrake shook his head. "I don't know. He seems to have a personal issue with this Erickson."

"Personal?" The old woman cocked a salon-shaped eyebrow. "Haden Koschei doesn't have *personal* issues."

"Koschei is a mystery. To know him is to understand that his secrets are lies and hidden in a darkness no one can plumb." Dendrake shrugged his shoulders, and his whole torso jiggled. "What's important right now is that this single individual be dealt with. We need to apprehend him, determine what he knows about Siren Song, and then make sure everything disappears."

Everyone in the room agreed. Still, the Texan wondered, "It's just one man. How hard can it be?"

"He's eluded Koschei so far," Dendrake said. "And that's the dicey thing in all of this. Koschei wants him too."

"We can't accommodate anyone at a risk to ourselves," the old woman said. "Not even Haden."

Dendrake seemed relieved by the old woman's comments. "I've contacted the appropriate contractors."

The Texan nodded approvingly. "It's a government job then?"

"No." Dendrake answered. "Our friends in the government have assisted us with Siren Song from time to time. Hell, they probably benefit from our work as much as we do, but I've chosen to keep this matter within the Council. I've decided to use private contractors."

CHAPTER THIRTEEN

What's Going On

With the exception of the occasional jogger and a Park Service worker or two, the path around the Reflecting Pool was completely deserted, and the solitude only heightened the solemnity of the surroundings.

Both Daniel and Moog slowed their pace to keep step with Atibon. The old man drifted along, but it was sentiment, not age, that held him back.

"I was here, you know. There was such hope in the air. Even I believed." Atibon looked off across the empty space, but his eyes twinkled as though he could still see every face in that crowd.

"With Dr. King?" Moog asked.

"You'd think someone like me would've known better." Atibon's voice dropped in volume and spirit. "*Believe*—the goddamn word has a lie right in the middle of it. I shoulda known they would've killed him."

The three walked in silence for a while before Atibon could continue. "Before him, they killed poor Sam Cooke. But just killin' him weren't enough. The bastards had to humiliate him by stealing the poor man's pants and making up some goddamn lie about him attacking the woman behind the desk at a motel." He shook his head in disgust.

"Them that saw the body could see for themselves that he'd been beaten half to death, nose all busted, hands mangled up. Still, they just call it justifiable homicide and let it slide, without lookin' for things they don't wanna find 'cause there ain't nothin' scarier to them than a black man with no pants on."

"My gramma loved Sam Cooke," Moog remembered wistfully.

"Voice of an angel," Atibon agreed, although his tone indicated his thoughts were far away from heaven. "Poor Otis Redding's plane dropped into a goddamn lake, but they never explained just exactly what brought it down, and they ain't never recovered the engine or propeller. Now days they don't need to kill no one, 'cause we do the dirty work for them. Just keep killin' ourselves. Tupac. Biggie. Jam Master Jay. Big L."

"It's a long, sad list of brothers," Moog said.

"A lot of folks struggled and died in the fight to be free. And just when we get close to realizing that dream, they find a way to slip those shackles back on. They got us listening to music 'bout killin' one another, 'bout poisonin' one another with that shit they brew." Atibon shook his head in disgust. "Who the hell you think gettin' rich off that poison? It ain't no one you know."

There was no stopping Atibon, and neither Daniel nor Moog tried.

"They strip our women of dignity and respect. They talk to our babies about bein' souljas in a war they ain't never gonna win. They got us glorifyin' a life that can only lead to incarceration 'cause they made prisons a corporate profit center. They have us laughing and joking and using the same word they use. Make me sick." He stopped to take a breath and collect himself. "Don't matter if they're steel or gold, wearing chains is wearing chains."

Moog felt like he should say something, but he didn't. Daniel felt like he should just shut up, and he did.

"That's why they killed Jimi, you know," Atibon continued. "He was a beautiful man, singing about peace and love, so they woulda gotten 'round to it sooner or later. But Jimi was a black man who loved the ladies, and he didn't care nothin' 'bout color." Atibon shook his head sadly. "So they killed my boy."

"They?" Daniel asked. "I thought you didn't know who killed Hendrix. I thought that was the whole point of the quest you sent me on?"

It took a lot to stop Mr. Atibon in his tracks, but Daniel's question did the trick. "It wasn't so much the identity, as—"

"I told you the man who killed him was named Feodor Pushkin," Daniel said, searching Atibon's face for a sign of recognition—and finding it. "But you know something more."

"I know that names don't mean much."

Daniel was too used to Atibon's riddles to be thrown by them any longer. "But you know something that does."

Atibon's eyes darted to the left, but even he knew there was no point in lying. Not any longer. "Whatever his name was—or is—the one who killed Jimi, he took something from him. Something that belonged to me."

Both Daniel and Moog were thinking it, but Daniel was the one who asked, "What the hell are you talking about?"

Atibon sighed, knowing that he had a long story to tell and that neither man would accept its length as a reason not to tell it. "Jimi Hendrix wasn't always Jimi Hendrix."

Daniel had been around Atibon long enough to know that *anything* was possible. "Just who was he?"

"He came into this world as Johnny Allen Hendrix. He was a scrawny, troubled kid when I first found him. Just fifteen years old." He paused like he could see the boy standing in front of him then and there.

"And?" Daniel prompted

"What you think, *mi key*? We made a deal."

"You and this kid?"

"Me and the greatest guitar player that ever lived. Even better than my Robert."

"That was the deal?" Daniel guessed. "The greatest part."

Atibon just smiled. "Let's just say I gave him a little somethin' extra."

"And what exactly was that?"

"What I gave him—what your Mr. Pushkin, was it—it's what he stole when he killed Jimi. It's mine. And I want it back."

"You used me." Daniel was incensed.

"I made a deal with you," Atibon answered.

"You knew all along who you were after. You didn't need me to find the killer, you needed me . . ." Daniel didn't quite have that part figured out. "For what?"

Atibon didn't have an answer. Or, at least, not one he was willing to share.

But in the moment of silence, Daniel found the answer all by himself. "I was your stalking horse."

Atibon didn't say a word, but pretended not to understand.

"You sent me out there to . . ." Not all of the pieces were clear to him yet. But he was putting them together as quickly as he could. "To draw someone out. Who?"

It almost seemed as if Atibon blushed. "You're making more out of it than there is, *mi key*."

"Who is it?" Daniel asked as he searched his mind. "Who would want anything to do with me? Or was it Jimi?"

"It wasn't just Jimi," Atibon confessed in an uncharacteristic moment where emotion got the better of scheming. "There've been a lot over the years. Too damn many." His mind drifted to a list he kept in his head. "Poor Duane. Al Jackson Jr., Bob Marley."

It wasn't the first time that Daniel had heard the reggae star's name in connection with whatever was unfolding, but the mention filled Moog with boyish enthusiasm. "Marley?! Man, Marley is the greatest."

Atibon agreed. "Son, you have no idea. He was the face of Jamaica and when *they* were fighting over the scraps of her soul, they sent men to his home, shot him in the chest. Left him for dead.

"But I'll be damned if Bob didn't stand up for his rights and play the prime minister's concert for peace two days later anyway. He said, 'People trying to make this world a worse place don't take no day off, how can I?'"

"He was something special," Moog said in eager agreement.

"They say he died of a skin cancer under his damn toenail." Atibon didn't make any attempt to contain the scoff in his comment. "But they poisoned him straightaway." His voice caught for a minute. "Last thing he said was 'Money can't buy life,' and I'll be goddamned if that ain't a truth you can't avoid."

"And the . . . *thing* you gave him," Daniel wondered. "That you gave Jimi and the others."

"They're mine," Atibon declared. "Someone took them and I want them back."

"And the someone?"

Atibon smiled. "Well, that's for you to find out, isn't it, *mi key*?"

"You pretend you don't understand what a stalking horse is." Daniel thought he understood everything now. "But I'm guessing you know all about bait."

Atibon's grin grew. "Can't go fishin' without it."

"And that's me you've got hanging from your hook?"

"Ain't like that, son. A worm ain't got no bite." He looked at Daniel with a gleam of paternal pride in his deep brown eyes. "An' you got all sortsa bite in you."

Atibon looked over at Moog. "An' you ain't nothin' *but* bite."

"How this got anything to do with me?" the big man asked.

A Park Service worker drove by in a cart, and it seemed to Daniel that he took special notice of the trio as he putt-putted past them. Daniel made a mental note, but was too tired and his thoughts were still too blurry to do anything about it.

"You still want your girl back?" Atibon seemed surprised that he had to explain the point.

"We had a deal." Moog jumped. "You said you'd get her—"

Atibon stopped him quickly. "I said if you brought me my boy back, I'd *help* you get your daughter." He smiled and gestured to Daniel. "And here's your help."

Moog shook his head. "He's a lot of things, but he ain't help."

"And I'm out of this all the way around," Daniel insisted. "I've got nothing in this fight."

Atibon laughed. "You can't stop lying to yourself, can you, boy?"

"I'm grateful to Moog for everything he's done, but all I want right now is to get free of all of this."

"You ain't never gonna be free, boy." The old man's voice sounded sincerely sad to deliver the news.

The somber timbre took Daniel a bit off guard. "No, I'm—"

"You got every bit as much at stake as your friend there." Atibon nodded toward the big man. "Maybe more."

"Oh no," Daniel insisted. "I did what you asked. Our deal is done, and you and I are jake!"

Atibon wasn't impressed. "Maybe. But that don't change the fact that the same man gots his daughter, gots your woman too."

"First, she's not my woman." Daniel counted off emphatically. "Second, he doesn't *have* her. She's there because she wants to be."

"You don't know nuthin' 'bout women, do ya, son? Sometimes a woman will do things that she knows is gonna hurt her, just 'cause she feels bad 'bout herself and thinks she deserves it. Sometimes they're just lookin' to hurt you back. Sometimes they wanna see if you'll save them. And sometimes they just do stupid shit. None of that matters. The only thing that's important now is that you love her."

The accusation was outrageous, and Daniel wanted to tell him as much—but he couldn't say a word.

"You love her more than anything. And you know you're not going to just walk away and leave her where she is."

Daniel didn't have any words of denial for that either.

"There's a reason I brought you both here." Atibon looked at the pair as though he were a disappointed dad. "If the two of you can't put your past behind you and come together, then you don't have a goddamn future. And if the two of you fail now, then everything you done was for nuthin', and what you've fought against will rise up. If you ain't brothers, then you're nothing. And everything that matters to both of you—everything that matters in any way, at all—*everything* will all just go to hell."

Daniel and Moog both had something to say to that, and they might've continued walking and talking if all three of them hadn't noticed that the Mall had suddenly become crowded with men in

Park Service uniforms. A dozen men in ranger uniforms circled around them and closed in fast, keying walkie-talkies and calling in even more backup as they raced forward to close their trap.

"What's this?" Daniel wondered aloud, before he could react.

"This," the old man said with such certainty that it was almost as if he'd been expecting a confrontation, "this is the beginning."

"The beginning of what?"

"The end," Atibon said with resignation. Then he turned toward the advancing men and screamed back to Daniel and Moog, "Run!"

CHAPTER FOURTEEN

You Better Run

The initial contact team of twelve hired guns dressed as US Park Rangers had done their best to set up a perimeter around their subjects and gradually tighten it while they pretended to rake leaves and pick up litter. Slowly but surely, they had each worked closer and closer toward the trio until one of the three looked up and called out, "Run!"

Daniel turned on his heels, but everywhere he turned there were men running toward him.

"Run!" Atibon screamed again.

The word echoed in Daniel's ears, but he couldn't place its origin. Not until he felt the slap hit the back of his head. He turned around to find the old man pointing down toward the end of the mall. "Run!"

Daniel didn't take a step. "What about you?"

"Don't you worry 'bout me," Atibon yelled as he pushed Moog toward Daniel as if the big man were merely a recalcitrant child in his care. "I'm like catching a black cat's shadow on a moonless night. I'll buy you time, but you better get the hell out of here."

Daniel and Moog knew better than to argue. They turned and did as they were told. Without a word, they both picked the same hole in the tightening circle and ran toward it as hard as they could.

The approaching ranger blocking that gap caught the force of Moog's lowered shoulder before he could defend himself. The impact drove the man off of his feet, and he sailed backward ten feet before landing flat on his back.

Daniel and Moog ran past him, not slowing to look back at the growing numbers that were now joining the pursuit. They ran as hard as they could, but that wasn't really very hard at all. They'd each lived their life on the run, but ironically that hadn't included a lot of actual running. By the time the pair had made the lawns of the Washington Monument, there were six younger and much fitter men behind them and closing fast.

Daniel and Moog started across the street, neither of them paying the slightest attention to the oncoming cars that sounded their horns and squealed their brakes. They both kept moving, though their burning legs and heaving chests had slowed them to something less than a sprint.

"It's. No. Use," Moog exhaled between pained, labored breaths.

Daniel didn't have the wind necessary to disagree.

They reached the sidewalk safely enough, but each was silently resigned that there was little point in fighting, and even less in running. They pulled up and prepared themselves for a last stand of heavy-breathing fisticuffs on the sidewalk.

They turned to each other without wasting their breath on a sentimental expression of brotherhood that was really unnecessary with the fight of their lives imminent.

Thirty feet away.

Now twenty.

Now, there were a dozen men chasing after them, sprinting in unison across the street in matched, athletic strides that betrayed their military training.

Ten feet.

Moog and Daniel readied themselves for the opponents they knew they couldn't outlast. Each of them picked the one man they planned on hitting first. From there, they both knew, it would only be a matter of time.

What happened next took place so quickly that no one had a clear picture of exactly what happened.

The truck came out of nowhere.

Just as the first of the men was about to clear the street and reach the sidewalk where Daniel and Moog stood ready to fight, a Peterbilt tractor trailer hauling a load of restaurant supplies inexplicably ran the red light and seemed to accelerate. It struck three sedans and an SUV that had stopped for the light, and then pushed the automotive Twister pile straight toward and then over the dozen men who were rushing toward Daniel and Moog. None of them escaped the metal death trap as the tractor trailer shuddered to a stop, brakes squealing and tires smoking.

There were screams from some of the tourists who witnessed the event. Some yelled, "Someone call 911!" Others actually did. There were even more who simply stood by, stunned into silence by what they'd seen, and more than a few who reflexively pulled out their smart phones to be the first to get the carnage on the Internet.

Daniel and Moog took off again. Adrenaline-fueled, they made it to the Smithsonian Metro station without stopping.

"Come on," Daniel called as they started down the escalator that led into the bowels of Washington's subway system.

Moog took a step or two, but then hesitated. He understood the need to get as far away as possible and to do it as quickly as possible, but he hated the idea of heading down into the subway tunnel, where their movement would be restricted and they could be so easily trapped.

Daniel sensed he was alone in his descent and turned back to his friend. "Come on," he called, this time more than halfway down the escalator steps.

Moog took another step, but couldn't convince himself to commit. It was all too easy and obvious. "It's a trap," he called down to Daniel. But his friend was too far down the hole to hear.

"What?"

"It's a trap," Moog shouted even as he struggled to move up the down escalator. "Otherwise they would have had people posted here just in case—" He stopped midwarning.

Moving in on the station were a pair of black SUVs and all of the tactical personnel he'd expected to be there. Whatever escape route they had back out on the Mall was now closed.

Moog turned on the steps. There was only one way out now, and he headed down the escalator as quickly as he could, taking the steps four and five at a time. He was only halfway down when he realized that it was already over.

At the bottom of the escalator, Daniel stood with his hands high above his head, surrounded by six men.

Two of them turned and began to move toward Moog, almost nonchalantly, as if they were expecting the big man to realize that there was no longer any point in running. Or fighting.

Moog thought otherwise. The big man hit the complacent pair like Adrian Peterson moving through a prepubescent D-line in a Pop Warner game, sending them both flying across the station platform.

The four still guarding Daniel turned, genuinely surprised by the speed that such a big man could generate under the circumstances.

In the near distance, three tones signaled that a train was leaving the platform below. Without stopping, Moog rushed toward the group, wrapped his arm around Daniel's waist and took him along as if he were merely a bag of groceries.

The big man ran straight for the concourse wall. Behind him he heard somebody holler, "Stop!" Instead, Moog leapt into the air, still carrying his friend tucked under his arm. The pair cleared the concourse wall easily, and then began to fall.

Daniel screamed as they dropped through the air.

And then just as suddenly, they hit the steel roof of the metro train as it started out of the station. The impact was jarring, and Daniel rolled free of his friend's embrace. He slid across the smooth metal, unable to gain a handhold to stop himself from falling free of the car.

Moog's hand caught Daniel's just as the rest of his body slid over the edge. He dangled for a second, looking first through the windows at the startled passengers inside the car, then in the direction they were headed—straight into the tunnel.

Daniel scrambled to climb up as Moog struggled to pull him. Together they just managed to get Daniel to the top of the car as it plunged into the dark confines of the tunnel.

Both men flattened themselves against the roof of the car to avoid the formed cement ceiling passing overhead at sixty miles an hour.

"Are you sure about this?" Daniel screamed over the noise of the subway train as it shot through the darkness.

"You rather be standing back there with your hands all up in the air?"

"I'm just saying—"

A light became visible at the end of the tunnel as the train began to slow for its arrival at the next station. A voice called over the PA system: "Next stop Metro Center." But the doors of the train never opened.

Instead, the waiting platform was lined with men in full tactical dress. All of them held automatic weapons aimed at the roof of the train.

Daniel and Moog looked down at the scene and calculated the odds of continuing their improbable escape.

Moog shook his head. "This shit the end of the line."

"Yeah," Daniel agreed, but then smiled. "But the mojo will make something happen." He was certain of that. "It always does."

CHAPTER FIFTEEN

How to Write a Pop Song

Vicki had gotten used to Haden Koschei's "visits."

Maybe even learned to look forward to them. To long for them. To fantasize about them in all the ways that were possible to lose herself—and find some brief respite from the darkness she tried so desperately to contain within herself—during that time when she was freed from the burden of being herself and reduced to nothing more than a something that someone else used for their own pleasure.

She was aware that some people would've found the relationship degrading. Daniel, with all of his overly simplistic moral judgments about right and wrong and good and evil, would've looked down on her in that condescending way she hated him for. He would have told her she'd made herself a servant or a slave, maybe even a whore.

She *knew* that's what Daniel would think. And she hated him for it.

He'd said he'd loved her, but that wasn't how it turned out in the end. He was too small-minded and full of fear to really love her, to love the *real* her. Instead, he shone a light on all of the things she hated about herself. She couldn't help but see herself through his eyes. And she hated him for that more than anything.

And the more she hated Daniel, the more pleasure and release she found beneath her new master. If Daniel couldn't love the real her, at least Haden Koschei would fuck it.

"What are they doing here?" Vicki asked, making zero effort to hide either her disappointment or annoyance that Haden Koschei had arrived for their usual session with two shapely friends in tow.

Vicki knew the brunette as Angelina Silvano, Koschei's mistress—which was to say the woman he took out to dinner before he fucked her. Vicki had met her a few times at this party or that event, and the two women had developed an instant enmity for one another.

The surgically enhanced blond was another of Koschei's protégées, whom Vicki knew only by her stage name: Hellena. Her airbrushed image and Auto-Tuned voice were everywhere. Vicki didn't like anything about her either.

"Right now," Angelina muttered as she walked past her inhospitable hostess and looked disapprovingly around the monochromatic apartment, "I'm being bored to death." She turned to the old man and purred, "Can we go now, Haden? There's nothing here of any interest."

Hellena looked about the place and reached a different conclusion. "Oh, I love it. It's so . . ." She looked straight at Vicki and flashed a capped smile. "You."

Besides a fierce pout, Angelina wore red Manolo Blahnik heels and a red bandage dress that, while fitted to accentuate her curves, seemed designed to be taken off. Hellena was (barely) dressed in a white peignoir-inspired dress that was mostly lace and very little else.

Individually, either woman would have been intimidating. Together, as arm candy bookends, they made Vicki feel more than a little frumpish in her well-worn jeans and ribbed, white wifebeater, and she couldn't help but pick and fuss at her cuticles and nails.

"Now, now, my dear." Koschei went over to Angelina and petted her long, black hair as though her head were a cat in his lap. "Play nice."

She turned to him and let the very corners of her scarlet-painted lips turn seductively. "I'd rather play naughty."

Vicki rolled her eyes pointedly, but neither of them seemed to notice. Or, at least, let on.

"There's time enough for all that," Koschei assured her, ignoring the flash of jealousy in Vicki's eyes but noting it with pleasure. "Let's hear what she has to play before we dismiss her so quickly." He returned the same sort of wickedly knowing smirk. "Or rush on to the festivities."

Koschei turned to Vicki. "You go into the studio next week, and I thought Angelina and Hellena might have different perspectives to bring to your music." He flashed them both a knowing glance, which Vicki read as an implication that there was some need for a different perspective. "What do you have to play for us?"

Environment is an essential component of every singer's performance. Six eyes staring up at her from her corporate-rental couch was not what Vicki would've considered a performance-enhancing environment. Still, what was there to do? The rent had to be paid—one way or another.

As soon as Vicki reached for her acoustic guitar, Angelina let out a strained sigh.

"What?" Vicki asked, self-consciously adjusting the instrument's strap around her shoulder.

"1997 called. It wants you to grow your pits and get back for Lilith," Angelina sniped.

"What are you talking about?" Vicki knew exactly what she meant, but it was the first (and best) retort she could think of under the circumstances.

"I mean, it's the twenty-first century, for God's sake. Playing an instrument is so . . ." She paused to find just the right word. "Unnecessary."

"You mean unnecessary to make music?" Vicki meant her question to underscore the absurdity of Angelina's comment, but it did not have the desired effect.

"Yes," she answered matter-of-factly. "From the crows' feet around your eyes, I can understand that maybe they're a little *after* your time, but they have these things these days called com . . . pu . . . ters." She sounded it all out in case Vicki was slow on the uptake. "*That's* how we make music today."

"It's really easy," Hellena agreed. "You don't even have to worry about singing the right notes or anything." She laughed a bubbly laugh, and Koschei patted her on the thigh as a reward for being a good girl.

Angelina looked Vicki up and down. "I suppose if you wanted an electric guitar, as a prop, I mean. You know, like Madonna uses sometimes. An electric guitar looks like a big phallus. I suppose they could do something with you swinging a big dick in front of you. But that big wooden thing you've got there just makes you look like . . ." She paused again for a vocabulary search. "Like you belong at a Renaissance fair or something."

Koschei was clearly amused, and his sly smile was more aggravating (and hurtful) to Vicki than any of the things that

Angelina had said. He patted the significant portion of thigh that was left uncovered by her dress. "Now, now. Pull your claws in, kitty. Why don't we just let Vicki play us something before we get all scratch post on her."

Angelina tossed her head as both a concession and a statement of her complete lack of interest in whatever was about to happen next.

Koschei nodded at Vicki and offered her a glance that silently challenged her to impress him.

Vicki plucked the strings one by one. E. A. D. G. B. E. If a tone didn't strike her ear correctly, she twisted the corresponding tuning peg until her instrument was tuned to her liking.

"This sucks," Angelina hissed. "Can we go now?"

Koschei smiled and tightened his grip on her thigh. "Just give her a chance."

Vicki grimaced, but tried not to let on that the display bothered her.

She took a few deep breaths to try to lessen her mounting nerves, but the tactic didn't work. The tension mounted, and the first few chords she played squeaked beneath her trembling fingers. Her attempts to find the key with her voice led to a series of unintended notes that cracked and strayed in the most embarrassing way.

"Was that the song?" Angelina asked.

"I don't think that was the song," Koschei mock-answered, and then playfully turned to Vicki. "That wasn't the song, was it?"

"No." Whatever positive energy she'd been able to generate for her command performance had leaked out of her like the air from a birthday balloon ten days after the candles have been blown out.

"Then why don't you play it for us now?"

Without wasting words, she adjusted the guitar strap and began to play again, this time with a recognizable sense of purpose. "I call this one 'My Ink.'"

Angelina groaned for effect. Koschei patted her thigh and nodded a request for continued patience. And silence.

Vicki didn't see the gesture. Her eyes were closed, and she began to sing.

Some of my triumphs, most of my sins
They are etched here on my skin
For any of my lovers to see
But when taken as a whole
They sing a song that stirs my soul
Yeah, my ink, it tells the story of me.

There's a little girl I used to know
And one I used to be
There's a flower for one that never was.
There's—

"Oh my God," Angelina erupted. "Is this for real?"

"It's kinda good. I guess," Hellena offered, but it was clear her opinion was as fake as almost everything else about her.

Koschei smiled patiently and prompted her to silence. "It does seem a little too . . ." He turned to Vicki. "Sincere."

Of all of the songs she'd written in her life—and she'd written hundreds —Vicki had never penned one to which she felt such a strong emotional connection. The lyrics were a confession she'd never thought she'd have the courage to say aloud, much less share with the world in song. She recoiled at the critique. "Sincerity's a bad thing?"

"No," Angelina hissed sarcastically. "It's the *worst* thing. No one does sincerity anymore." She reconsidered. "I mean, unless you're trying to win *Idol* or *X-Factor* or *The Voice*. Or I suppose if you're working that Jesus con like Carrie Underwood. Then you've gotta be overly sincere, but that's not *real* sincerity. Nobody does that today."

"I think sincere is really hard to do," the blond offered.

Koschei pretended to understand how the cruel words stung Vicki. He got up from the couch, put his arm around her, and led her back to a position uncomfortably close to her musical nemesis.

"Making a pop song," he said with patronizing patience, "is like making anything else of value. There's a blueprint, a recipe, a formula that must be followed."

"There's no recipe for art," Vicki objected.

"We're not talking about art," Koschei corrected sharply. "There's no money in art. We're talking about commerce. And there's a definite blueprint to writing a pop song."

"And just what is the formula?" Vicki asked, though her question was more a statement of disagreement than a genuine inquiry.

"It varies from performer to performer," he admitted. "But, with women, we always build on sex." Koschei stated the principle like it should've been understood all along. "And in today's market the key is to ratchet the sex up a notch or two."

"And what exactly does that mean?"

"It means a couple years ago you could get a hit just by kissing a girl or pretending you get off with whips and chains. But that's all been done now. There's little pageant girls and Kidz with a *z* singing that ass-stuffing 'Can't Stop' twerk shit. If you want to have a hit today, you're going to need to take the sexual taboo even further."

"My single is called, 'Gotta Do Me,'" Hellena volunteered cheerfully.

Vicki was more than a little uncomfortable with the turn of the conversation. "You say all of this like you've got something in mind."

"We do," Angelina said, reaching into her purse and retrieving a piece of paper.

Its appearance concerned Vicki. "What's that?"

"Perhaps we should have handled things a little more delicately," Koschei advised his friend as he took the paper from her and handed it to Vicki. "This is a little something that I had written for you."

"I wrote it," Angelina stressed. "So I'm going to get sole writing credit on it."

"Sole writing credit on what?" Vicki asked before realizing she was holding a lyric sheet.

"What do you think?" Koschei asked hopefully.

"What do I think?" Vicki couldn't believe the old man could have any question about how she'd feel.

"That's what he asked you."

Vicki shook her head in disbelief and read from the lyric sheet in the most distressed, monotonous voice she could manage.

Boy, you know I like you. I like your friend too.
I like all your bad boys and I know what we can do.
I want to get filthy. Yeah, I want to get insane.
Get your bros together and I'll pull the love train.
Love train.
Love train.
I'll pull the love train.

Vicki looked up from the paper. "Love train?"

"It's a little different from the O'Jays song," Koschei admitted. "But this is *hot*. It's today."

"You think this is hot?" Vicki asked, with a mixture of disbelief and uncertainty.

"I think it's hot," Hellena said, which explained at last to Vicki why Koschei had brought her along.

"The important thing is what do *you* think?" Koschei asked with uncharacteristic enthusiasm. "Isn't it great?"

"No," Vicki said. "It's not great."

"All right, it's not great," he conceded, and he patted Angelina's hand before she could disrupt the discussion with her objections. "Maybe it's not great, but it's a guaranteed hit. And that's more important than great."

"A lot more important," Angelina concurred.

"I'll sing it if she doesn't want it," Hellena chirped.

Vicki was far from convinced. "Are you kidding me with this?"

"Don't you get it?" Koschei seemed genuinely concerned that she might not have grasped his marketing angle. "We've already had all the naughty girl songs we can take. That's tame now. We've done *ménage à trois* and S and M. There's more women rapping about anal than anyone knows what to do with. There's really not all that much that's left untouched." He smiled, "No pun intended."

Angelina laughed. Vicki didn't.

"Anyway, if you're going to have a hit you're going to need something that's going to not only shock but titillate the public, and that's almost impossible to do anymore. But,"—he raised his long, thin finger for emphasis—"a woman having sex simultaneously with a lot of men—"

"I know what pulling a train is," Vicki interrupted impatiently.

"I'll bet you do," Angelina sneered.

Vicki had had enough, and she turned to the woman, intending to make her objections—and maybe her fist—felt.

Koschei raised a hand to stop her. "The point is that you'll be recording it—"

"I won't be recording this," Vicki assured him.

"Really? Then I'd advise you to take a look at the contract you signed. I'm paying the bills and *I* determine what you record. So I'm telling you that not only are you going to record 'Love Train,' but it's going to be your first single."

"I'm not going to record this," Vicki insisted.

Koschei didn't seem so sure. "Really?"

Vicki was adamant. "Really."

"Well, then I'll have to terminate our agreement and look into remedies provided for in the contract. I assume you have the money necessary to make the payment." His eyes made clear that he wasn't joking. Or bluffing. "And I assume that you won't mind saying good-bye to all of this," he gestured around the luxury apartment. "And killing your dreams."

Vicki didn't have the money. The words to respond. Or any other dream to substitute for the one she'd been pursuing for what seemed like her entire life. "No."

Koschei acknowledged their understanding with a smile and walked over to her. He took the guitar from around her neck and tossed it to the ground, not caring that it landed with a terrible clang and a crash. "Then I would study those lyrics." He put his hands on her hips and pulled her to him. She felt him hard against her, and the sensation filled her with an ecstasy that wiped all other concerns from her mind.

"OK," she said, and then let his mouth fill hers.

He pulled his lips from hers and whispered, "And I would be ready to record that first."

"OK." She returned her mouth to his, triumphant that he'd chosen her over Angelina.

And then Angelina's hands were on Vicki too. And then Hellena's. It was an odd sensation—three sets of hands exploring her at once—but not unwelcome. She still hated Angelina, and thought Hellena was an idiot, but the kisses and nibbles on the nape of her neck made her let out a low moan.

"You'll need to really sell that song," Koschei said, his hands ably working the buttons of her jeans.

"I will," Vicki said as she let him.

"Really sell it," Angelina stressed.

"I will," she said in something of a pleasured groan.

"Well, just to be sure," Angelina purred, as her hands ran under Vicki's tank top, "we've prepared a little surprise for you."

Vicki had completely surrendered to the moment. And to all three of her houseguests. "Surprise?"

Angelina pulled away from the writhing entanglement long enough to retrieve her iPhone from her purse. She made her call and waited for the connection. "Yeah," she said to the lucky person who answered. "It's me. Send up the boys."

Vicki pulled away from Koschei and Hellena, startled but not alarmed. "What?"

Angelina tossed the phone to the couch and sauntered back to the trio. She pulled off Vicki's top, then smiled wickedly. "Choo-choo!"

CHAPTER SIXTEEN

Tied Up, Taken Away

The sharp ache at the base of his skull was almost excruciating enough to convince Daniel he'd finally returned to some level of awareness. On the other hand, the total darkness in which he was immersed argued that the pain had merely invaded the black hole of unconsciousness.

Somewhere in between the two there were fleeting memories of a Metro station platform and one last mad dash toward what he'd hoped was freedom. Then came a fuzzier image of men in tactical gear appearing at the top of the escalator Daniel was climbing. There was a boot to Daniel's chest, and then a long, bumpy ride down the up escalator. A stinging, sharp pain in his right arm, and then . . .

Daniel couldn't recall anything more. Just the shot in the arm.

The debate over the state of his senses was settled once and for all by the sensation of something rough rubbing against his face. It wasn't stiff like a concrete floor or the boards of a crate, but flexible like fabric. The realization convinced him that he was now very much awake—with a cloth bag over his head.

Although still disoriented, his senses were returning gradually. First, with a sharp pain in his wrists that let him know his hands were bound behind him. The restraints were sharp and had cut off his circulation, but they weren't cold like handcuffs. He assumed they'd secured him with zip ties.

Next came the realization that he was lying down. On his side.

The surface beneath him was smooth and cool like metal. And every once in a while there was a sharp jolt that would bounce him up in the air and allow him to fall back down.

His ears were ringing with a loud droning sound that rarely changed tone. *An engine*, he thought.

Underneath the unwavering hum, he could detect a sharp, sibilant hissing. It made him think of tires on wet pavement.

Daniel put all of the pieces together and came to the conclusion that he was in a van—maybe, the back of a truck, although he didn't think so—rolling along at highway speed over wet pavement.

What Daniel couldn't tell from any of the sensory clues around him was whether he was alone. "Moog!" he shouted as loudly as his dry throat would let him.

The only reply was a sharp kick in the back. The pain convinced Daniel that, whether or not his friend was along for the ride, he was most certainly not alone.

A second or two later: "I'm here, man!"

Daniel was relieved to hear the big man's voice. But pained by the groan that followed a moment later.

"Two of you shut up!" The voice was loud, but not strained by the volume, like it was used to shouting. *Military*, Daniel thought. Another kick in the gut seemed to confirm his deduction.

Bound and bagged, there was nothing Daniel could do but lie as still as possible and try to regain the breath that the boot had knocked out of him. He forced himself to take short, steady breaths and, as he did, he focused on the future.

A time was coming. Daniel was certain of that.

Maybe it would arrive soon. Perhaps it would take a little longer. But a time was coming when the restraints would be loosed and the bag removed. If he was patient and waited for the mojo, an opportunity would present itself, and he—and Moog—would have the chance to take up their grievances with Sergeant Shouty. And when that time came, Daniel was determined to make the most of it.

* * *

He heard the squeal of breaks beneath him, and the numbing drone of the engine gave way to silence.

It was almost impossible for Daniel to maintain a reliable sense of time with a sack over his head. He had no idea whether it was day or night, but he guessed that an hour (maybe two) had passed since his painful interaction with Sergeant Shouty.

Booted feet stomped to attention as men—more than just Sergeant Shouty—stood up. A second later a metal door clanked open, letting in a blast of fresh air. Wherever they were, it was colder than DC, and the air was much sweeter. Even with a sack over his head, Daniel could tell the air smelled impossibly sweet.

"Get up!" Sergeant Shouty screamed.

Hands grabbed Daniel's arms and lifted them until he had little choice but to comply with the barked orders or have his limbs pulled from their sockets. Another hand landed on the top of his head and forced him to bend down and forward as he was led off of whatever type of vehicle he'd been transported in.

He took a step forward, but it was a real bitch. Hours of lying in such an uncomfortable position had left his legs riddled with pins and needles. Daniel put a tingling foot down, but his numbed legs couldn't support his weight and he tumbled forward.

Instinctively, Daniel's body tensed and twisted in midair to avoid a straight face-plant, but he still hit the ground hard, landing on his side with a thud.

The ground beneath him was wet. His pants and shirt were soaked in an instant, and a second later, his body was chilled.

"On your feet, asshole!" Sergeant Shouty's voice again.

More hands picked Daniel up, set him on his feet, and pushed him forward.

He took a staggering step, then another, shuffling along not to keep up but merely to keep from falling. Every uncertain step was an effort, but a hand repeatedly pushed him from behind to make him move faster.

"Get moving, asshole!"

A time was coming.

And when it came, Daniel was going to hurt Sergeant Shouty. Bad.

* * *

The sweetness in the air was suddenly replaced with the stale scent of air conditioning, and Daniel realized he'd been led into a building of some sort. He heard several locks click. Big locks. Institutional locks.

He felt like they were moving down long hallways. There was at least one trip on an elevator. A final hallway. Then the slamming of a door.

The edge of a chair hit Daniel in the back of the knees, and he fell helplessly back into the seat. A hand pushed him forward and another grabbed his bound hands. Snip. His hands were free for a moment, but then seized again and secured to the arms of the chair.

Next, the sack came off, and it seemed like the room was suddenly filled with the light of a thousand suns. Daniel slammed his straining eyes shut, but he couldn't squeeze them tightly enough to keep them burning from the brightness.

"Open your eyes!" Sergeant Shouty ordered.

Daniel squinted, not in compliance, but just to sneak a peek at the face he was going to step on before much longer. "Who the hell are you?"

The face came closer until its nose was just about touching Daniel's. "Take a good look and tell me you don't know me."

The features seemed too soft to be military, even with a large burn scar over the left half of the face. There was an arrogant air to the man that made Daniel rethink his initial assessment. Not military. Feds.

"Never saw you before in my life," Daniel answered. "And with that char-grilled, DQ Brazier burger thing you got going on with your face there, I think I'd remember."

The comment earned Daniel a fist to his already swollen nose.

"Take a good look," the man insisted, his anger leashed—but just barely.

Daniel took a closer look. "Still got nothing for you."

"My name is Tom Connors," the man said, clearly thinking the name would jog his memory.

"Like the drink?" Daniel asked, just to see what would happen if the anger slipped its leash.

Another fist.

"Not Collins. Connors. Tom Connors," the man stressed.

"Come on," Daniel groaned. "Even you have to admit that's a generic name. How am I supposed to remember . . . ?"

The man pointed to the scar that covered half of his face. "Because you did *this*."

Daniel shook his head, not to be antagonistic, but because he truly had no idea what the man was talking about. "I think I'd remember something like that."

"Do you remember a house in St. Thomas?"

Daniel's silence was an unintended admission.

"And a task force raid on that house?"

More incriminating silence.

"A house that you rigged with explosives to detonate—"

"Slow down, Joe False Flag," Daniel protested. "I couldn't rig a bottle rocket to go off on the Fourth of July. The place had a stove with a lousy gas line, and you had a pudgy guy on your team with an itchy trigger finger. If you've got a score to settle with someone for flash frying your face, it's with Porky, not me."

If Connor's convictions were shaken by Daniel's disclosure, it only made him yell even louder. "You're the reason I was there, Erickson."

"I didn't invite you over for drinks," Daniel pointed out. "You guys showed up all on your own. And then one of your own goes and blows my house up, and you're walking around all this time with a hard-on for me?" There was no effort to conceal the ridiculousness he found in the situation. "You've gotta be kidding me."

"No. I'm not kidding you." The stern sneer that stretched the scar tissue across the man's face was proof of that. "And there's nothing I'd rather do than drop you in a hole right now."

"Nothing?" Daniel shook his head in mock disappointment. "This world would be so much better off if all you assholes with guns and agendas just wanted to do something fun and reasonable, like dance with a pretty girl or walk a damn dog on the beach."

"You think you're funny?"

"No, not funny. I'm blessed. Or cursed. Depends how you look at it." Daniel had more or less given up on figuring out the elusive difference between the two. "But I'm sealed in a bargain with this guy who stepped from the shadows down the Crossroads—you know with Robert Johnson and all that."

If the reference registered with Connors, the recognition didn't show on his face.

"The guy's a real mojo magic dude, I promise you," Daniel said, as if it were all that simple.

Connors was equally unimpressed.

"Anyway," Daniel continued. "All I can tell you is that at any moment *something* is going to happen. I've got absolutely no idea *what*, but something. And when that shit goes down, it's going to turn all of this upside down."

"Is that right?"

Daniel nodded confidently. "It's guaran-goddamn-teed. And that's why the other thing you need to be aware of right now is that—while I know I don't look all that menacing to someone like you, with the badass combat scar and the Nick Fury wardrobe—that man's mojo has made me scary good at hurting people. And if I'm completely honest with you, your little temper tantrum here has landed you on my Top Ten Fools I'm Going to Put in Traction list."

Connors struck him with a tightly closed fist. "How about now?"

Daniel tried to shake the dizziness from his head and casually spit blood on the floor. "You just made Number One. With a bullet."

"Oh, you've got a bullet in your future, but the only thing that's going to happen now is that I'm going to ask you some questions and you're going to tell me everything I want to know, not because you're afraid I'm going to kill you, but because you're trying to get in my good graces so that I will. I'm going to hurt you so bad and so long that you're going to forget what it was ever like to not be screaming."

"I understand that you think so. But you're not going to get that chance." Daniel smiled self-consciously, like he owed his interrogator an apology for what was about to happen. "It's just the mojo."

"Trust me," Connors hissed. "There is nothing of heaven or earth that could save you from me right now."

"Maybe not heaven or earth." Daniel was willing to concede. "But there's a third option you're overlooking." Daniel's grin grew and his eyes grew wide with wonderment. "Something is about to happen. And it's gonna be a motherfucker."

CHAPTER SEVENTEEN

No More Mr. Nice Guy

The brick building sat not quite out of sight at the end of a long, winding drive, tucked behind a thick stand of blue spruce. A concertina wire–topped chain-link fence ran along the perimeter of the five-acre property to keep out the nosier neighbors. The only clue to what went on within the mysterious walls was a simple sign near the front gate that read "Teller Tech."

In the absence of any facts about the actual nature of the activities within the compound, the good folks of Scott Township simply created rumors.

The most popular story was that it was a medical research facility, and more than a few of the regulars who gathered every morning at the counter of the Scott Sixty Truck Stop for a cup of coffee and a spot of conversation claimed to have seen one cryptic monstrosity or another in the woods adjacent to the place.

A younger crowd swore the place was a drug lab where crack and meth first had been invented, and later produced in order to fund black bag operations that even Congress couldn't countenance. And still others were certain that the facility was a mind control center funded by the New World Order. Or Scientologists. Or aliens? Or was it the Alien Scientologists' New World Order?

Still, for all the locals' conjecturing and creative hypotheses, not even the woman who sat at the receptionist desk in the building's outer office was entirely certain what went on beyond the door behind her station. Instead, Linda Krushinsky kept her focus (and curiosity) contained to the small reception area she oversaw.

The space was no bigger than forty square feet and occupied by nothing more than Linda at the receptionist's desk and three molded plastic chairs placed against the far wall. It wasn't much, but it was her domain and she took overseeing the space very, very seriously.

So, when a man who wasn't on her visitor log (it was completely empty for the entire week) walked into her waiting room, she straightened her back and greeted him with a "May I help you?" that really meant "You're in the wrong goddamn place, and you need to turn yourself around and get the hell out of here."

Gerald Feller ignored the clear instruction contained in her tone, and instead smiled brightly. "Actually, I'm here to help you."

She found the stranger's cheerfulness unnerving. "Excuse me?"

Feller was pleased to have captured her interest and full attention. "You have a family."

"Whether I have a family's not really any of your business." Her thick hand dropped to her lap as casually as someone reaching for an under-the-desk alarm button could manage.

Feller took note, but seemed unconcerned. "That wasn't really a question, Linda."

She froze, knowing she hadn't told him her name and certain that there wasn't any good way he could have known on his own.

"That was a statement of fact." His chilling smile turned into a cruel sneer. "Just like it's a fact that if you touch that Honeywell 5869 wireless panic switch under your desk, I'm going back out that door to empty my Springfield .45 into the trunk of my car." He pulled back his suit coat to reveal the piece he was talking about.

"And that would be a personal tragedy for you because your husband, Jack, perky Bethany-Anne, and little Jack Jr. are all bound and gagged in there." He took a minute for the shock to hit her like a sledgehammer between an aged cow's eyes. "That's not a threat. Just another statement of fact."

Linda's hand trembled just above the alarm button. "What do you want?"

"I gave up a long time ago on what I *want*," Feller said. "This is more a matter of *need*. And right now I need something behind Door Number One." He nodded at the door behind her which she'd never opened.

"I don't know what you're talking about."

He smiled and nodded. "I understand." He pulled his pistol as promised and turned to go. "I only hope your family does, because I'm going to tell them 'Mommy sent me!' right before I start shooting."

Linda's heart raced faster than her thoughts. "No, wait. Stop."

He did.

"What is it, Linda? Do you know what I'm talking about or shall I set you free from the ball and chain of a husband and kids?"

"A truck came in this morning," she offered him. "That's all I know."

He shook his head in mock regret. "Well, that's too bad for hubby and the rug rats because I already know that."

"I don't know what's in there," she pleaded. "I swear to God."

"All the way to God?" He sneered. "Well, suppose you let me have a look for myself."

"I . . . can't . . . do . . . that." Her shoulders shook with great sobs gasped out between her words.

"We both know that's a lie." He stared at her with dead-certain eyes. "It'd be a shame to lose your family for nothing more than a stupid little lie."

She mumbled something beneath her tears, but it was clear she understood. Her trembling hands reached for a button.

Feller raised his pistol as a warning. "No alarms, Linda."

She took her finger away from the panic switch and reached instead for the Cobra electric "Buzz In" door-lock release.

The door behind her buzzed and, for the first time in the six years she'd worked there, swung partly open.

Feller crossed the room to it and pushed it open. "See, it was all *this* simple."

She couldn't stop crying.

"And it all worked out just fine in the end. Didn't it?" He smiled. "And just so you know"—a pregnant pause—"I don't have Jack or your kids in my car." He laughed like it had all been a joke that she should have seen through from the moment he'd first told it.

She laughed nervously too. Not because she found any humor in her terror, but because she was overcome with relief.

"I mean, really, what kind of monster do you think I am?"

Before she could answer, he shot her once in the chest.

He stepped through the door and left her to die alone.

CHAPTER EIGHTEEN

Set You Free

Daniel spit blood on the concrete floor and tried to pretend the last blow across his face hadn't hurt any worse than the dozen before. "What alphabet agency did you say was responsible for violating my constitutional rights right now?"

Connors's scar twisted with his smile. "Oh, you *wish* we were government."

"Why's that?"

"Because the government has rules to follow. Limits on what it can do. And what it can't." Another blow to the face made his point. "That's why the government is transitioning out of high value interrogations and privatizing."

Daniel tried to act nonchalant as he spit out more blood, but the thick red stuff sliding down the back of his throat only added to his growing nausea. He stifled a gag reflex and forced himself to ask, "If you're not law enforcement?"

"Consider us more *policy* enforcement. Private consultants."

"Like a think tank for thugs."

Connors smiled. "Exactly." And then he hit Daniel again.

The interrogation began in earnest. "You've been in some rather odd places lately."

"You have no idea."

"Asking some rather odd questions."

Daniel was exhausted, almost too tired to speak. "You can't learn if you don't ask."

"And just what exactly have you learned?"

"That a lot of terribly talented people have died a lot of terribly suspicious deaths."

Connors nodded. "And who have you talked to about this?"

"I told the man who sent me."

This seemed to be of great interest to Connors. "And who is that?"

"I'm not sure I know," Daniel answered without any intent to be deceitful. "I'm only sure that you wouldn't believe me if I told you."

"Tell me what you know about Siren Song," Connors demanded.

There was a knock at the door, three simple raps as if a neighbor had come to borrow sugar. Connors turned and went to answer, obviously annoyed by the unexpected interruption. "What is it?"

Connors opened the door and was shocked to find that the St. Thomas reunion in Interrogation Room Number One had been joined by another familiar face. "Feller?" The name was spoken with equal parts shock and disgust, as if it were the diagnosis of a social disease Connors had contracted.

"Oh my God!" Feller exclaimed, his voice lilting like an excited sorority girl. "Tom Connors. I totally did not expect to find you here. I thought you were still with the Bureau."

"I left. Six months ago." Connors was clearly stunned by the appearance of the man who had led him into that hellish house in St. Thomas. "What are you doing here? There's no way that Cold Water hired you." He'd intended it as a definitive statement, but it conveyed a good deal of confusion about what exactly was unfolding.

Daniel, however, was completely certain. "Mojo. I told you so."

Connors looked back at him in reproach.

"Here we go." Daniel nodded toward the visitor at the door, enjoying the realization in his inquisitor's eyes that the situation had veered inexplicably and dangerously out of his control.

Connors only stared back at him, as if he were waiting for Daniel to offer up a new prophecy that would tell him what to do.

Daniel had one. "I'm pretty sure he's going to kill you now."

Connors instinctively reached for his sidearm, but Cold Water Corporate Protocol AA-0.36 required personal firearms to be locked up during all private subject-interview sessions. His hand made it to the holster at the small of his back, but came away empty.

It probably wouldn't have made any difference. The shot from Feller's .45 had torn through Connor's gut before he ever would've had the chance to fire his weapon.

"You're gut shot," Feller announced as he looked down at the man squealing and squirming on the ground at his feet. "Real bad. You're going to die soon, but it's going to hurt worse and worse until you do."

Blood was already pooling in his mouth, but Connors still managed to force out a "Help" and a "me." It was excruciating to mutter each word, and taken together they were absolutely pointless.

"Help you?" Feller asked, enjoying every sadistic moment. "Like you helped me when you demanded they discipline me? Like when you pushed me out of the Bureau? When they took everything I ever had? When my wife left me?"

Connors wasn't in any shape to answer any of the questions.

"Yeah, I'll help you. Just like you helped me." Feller put his right foot on the scarred side of the fallen man's face.

At first, Connors struggled to free himself from beneath the cordovan lace-up, but Feller steadily put more and more of his weight down until, at last, his full weight was on the man's head.

Tom Connors died that way, under the foot of Gerald Feller.

Daniel wasn't frightened by what had just played out in front of him, but he was curious. "Now what?"

"Now," Feller said as he pulled a knife from his coat pocket, "you meet a fate far worse than poor Tom there." He went over to the chair and cut the zip ties securing Daniel's wrists to the arms of the chair. "Now we go see a mutual friend."

Daniel rubbed his wrists, though he knew it would be a while until the circulation returned—and that it would hurt like hell when it did. "And just who would that be?"

Feller smiled. "Haden Koschei."

"He's not really a friend of mine."

"No." That they agreed on this point pleased Feller more than anything. "No, he's not."

CHAPTER NINETEEN

They've Come to Take Me Home

"Where the hell do you think you're going?" Feller called after Daniel, who was headed in the opposite direction down the hall.

"I'm looking for my friend." The answer was a simple one and didn't distract Daniel from checking each locked door as he passed.

"Well, quit it and get your ass back here." Feller reached for the pistol he'd only just holstered. "I've got nothing to do with anyone but you, and you're coming with me."

Daniel wasn't concerned about the gun or the man carrying it. "I have no idea what your loco honcho wants with me or why he's gone to such lengths to take me alive."

Feller's eyes widened at the realization that he'd been uncovered.

"Don't look surprised." Daniel shook the locked knob of yet another door. "It's a real challenge for a pudgy guy like you to get all stealthy. Being followed by you all around England was like getting stalked by an overfed groundhog."

Feller silently bristled.

"I know you tried your best," Daniel consoled him. "Of course, that still isn't very good. But right now, what we need to focus on is that we both know you can't afford to shoot me. That's just a fact."

There was no point in arguing the point, and Feller didn't try.

"And *that* means that you can't afford to have anyone *else* shoot me," Daniel pointed out. "So I'm going to charge along these corridors, banging on doors and whatnot, trying to find my friend, because I'm not leaving this place without him."

"Oh, you're leaving here all right."

Daniel called the bluff by banging on another door. "But seeing as I don't have a gun, there's a strong likelihood that I'm going to get killed if one of these doors opens up and one of Connors's playmates finds me here." He paused for Feller to calculate the ramifications. "And that brings us right back to the part of our story where you need me alive for Koschei."

Feller tried to pretend the point wasn't checkmate.

"Now I don't know your boss much better than I'm betting you do," Daniel continued. "But we both know you don't want to disappoint him. So, if I were you, I'd hurry up and take the point, and help me find my friend, because we're running out of time to get gone before someone sends in a badass cleanup crew."

Feller wanted time to think everything over, but there wasn't a minute to be had. The big prize was behind Door Number Four. Daniel banged on it and a second later a man in a polo shirt just like Connors's came storming out.

"What the hell?" the man exclaimed as he reached for Daniel. Just then, his peripheral vision caught the figure standing twenty feet down the hall. He turned, but it was already too late.

Feller's shot took the man square in the chest.

A second later, Daniel instinctively dropped to the floor beside the corpse. Bits of concrete and dust flew in the air as a shot from inside the interrogation room bit into the wall where Daniel had been standing a heartbeat earlier.

The shooter moved out into the hall, assuming that he'd hit Daniel and that there'd only been one shooter down in the maze.

It was a fatal mistake. Feller's shot hit the man in the left temple and exited the right.

When the smoke cleared, Daniel got to his feet. He looked down the hall toward Feller, and then cautiously poked his head into the interrogation room.

Only Moog was inside, tethered to a chair with zip ties.

"What the hell been keeping you?" the big man snapped, making clear he'd expected the rescue but was annoyed by the time it'd taken.

"I ran into an old friend and stopped to talk." Daniel undid the restraint holding Moog's left wrist.

"How'd that work out for him?"

Daniel turned his attention to the other wrist restraint. "Same way it does for most of my friends."

Moog tried to rub the circulation back into his wrists as Daniel worked the belt holding the big man to the chair. "What happened to the guy?"

"He ran into a mutual friend of ours."

The open buckle fell from the big man's lap, and he rose uncertainly to his feet. "And now?"

"We gotta ride, ride like the wind."

"You know I hate it when you talk in pop songs."

"It's the universal language," Daniel assured him. "But we gotta get outta this place if it's the last thing we ever do."

"Shit!" Moog called out when Feller appeared. "Get down!"

Before Daniel could explain, there was three hundred and fifty pounds of loyalty on top of him, shielding him from the man in the doorway.

"*That*," Daniel explained as he struggled to push Moog off of him and direct his attention back toward Feller, "is our mutual friend."

"He's the fucking FBI agent," Moog asserted with disbelief.

"Not anymore."

Moog seemed relieved. "No?"

Daniel shook his head. "Oh no. It's so much worse than that."

"Worse than the Feds?"

A nod. "He seems to have devolved into Koschei's slightly psychotic minion."

Moog had a few points he needed filled in. "And the reason we ain't killing him?"

"Aside from the fact that we're both lying here stretched out on the floor?" Uncomfortable with the position once he'd described it, Daniel struggled to his feet. "And the fact that he's got a gun and we don't?"

"Yeah. Besides all that?"

"Well, besides that, he wants exactly what we want?"

The big man got to his feet. "To kill Koschei?"

"Well, all right, not *exactly* what we want. But he wants to take us back to his boss, and right now that makes him our E ticket to the Send Koschei Straight to Hell fun ride."

"I say we kill him," Moog voted aloud.

"I'm standing right here," Feller objected. "With a gun."

"This don't concern you," Moog countered before turning back to his friend. "Seriously, I say we just off him, here and now."

"He's the quickest way to Koschei, and we don't have time to waste," Daniel stressed. "*Malaika* doesn't have time to waste."

Moog's deep brown eyes looked hard at the only man he trusted. "You sure about this?"

"I'm sure that I don't know a better way right now."

Moog silently considered their situation, and then gave an affirmative nod. "OK."

"If you two young lovers are done whispering in one another's ears," Feller called out, "we can stop at the chapel of love once we're on the road, but we really should get out of here."

Moog had one last thing to share with Daniel. "You know I'm going to kill him."

"Yes." Daniel nodded. And smiled. "I'm sure of that too. But for right now, he's right."

With that, Feller turned and led the way down the hall. "Follow me, ladies."

With a stifled growl, Moog did.

Daniel did too, but not before stripping the corpse at the doorway of its pistol.

CHAPTER TWENTY

Mother

Everything happens for a reason.

Life's patterns repeat themselves over and over again. The same situations return and present themselves, refusing to grant any progress in life until a solution is found or a compromise made.

The Teller Tech facility (and the carnage they'd left there) wasn't more than five miles behind them. There was no reason to relax yet, but Daniel could feel himself settling into a long forgotten sense of calm. He sat silently beside Moog in the backseat of Feller's sedan and simply watched the scenery go past. It was nice. And normal. Relatively speaking.

The last moment of relative normalcy that Daniel could recall had been the early morning walk down empty residential streets on his way to pay a visit to the poor departed Mr. Dredsley. That had been nice too. But days ago. And countless druggings and beatings ago. Yet another lifetime ago.

On the right, Daniel noticed the strip mall they drove past and noted that it'd changed since he'd seen it last. He sat up straight, aware that this was a stray thought that had slipped into his head.

For a mile or two, Daniel consoled himself with the thought that the intensifying feeling of familiarity must be an aftereffect of everything he'd experienced in the past few days: the bumps on the head, the controlled substances washing through his brain. Maybe it was all just a willing delusion, created by his subconscious to lure him into a contented resignation that everything was all right, when—given the chauffeur and the destination—everything was decidedly not OK.

There were plenty of plausible explanations for why his mind might have contorted to produce a feeling of relative stability, but none to explain how he could have known that the Dairy Bar was just up ahead on the road or that the Homestead Family Restaurant was just beyond it. No, every passing mile made it clearer and clearer that the real delusion would be for him to deny that these were *not* surroundings he knew well.

"Don't turn here," Daniel told Feller, who'd signaled to turn off to the right.

From behind the wheel, Feller turned to his backseat driver. "This is the way to the highway."

"This is the way back to the highway and takes you straight through the center of town," Daniel said with such certainty that Feller canceled the signal and drove on straight ahead. "Too many bored townie cops. You'll never get past them. Keep on straight here," he directed, "and in about five miles we can take a right. That'll take us out past the state park. That's the best way to get to the highway without being seen. And with what we've just left behind, I'm guessing none of us are interested in making any new friends right now."

"New friends," Moog cracked. "I don't even like *you* all that much right now."

Daniel smiled, thankful that a shooting or two had seemingly begun the repairs on their fractured friendship. "You weren't saying that twenty minutes ago when I was pulling your ass out of that—"

"You didn't pull my ass outta nuthin'. I had those suckers right where I wanted them."

"You mean beating your ass while you were tied to a chair?"

"It's called giving your opponent a false sense of security. You should read some strategy sometime," Moog advised. "Some Sun Tzu or some Musashi. That'd straighten you out."

"I didn't know you were so international in your reading tastes."

"There's a lot you don't know about me," the big man said defensively.

"Like, apparently, you think being tied to a chair and getting your ass beaten is a strategy."

"I hate to interrupt your marital banter," Feller said to cut them off. "And it's not that I don't appreciate the backseat Garmin, but how exactly do you know the back road to the highway?"

"Because I've taken it before." Daniel looked out at the passing landmarks, now confident that he knew every one of them.

"You've been in that particular facility before?"

"No, that was a first for me."

"Then how?" Feller felt he was missing something.

And he was. "I was raised here," Daniel said.

"Get outta here," Moog was the first to say, but Feller was thinking it too.

"Freaks me out too," Daniel admitted. "I haven't been back here in . . ." He stopped to calculate how long ago it was that he and Connie had brought Zack for a visit. Zack had just been a toddler, no more than two or three. "Fifteen years. Maybe a little more."

"And the shadow base?" Feller asked, wondering where Teller Tech fit into the emerging story.

It didn't. Daniel shook his head. "After my time. I never knew anything about it."

"Coincidence?" Moog wanted to know.

"I don't think I believe in them anymore," Daniel said. "But I don't have a better explanation for it either. We're in northeastern Pennsylvania. Close to Manhattan, not far from DC. Access to all the highways of the east coast. A couple of Army bases nearby. And yet there's nothing around here but fallow family farms and suburban track homes. It's really the perfect site for a place like that."

Daniel shifted his attention to the driver. "Which brings us to you, Feller."

"What do you mean?"

"I mean was it a coincidence that you just happened to bring your murder and mayhem our way?"

"I told you, Koschei wants you."

"And he told you where we were?"

Feller nodded.

"And how did he know?"

"I assume the people who had you told him. Or they told someone who told him. Lots of people tell him lots of things."

Daniel shrugged. "I guess the murder and mayhem *were* all part of his strategy."

"So what now?" Moog asked. "We stop by your folks' place for a hot cooked meal?"

"They wouldn't have you," Daniel said, without a note of sadness to his voice. "Or at least they wouldn't have me."

"Whatchu do?" Moog wanted to know.

"It's a long story."

"Don't we have enough time?"

"You wouldn't believe me if I told you."

"Are you kidding me?"

"When I was a child, I got sick. I had a fever."

"And?"

"And the doctors told my mother that I was probably going to die, but that if I didn't . . ." Daniel's voice trailed off to silence.

"Yeah?"

"They told her that if I didn't die, she'd wish I did. There was too much brain damage from the fever, they said."

"That explains it," Moog said, but even he realized it wasn't as funny as he thought it would be.

"Three days later the doctors tell my mom they've got good news. The fever is broken and I'm not dead and I'm not the potted plant they'd told her I'd be. I'm perfect. And they hand me to her. And she takes me in her arms. And she cries. Not tears of joy, but anguish. And she hands me back to the doctors and tells them that I'm not her son."

"You're kidding me."

Even in the dark of the car's interior, Daniel's face made it clear that he wasn't. "When I was about ten years old, I remember sitting out on the porch with her one summer afternoon and she told me that she'd known the whole time that she lost her son to that fever and that whatever I was, I wasn't hers."

"That's some messed-up shit, man."

"I used to think so, but now I'm not so certain. Maybe she was right."

"Man, that's just crazy."

"The whole world is made up of crazy," Daniel said. His voice sounded like it was coming from far away.

They found the back way to the highway and drove on through the night.

CHAPTER TWENTY-ONE

The Raccoon and That Mustard Guy

From Pavlov to Freud, Skinner to Rorschach, science has endeavored to uncover and comprehend the infinite mysteries of human behavior. All these efforts have been a complete waste of time and effort.

To truly understand the shadowy workings of how humans think and behave and interact doesn't require any more than a couple of willing (or not) subjects, a car, and an endless stretch of highway. There is simply no surer way to determine an individual's disposition, tastes, and character than to take them on an extended road trip.

With Gerald Feller at the wheel, and Daniel and Moog occupying the backseat, it took less than five hundred miles for the gamut of behavioral abnormalities to evidence themselves among the traveling trio.

"Oh my God," Daniel groaned. "I wish I was back in their bunker, tied to a chair, and getting hit in the face."

The comment was surprising to Feller, who hadn't spent this much uninterrupted time with other people since he and his estranged wife had decided to drive from Peoria to Pensacola for her second cousin's third wedding—and was enjoying this trip and company much more. "What are you talking about?"

"This music," Daniel explained. "Can we just put something else on?"

"Oh, thank God." Moog had been tolerating the trip's soundtrack, but now that a complaint had been registered, he was eager to add his voice to the dissent. "Man, I thought this was a white thing, and I was the only one felt like they had a nail being driven into their forehead."

"What are you talking about?" While the revelation that his traveling companions weren't enjoying themselves came as a surprise, he found the nature of their complaints completely befuddling. "This is the Beatles."

"I know it's the Beatles." Daniel wondered if it was even possible to not know it was the Beatles. "But eight solid hours of this shit has me wishing I was Paul so that *I* could blow my mind out in a car."

"Shit?" Feller repeated the word as though he couldn't even define it, given the context in which it'd been used. "The Beatles are the greatest rock band in history."

Daniel's patience had abandoned him about a dozen exits back, and he was anxious to make the necessary corrections. "First off, they're not a band. Bands are groups of musicians that go out on the road and play actual shows. Guys who are huddled in studios indulging fetishes with overdubs and tech tricks are rightfully known as *projects*. *See* Alan Parsons. Maybe, if they've got so much funk that they're gonna make you sweat, they might qualify as *music factories*, but they're not bands."

"The Beatles played live." Feller was quick to the defense. "They had to stop playing shows because the crowds got too loud."

"Public appearances where the shrieks of teenage girls drown out the amps don't count as shows," Daniel insisted. "The Stones played over teenage squeals. The Who and The Doors did too. Hell, Lemmy Kilmister never complained that the teenage girls were louder than his rig."

"The Beatles played live lots. They were a great live band. Everyone says so."

"Everyone says the emperor has a ballin' set of clothes, but that don't mean his raggedy ass ain't sticking out," Moog offered.

"The business machine behind the Beatles is like a musical hog processor," Daniel added. "They've sold everything but the oink, and wrung every possible penny out of that enterprise. You think they've got their greedy, little hands on any listenable live material and just decided not to release it?"

"There's *Live at the Hollywood Bowl*," Feller responded.

"The fact that they've been used to shill everything from bobbleheads to pj's, yet they only milked out one live album just proves my point. If there was anything there, someone would've put it out and sold it."

"There's *Live at the BBC*. Two volumes."

"Studio," Daniel countered. "Doesn't count."

Daniel wasn't finished. "And second, they weren't even a rock band."

Feller was tempted to stop the car in the middle of the interstate. The offending comment was so sacrilegious that he had to repeat it in his incredulous, dumbfounded voice. "The Beatles were not a rock band?"

The vocal affectation didn't sway Daniel at all. "No. They were not. Rock music is rebellious music."

"The Beatles were rebellious," Feller answered immediately. "They have two whole songs called 'Revolution.'"

"One's a tape loop of an English guy saying 'number nine' over and over again. The other has a 'Shoo-bee-doo-wah' chorus. There's nothing revolutionary in 'Shoo-bee-doo-wah.'"

To Feller the conversation was as if someone were criticizing gravity or oxygen or something else that was fundamental and necessary to all life. "Anyone will tell you that the Beatles are the greatest rock band *ever*."

"Many people will," Daniel easily conceded. "But they're all wrong. Listen, if everyone in the group has matching haircuts and outfits, if you've got a Saturday morning cartoon show *and* an animated movie, and there's a raging international debate over which one is the cute one, then you're not a rock-and-roll band. Rock-and-roll bands are not the stuff of Vegas Cirque du Soleil shows. So, move on with it already. Not only aren't the Beatles the greatest rock-and-roll band, they're not even *a* rock-and-roll band." Daniel took a moment to consider if he'd been too harsh or brash. "I will, however, give you the world's greatest boy band."

"Jackson Five." Moog was quick to nominate.

"All right," Daniel conceded. "Beatles are the second-greatest boy band."

Moog folded his thick arms across his massive chest and sat back in his seat, satisfied that he'd made his point without needing to use too many words.

"They are not a boy band." The grim tone of Feller's voice made it clear that the criticism really mattered to him.

"How about world's greatest pop band, then?" Daniel was almost conciliatory.

Feller was apoplectic. And silent.

"That's something to hold on to," Daniel coaxed. "World's greatest pop band. What's wrong with that? 'When I'm Sixty Four.' 'Mean Mr. Mustard.' Half their stuff is vaudeville, for God's sake. 'Rocky Raccoon.' Really? The best stuff they nicked off of Little Richard."

"Do you have any idea how many records they've sold?"

"What the hell does that have to do with anything?"

"It means everything. Record sales are how they keep score."

"You can't keep score with music," Daniel said, although he realized that he'd played that particular game for his entire life. He justified the hypocrisy by telling himself it had been another existence.

"Listen, no one in the world sells more burgers than McDonald's." He continued. "But that doesn't mean it's good food. To get lots of people to agree on the same thing you have to make it as palatable as possible to as many people as possible. In food that means making what you serve as bland as you can. With music, it means writing a song with a hook like an advertising jingle." Daniel thought back to his own transgressions. "Trust me, I know."

Feller was left with only one response: an angry "You're a fucking asshole."

"Why does it always have to go there for you Fab Four fans?" Daniel wondered aloud. "For people who don't need anything but love, there's no one quicker to righteous outrage than a Beatles fan."

"You're a fucking asshole."

Daniel laughed. Moog joined him.

For Feller there wasn't anything funny about it. "It's going to be a pleasure to kill you."

"Maybe," Daniel acknowledged without losing his smile. "But don't go fooling yourself into thinking it's going to be yours."

Feller let the comment pass. And he didn't acknowledge that it sent a shiver down his spine.

"Now can we please get some decent tunes on in here?"

"It would be nice," Moog agreed.

Feller looked at them in stony silence, then turned the music up louder. It was overdubs over overdubs and syrupy orchestral strings for another hundred miles.

CHAPTER TWENTY-TWO

The St. Louis Blues

Ever since Meriwether Lewis and William Clark staged the granddaddy of badass road trips, St. Louis has been a stopover for hundreds of thousands of pilgrimages, migrations, and sojourns. From early pioneers following their fortunes westward to newly freed slaves seeking refuge and opportunity in the North, the Lou has offered road-weary travelers an opportunity to rest and reload.

By the time they saw the Arch illuminating the night sky and looming on the far prairie horizon, it was almost midnight, and Daniel and his companions were ready to join in the city's tradition of hospitality. And ready refuge.

"I've got to get some sleep." Behind the wheel, Feller had reached that tipping point where the highway goes from a mere strip of pavement to a living thing, an asphalt monster that distorts what's left of perception and drains that last store of energy with every mile that passes.

"Then get some sleep." Moog made it sound simple. "I'll take the wheel for a while, and you can crawl in the back here and drift off to little psycho slumberland."

"First off," Feller started to count down, "you don't know where we're going, so it's not like you can drive us there."

"You could tell me." Easy enough.

"I could," Feller admitted, while also making it clear that wasn't an option he was considering. "But I'm not looking to find my bones buried in a shallow grave at the side of the road just yet, so I think I'm going to keep that little bit of information to myself."

"Suit yourself." Moog folded his arms across his chest like a kid who didn't care.

"I'm going to find a place to stop and get a couple of hours' sleep." Feller rubbed his face, wiping fatigue from his squinting eyes. "And to get that done, I'm going to have to do something with the two of you."

Suddenly, Moog was a kid who cared again. "What you thinkin' about, fool?"

Feller had spent a mile or two working that out. "I'm just going to bind the two of you up and leave you in the car."

The big man had objections. "You're not binding anyone to anything, asshole."

"It's not a race thing," Feller tried to explain awkwardly.

"It's not a *what*? Did you seriously just say—"

"Not everything is a race thing," Feller protested. "Why do you people have to make such a big deal out of every little thing?"

"*You people?*" That concluded the conversation portion of the evening for Moog, who started the process of gathering himself up to get over the seat in front of him. "You cracker motherfucker! I'm gonna fuck you up like—"

"Hey, hey." Daniel held back his friend, knowing that none of them wanted fisticuffs at seventy-five miles per hour.

"I told you not to talk to me like that," Feller screamed, producing what he thought was the only gun in the car. "I don't let *anyone* talk to me like that anymore."

"Whoa, whoa!" Daniel pushed the barrel of Feller's pistol away from its oversize target while he struggled to control his friend. "Put the gun away."

"I'll put the gun away," Moog offered, reaching for the piece himself.

Daniel grabbed his friend's wrist. "I got this."

"Did you hear what that cracker said to—"

Daniel looked deep into Moog's wild eyes and demanded control. "I got this."

Moog took a deep breath and threw himself back in his seat, silently stewing. He had enough fury for both of them, and his flaring eyes made it clear he was close to spreading it between the two of them.

Daniel widened his eyes, trying to wordlessly communicate to his partner that he had a long game to play. Then he turned his attention back to Feller, who was breathing hard behind the steering wheel. "Listen, no one appreciates your middle-aged line-in-the-sand more than me. But if you haven't figured it out, we *want* to go see Koschei. That's the only reason we're traveling with you. And forget the shallow graves. That's the only reason you're not in a rest stop Dumpster."

"Damn straight," Moog agreed, like he was giving a shout-out at a gospel service.

Daniel kept preaching. "We're not your prisoners, Feller. And you're not calling any shots."

"No?" Without taking his hand from the wheel or his bloodshot eyes from the road, Feller confidently held up his pistol. "Gun makes the rules. And I got the gun."

"This is America, Feller. There's never any shortage of guns." Daniel had been waiting for a better opportunity to produce the pistol he'd sneaked out of the Teller Tech facility, but he knew that the immediate situation was liable to escalate if he didn't act decisively. In a flash, he pulled the weapon and put its barrel against the back of Feller's head. "And more guns just make for a bigger mess."

Suddenly, Feller wasn't tired anymore. He knew he needed to say something, but it's awfully hard—damn near impossible—to find the right words with a piece of blued steel pressed hard against your skull.

"Don't feel bad about it." Daniel's voice was soft and conciliatory, his eyes filled with the cold purpose of one who'd given up counting the deaths he'd seen—or caused. "It's not that you've failed in any way. It's just that I'm a helluva lot harder to kill than you think. And you're . . . not."

"Not hard at all," Moog added.

Daniel gave him a reproachful look. "I've got this." He pulled the pistol away from its point-blank target. "So find a place to stop. I think we could all use the rest, because I get the feeling we've still got some miles to go. But there's no way in hell you're going to make your destination unless you give up on trying to run everything with nothing but a gun."

"Do whatever you want." Even Feller was aware that his near-adolescent response wasn't much of a comeback, but it was all that he had.

"That's exactly what we're going to do," Daniel assured him.

A strained silence filled the car as they passed an exit or two, and it didn't break until they'd found a hotel where no one questioned three men—with more than enough cash and not a piece of ID among them—looking for rooms.

Feller stopped at his room and unlocked the door with the key the whoremonger behind the registration desk had given him. Without looking directly at either Daniel or Moog, he said simply, "I'll be pulling out of here in eight hours. If you're so eager to make the trip, you won't be late."

Neither Daniel nor Moog felt the need to make any response.

"We may be traveling to the same place. Maybe." Feller's eyes were still fixed on the door of his hotel room. "And maybe I can't deny that I'd be in a bad place with Mr. Koschei if I turn up there without you after all of this. But you're not the only ones who shouldn't be underestimated."

He turned to Daniel and Moog and there was no fear in his eyes. "Maybe you can slip me. Or do whatever you plan on doing. But you forget that I know that you're doing all of this for someone other than you. If I have to go looking for you in the morning, I promise you I'll see to it personally that it goes bad for you and yours before it ever gets back to me." He didn't wait for a response or an acknowledgment before slipping into his room and closing the door.

"We should kill him right now," Moog said with certainty.

Daniel shook his head. "We need him."

"Bullshit. I don't need nobody."

"Everybody needs somebody. Sometimes I think everybody needs everybody. You know?" He looked over at his friend, but it was clear Moog didn't. "Maybe everybody's got some part to play, and it's only when they don't play it that things get messed up. Like a musician who joins the band, but not on the right beat."

The big man shook his head. "Man, you need sleep more than anyone." Without another word, he stepped into his room and closed the door behind him.

Daniel walked into the third room. There was no sense in his old sleeping-in-the-closet trick anymore. He simply lay down on the lumpy mattress and kinda, sorta cleanish bedspread. He tried and tried, but he could find no rest there.

Hell, he couldn't find rest anywhere.

CHAPTER TWENTY-THREE

Nowhere Left to Run

Sleep and death.

For ages man has seen their similarities, compared and confused the two states: the surrender to stillness and a lack of awareness. The uncertain destination of those who slip into the shadow's embrace. And, maybe—for some lucky few—the feeling of rebirth that follows after.

If sleep is as close to death as one can get without passing beyond life's ephemeral borders, then those prolonged periods of unwanted sleeplessness that stretch a single night into an eternity are a purgatory for those living souls who are cursed to waking restlessness.

Fully clothed atop the bedcovers, Daniel tried in vain to lose himself in sleep's dark depths and clear his mind of the nightly collection of unatonable sins, aching regrets, and unshakable memories that rolled down his psyche like Mardi Gras floats on Bourbon Street. Macabre attendants threw treats and trinkets to the crowd: "what might have beens" and "if onlys."

When he could no longer stand the endless parade, Daniel rose from his bed like an undead from an open grave and stepped out into the night. With no destination but *out,* he headed off down the shady street, afraid of nothing but another moment of confinement with all the memories he'd learned he could elude by half a step—if he just kept moving. *Just keep moving.*

St. Louis's streets had fallen under the spell of that unbearably lonely hour when night has all but given up on all possibilities, but morning still seems too far off to offer any hope. Every block or two, Daniel passed a fellow traveler who was long overdue to return home or some unlucky soul who had no home to which to return. For the most part, however, Daniel was completely alone and his footsteps fell and echoed unanswered.

His aimless feet wandered block after block, until he finally found himself on Washington Avenue, in the heart of the Lou's revitalized MX district. He walked past closed restaurants and bars and strolled by hotels where the odd valet suspiciously watched him pass.

He stopped for a minute, aware of something standing off to his immediate right, and was surprised to find it was nothing more than his reflection. He turned to the storefront window in which his image was trapped and was taken aback by the man looking back. With the sun rising full and orange out of the east, the shadows cut across his face like scars and deepened the pools of black beneath his eyes.

It was not the man he was. Or, at least, not the man he wanted to be.

"This used to be the old Dillard's building."

Daniel had assumed he was alone, and the unexpected voice startled him. Still, he was long past being surprised by Atibon. The old bluesman stood beside him. "Now they turnin' it into a museum."

Daniel nodded politely, his eyes still fixed on the stranger looking back at him from the glass. The face was thin and lean, all angles that looked as if they'd been hand cut with a sharp blade. The eyes were tired, but mean and predatory. It was the face of a good man who was all too capable of very bad things.

He realized this was maybe the first time he'd ever really been satisfied with his reflection.

"Museum all about the blues," Atibon continued. "'Bout damn time, you ask me."

"Just like it's about time you showed up." Daniel turned from the window.

"I'm like the sun," Atibon chuckled. "Just 'cause you got yourself a cloudy day, don't mean I ain't there."

"And why are you here?"

"There ain't really no place I ain't." The old man grinned. "Leastwise, not where you're concerned."

"Or time?" Daniel wondered aloud.

"Whatchu talkin' 'bout, boy?"

"I had a dream," Daniel said, wondering even as he did why the images had bothered him so much. "Not really a dream. It was when Moog had me all doped up."

"What about it?"

"It was the night I tried to commit suicide." Daniel thought back and realized his vision was clearer than what remained in his memory of the actual event. "You were in it."

"Was I?"

Daniel wasn't sure anymore. "You weren't there, were you?"

"In your dream? You just said I was."

"No. I mean in my house. That night. Were you there? *Actually* there?"

The old man didn't blink. Or try to deny it. "I been watching you a long, long time, son."

"Why?"

"You know why."

"No. I don't."

"You ain't never gonna get where you need to go till you stop lying to yourself." Atibon flashed a look at his wrist but there wasn't a watch strapped there. "And you runnin' real close on time, *mi key*."

What disturbed Daniel most was that he knew Atibon was right. "And now?"

"You mean, why am I here now?"

"I mean right here, right now. I've known you long enough that you've cured me of believing in coincidences. Everything happens for a reason. So, when you show up, I know you want something. Or need it. There's a bottom line out there somewhere, I'm just trying to cut down to it."

"Puttin' it like that make it sound like we ain't got nuthin' between us but business. But the truth is, I grown fond of you, son. Not sure why, 'cause you ain't never give me no particular reason to think on you so." He scratched his tufts of gray hair and thought on it a minute. "You ain't never give me nuthin' but trouble, but I still would like to see all this end well for you."

The impenetrable prophecy didn't frighten Daniel. "I kinda feel I'm overdue for a happy ending too."

"Very least," Atibon continued, "I'd like to see you get the opportunity to end it on your terms. You know?"

Daniel did. "Me too."

Atibon nodded at the meeting of their minds. "Then now might be a good time to look back at that reflection of yours."

Daniel rolled his eyes. "Could you be any more cryptic?"

"What I'm sayin' ain't no riddle, fool." The old man's voice was tinged with frustration. "Take another look in the goddamn mirror."

Daniel was still protesting the inscrutable instruction when he returned his eyes to the glass and almost immediately noticed something besides his own face. There was a black Suburban, parked and idling across the street, doing a very poor job of inconspicuously observing him.

Without turning and revealing that he'd caught on to the tail, Daniel watched it for a minute in the glass. "These the same guys from DC?"

There was no answer.

Daniel turned and Atibon was gone. No surprise there.

Daniel collected himself and started walking at a casual Sunday-morning pace, stopping every now and again to look in a shop window and keep a tab on the SUV that was clearly following him at a bureaucratically discreet distance.

There were options to be weighed: running, fighting, simply ignoring. None of them were very good, but each of them was greatly reduced when Daniel looked farther ahead on Washington Avenue and saw another black Suburban parked down the block, waiting for him.

There was a third parked across the street from it.

Running was now pointless.

Fighting wouldn't achieve anything but a beating. His.

And there was no way for Daniel to continue the charade of pretending he hadn't noticed the three oversize SUVs closing in on him.

Whoever had gone to such lengths to hunt him down had created a box in which to trap him, and all he could do was wait for them to put a lid on it.

Then, as if it were an answer, he heard the chop-chop-chop of helicopter blades in the early morning sky above him. The lid.

Down the block, a man got out of one of the Suburbans and began walking down Washington toward Daniel. The man's perfectly styled silver hair looked as if it hadn't touched a pillow, and his tanned face looked none the worse for it. His suit was gray and, even from thirty yards, clearly bespoke and very expensive. He walked quickly and confidently, almost aggressively, like a lion who knew the kill was a certainty and only hoped his prey wouldn't insist on going through the tiresome trouble of making him actually run it down.

That, however, was exactly what Daniel intended.

"There's nowhere to run, Mr. Erickson," the man called out from fifteen yards away. He seemed unconcerned that anyone else might have overheard, as if he'd rented out the entire city for their private get-together. "And no point in fighting."

Daniel knew the man was probably right, but he looked back over his shoulder, and then to his left and right just to know where all the pawns were placed. "That doesn't leave me with a lot of good options."

"It doesn't leave you with any options at all, Mr. Erickson." The man closed the distance between them.

"I could make sure I don't die alone."

The threat only produced a bored chuckle. "You can't possibly mean me. You must be referring to your friends." With that, the man gestured, and one of the Suburbans broke from its not-so-secret hiding spot and pulled up to the curb. The tinted window rolled down, and Daniel wasn't surprised at all to find Moog and Feller seated inside. Neither appeared to be conscious.

"Only one of them is my friend," Daniel corrected. "And he and I don't see eye-to-eye all that often. So . . ."

"I understand. If they're of no importance to you, then they're of no use to me. I'll have them taken care of immediately." He gestured, and the window went back up.

"And by 'taken care of' I'm assuming you mean you'll take good care of them." Daniel hedged nervously.

"No. I mean there's a rather large landfill across the river in Granite City." The man gestured toward the eastern horizon as though he already knew the exact spot to drop the bodies. Then he stood and smiled triumphantly, aware that he'd just called the only bluff his opponent had left.

Daniel was aware he'd lost. "What the hell do you want?"

The man smiled as if he were raking in the pot after playing a winning hand. "Let's start with a moment of your time."

"You've already taken that."

"Then perhaps I'll need to take a moment or two more."

"And then what?"

"That all depends on you, Mr. Erickson."

"You just let us go on our way?"

"Possibly. If I'm satisfied."

"And if you're not?"

"Then you'll spend the tortured remainder of your life wishing that you'd been dropped in a landfill." The man grinned and summoned a Suburban with a single, subtle movement.

The SUV's rear passenger door opened, and Daniel reluctantly climbed inside.

There was a man in a polo shirt—just like the stiffs back at the facility had been wearing—seated beside him, but it was someone unnoticed in the third row of seats who immediately wrapped a muscular arm around Daniel's neck and pulled it taut as he injected the contents of a syringe into the exposed vein.

Daniel was out almost before he felt the needle's sting.

CHAPTER TWENTY-FOUR

Good to Be King

Consciousness hit Daniel like he was a slow moving armadillo crossing a Louisiana straightaway.

Wham!

It took a moment before he had sense enough to realize there was reason for the now familiar taste of blood in his mouth.

He was staring at a pair of shoes. Men's. Expensive. Black leather. Lace-ups. The kind bankers and other thieves wear.

They were standing on beige carpet.

And Daniel was lying on it. He was tied to a chair, his hands bound behind him, and the footwear and the carpeting were the only view.

"Set him back up."

Daniel couldn't be completely sure, but it seemed to him that the voice belonged to the man he'd met in the street.

Suddenly, an unknown number of hands took hold, and the chair that Daniel was lashed to was righted and set back on its legs. The sensation was nauseating, like when you take a dip in the road too fast, and Daniel had to catch himself to keep from choking on his own blood.

"I thought it was about time you woke up." It was the same voice. And the same man. He stood in front of the chair, rubbing his fist as a sort of explanation for why Daniel had come to be on the floor with a pain in his jaw and blood in his mouth.

"Wow," Daniel said, not worried about the social inappropriateness of spitting blood onto a carpeted floor. "It takes a certain kind of man to do the whole Sean Penn bit and hit someone tied to a chair. But hitting an *unconscious* person tied to a chair? That's something really special."

"Oh, you haven't begun to see special." The man seemed confident.

Daniel spit again. Not so much blood. "Asshole, I've seen all sorts of special." He was confident too.

"My name is J. Christopher Mallenthorpe." He approached Daniel and hit him again. "And before you and I are through, I'm going to hurt you. Hard. And in ways you'd never dreamed possible."

"Good to meet you, J. Chris-to-something." Daniel seemed to be choking on the name, but then just spit out more blood—on his host's expensive shoes. "I'm just going to call you Bitch. And your little speech doesn't scare me. Nothing about you scares me."

"You don't know me," the man sneered. "Yet."

"And I don't need to," Daniel said as he looked out of the window at the shapes and shadows that made up a city skyline (he was fairly certain it wasn't St. Louis's) silhouetted against a sky that was smeared to the far horizon with early-evening shades of Creamsicle orange and Twinkie yellow. "Because before that sun has set, you're going to be dead."

"You think so?" He arched his salon-shaped eyebrows to express his haughty disregard.

"I'm mojo-sure of it." And he was.

"What is this?" Daniel wondered. "Office building?"

"Hotel suite."

Daniel looked harder at the horizon visible through the wall of windows. "This isn't St. Louis."

"No." The man seemed caught off guard by the observation and turned as if he had to check to be sure. "It's New Orleans, actually."

"New Orleans? Why New Orleans?"

"Because New Orleans can keep its mouth shut," J. Christopher said proudly, as if he had something to do with it. "You can't go a dozen blocks in New York without being seen by half the damn Twitterverse. Chicago's a town of frauds and pretenders. LA is soulless, even to me. But New Orleans is like the perfect mistress: it understands the need to take care of business but never lets that get in the way of tempting you to surrender to your sins. And all the while it knows enough to keep its mouth shut about both."

"You strike me as a man that knows all about that," Daniel said.

His host was confused. "What's that?"

"Mistresses and all."

"I've had my share." J. Christopher smiled. "More than my share."

Daniel thought of his own wife and felt the long-surpassed rage begin to bubble and boil inside him. "Well, why don't you get on with whatever it is you've got planned here, because that sun's sinking fast and I'm running outta time to kill you."

"You're running out of time, but it's not to kill me."

"Let's agree to disagree."

The man seemed agreeable to that and began the planned portion of his performance. "You've been responsible for the deaths of a good number of people who were important to our organization, Mr. Erickson."

Daniel didn't have any apologies to offer. "I'm not sure I'm the one responsible. I prefer to think of them all as reaping the consequences of bad lifestyle choices."

"And you're just an instrument of fate?"

"I'm an instrument all right. But not fate's." Daniel tested the ropes that held him. Tight, but workable.

"Then whose?" The man seemed more than politely interested.

"That's a long story."

"Then I'd suggest you get started right away."

"Maybe later."

"I should remind you, Mr. Erickson, that you're not in much of a position for bargaining." His voice took on a menacing chill. "And no position at all for thinking in terms of later."

"I can see how you'd think that, but most of those people whom we were just talking about thought the exact same thing. For most of them, it was the last thing they ever thought. But the fact of the matter is that my future is far more certain than yours right now."

The man's cool demeanor showed the slightest fractures at the edges. "Is that right?"

"It's a goddamn fact of nature."

"Well, while we're waiting for your nonexistent cavalry to arrive, I'm going to ask you some questions. And Sanjay here," he paused and nodded toward a man who'd been standing behind Daniel and had gone unnoticed until his introduction, "Sanjay is going to make sure that you answer them."

Sanjay stepped forward and took a handful of Daniel's hair, pulled back his head, and put the twelve-inch blade of a Rampuri against his exposed throat.

Daniel knew better than to resist. "Well, when you put it that way, I'll tell you whatever you want to know."

J. Christopher seemed satisfied. "Not so cocky now, are you?"

"You know what they say." Daniel swallowed hard, and his Adam's apple rubbed uncomfortably against the weapon. "It's not bragging if you can back it up."

J. Christopher had apparently run out of patience and was ready to get down to business. "What can you tell me about Siren Song?"

"I can tell you that you're the second asshole that's asked me about it." Daniel paused for effect. "He died horribly too."

The man ignored the threat contained in the response. "You recently traveled to Great Britain."

"Wouldn't you rather ask something we both don't already know?"

"My question is why."

"We both know that too, don't we? I was looking into the death of Jimi Hendrix. I think he was murdered." Daniel noticed the man didn't seem surprised. "I think a lot of musicians have been killed over the years."

The additional allegation didn't seem to come as a shock to his interrogator.

"Tell me what you know about this"—choosing the right word here seemed very important to the man and required a slight pause—"theory?"

"Oh, it's more than a theory."

"Do you have any evidence?"

"Evidence is a funny thing. It's never about killing this man or that, is it? It's about altering the truth and changing history. That's the assignment. So is there evidence? Not of the act itself, only of the efforts to cover up the deed. There's no evidence of anything except that the story handed to the public doesn't make any sense. No evidence but the guilty consciences of old men grown worried in the face of approaching death."

It wasn't clear whether J. Christopher was satisfied by or resentful of the response, but Daniel's words left him temporarily silenced.

"Is that what this is all about? Protecting your legacy or paving your road to providence."

"We do what needs to be done."

"Really? Is that what you tell yourself?"

"What I tell myself is the truth." The man seemed oddly defensive, considering his status as inquisitor. "There's more to all this than someone like you could ever understand."

"You're probably right, because I'm betting you've got more money than anyone could spend in a thousand lifetimes. So what's the point? When do you have enough money?"

"That's a poor man's question," J. Christopher sneered, "asked by people who don't have enough money to realize there are two aspects to wealth. The easiest is getting it. The hardest is keeping it."

"That's what this is about? Keeping the money you've already got?" Daniel couldn't help but think it was a hollow purpose.

"You don't know much about history. Rome. France. Russia. History tells us that the minute those with money lose their focus, they lose their money too. And their heads."

"So you killed all of these talented people for no other reason than that their music might have inspired someone?"

"I didn't kill anyone," the old man protested.

"No. You had all of these talented people killed because you thought their songs would kill you?"

"You underestimate the power of the music you've fought so hard to preserve. Music is revolution. It spreads the seeds.

Provides the passion. If we hadn't stepped in to control it, there's no telling where it might have led."

"So that's it, huh?" Daniel couldn't help but be disappointed. "That's what this is all about? All of you one-percenters are just so petrified that the rest of us will wake up one day and realize that we're tired of your shit and want our stuff back." He would've shaken his head with exaggerated contempt if there hadn't been a blade pressed to his throat. "It must be so scary to be up on top, with the common ground that the rest of us pissants occupy so far below you. Such a long way to fall."

The old man didn't necessarily disagree. "It's a position I intend to keep."

"Well, I plan on ending our little talk here by pushing you from that perch. So, good luck with that."

"Luck has nothing to do with it. Now, who else did you tell about all of this?"

"That's the sixty-four-thousand-dollar question, isn't it? That's what you really need to know. There was a time when you and yours could control everything, but now there's too much information and too many ways of getting it out there." Even with a knife at his throat, Daniel couldn't help but grin. "The truth never stood a chance before, but now there's every possibility it could come dribbling out one drop at a time. Or come rushing out in a deluge of truth. How about that?"

J. Christopher struck a pose of entitled defiance, but didn't bother to interrupt.

"And what a steaming, hot pile of truth it would be if the world found out what you've done with their music. How you've leveraged their souls for a profit center. That's why you need to know what I did with my little pieces of the truth." Daniel grinned confidently. "You need to know. And you need to know *bad*."

"Not nearly as badly as your friends need you to tell me." J. Christopher nodded, and four men in black polo shirts marched Moog and Feller into the room. Both of them seemed to have received their own share of "hospitality" from Mr. Mallenthorpe.

"If this is your trump card, then you should take a lesson from Mr. Kenny Rogers and know when to fold 'em, fool," Daniel said. "The pudgy one's not my friend. And the big man there makes every day harder for me than it should be."

"And I'm not going to make 'em any easier after this shit," Moog managed to get out before one of the polo shirt–clad gorillas silenced him with a whack across the back of the head with the butt end of a collapsible baton.

"Now you gone and done it," Moog snapped over his shoulder.

Maybe J. Christopher was unimpressed by the scene. Maybe he realized that—against all odds—he was losing control of the situation. Whatever his reason, he snapped, "Shut up, boy."

And that was the beginning of the end.

"Boy?" The big man seemed more surprised by the stupidity of the comment than actually offended by it. "I'm going to jack you up like a car with four flats."

This time the baton struck with enough force to whip Moog's head around.

The only lasting effect of the blow, however, was that it pissed off Moog even more. He looked back at the polo-shirted gorilla, and then growled at Daniel, "Can you just hurry up with that mojo shit of yours, so I can get to killin' this motherfucker already?"

Another strike of the baton silenced Moog. But made him even angrier.

"That's mighty bold talk for a nigger on his knees," the polo shirt with the baton sneered.

"Oh, I'm gonna kill you, all right." The big man's mind was made up now. "My word of honor, I'm gonna kill you just as soon as his mojo comes down."

"What's he talking about?" J. Christopher was momentarily distracted by curiosity.

"It's this mojo thing I've got working for me," Daniel said almost apologetically. "In a minute or two something stupid is going to happen—something that you never could've prepared for—and it's going to turn your whole world upside down."

"Oh, I don't think so. I've prepared for everything." And J. Christopher honestly believed that in his heart.

Daniel knew better. "You've overlooked one thing."

"And what's that, Mr. Erickson?"

"You've overlooked the fact that I am a man powered by an unnatural hatred and guided by an everlasting love. And now I'm going to unleash one so that I don't fail the other."

And just like that, the time for talking was over.

Daniel leaned back in his chair just far enough so that when the legs came back down to the floor, one of them was right on Sanjay's instep.

The man roared in pain as the fragile bones of his foot broke beneath the force of Daniel leaning forward on the chair. The pain distracted Sanjay for one excruciating instant, but that was all Daniel needed.

Daniel leaned forward and opened his mouth. An adult male can generate a bite force of over five hundred pounds per square inch, and all of that came down on Sanjay's right thumb.

The man screamed again and dropped the Rampuri to the ground. Without releasing his wolflike vise on the man's hand, Daniel threw himself forward in the chair and tipped over, pinning Sanjay beneath him.

While Daniel had been bound with rope, Moog and Feller had their hands secured behind their backs by the plastic zip-tie handcuffs that many government and law enforcement agencies now favor as lighter, easier to apply, and more hygienic than standard metal cuffs. And while all of those advantages are valid enough, the zip-tie cuffs are prone to breaking if the restrained individual can exert sufficient force against them.

Moog's middle name was Sufficient Force. Or it should've been.

With a single, swift motion he bent forward, thrusting his buttocks backward as he pulled his arms forward. Before the racist polo shirt with the baton could utter a prayer, Moog was free.

A second later, the baton was in Moog's hand. A second after that, the racist polo shirt was dead. Another second, and so was his partner.

An angry Moog with a police baton was like an ADD kid on a sugar rush at a Whac-A-Mole: he swung at everything he saw, and even if he only hit half of it, there was nothing left standing when he was done.

Except Feller, who stood silently amazed at the carnage littering the ground all around him.

Two reinforcements came rushing into the room as what was clearly a last line of defense. One of them had a Mossberg 500 tactical shotgun to his shoulder.

He took aim at the big man with the baton, but an instant before he pulled the trigger Feller rushed at him. The shotgun blast went wide, shattering one of the windows.

Before the man could bring the barrel down, Feller moved in closer. The two men struggled over the weapon, but there was no real contest. The shooter was younger, stronger, better trained—and had his hands free. He pushed Feller to the ground and pulled the stock of his shotgun up to his shoulder so he could take aim on the fallen man's chest.

The would-be shooter's head exploded like an Independence Day watermelon with an M-80 pushed into the pulp. Moog stood behind him, his chest heaving with exertion, the baton in his hand dripping with blood.

On the floor, Daniel had exchanged his bite on Sanjay's hand for a piece of the poor man's nose. There was more screaming. And more blood.

No matter how hard he struggled, Sanjay still could not free himself from beneath Daniel. It would have been a foolish thing to do, because the area under the chair was probably the only safe spot in the room.

Moog came up behind them and a second later, Daniel's hands were free. And then they were on the fallen Rampuri. A single motion, and Sanjay stopped struggling forever.

The last member of the detail was the smartest of them all. He turned and ran back out the door.

"Dan—" was all that Moog could scream before the pistol went off.

The warning was enough to send Daniel diving to the ground just as the shot struck the floor where he'd been lying next to Sanjay's corpse.

J. Christopher stood at the head of the room with a pistol in his hand.

A second shot sent Moog diving for cover.

J. Christopher probably would've taken his third shot at Daniel, but before he could relocate his target, Daniel rolled toward him, popping up right in front of him with the Rampuri leading the way.

From his knees, Daniel drove the twelve-inch blade upward. It struck J. Christopher in the crotch, and Daniel kept driving it up until the weapon's handle was deep inside the man's pelvic cavity. Stunned and shocked, he stood for a moment with the weapon's bloody handle protruding from him like a strap-on belted to an impotent man. The 9mm slipped from his hand.

J. Christopher tilted his head slightly to the left, regarding Daniel with nothing more than curiosity, wondering how everything could have gone so horribly wrong—exactly as Daniel had predicted. He struggled to speak. "What are you?"

"J. Christopher Mallenthorpe, I am Daniel Erickson. And I'm the man that's going to send you straight to hell." With all his might, Daniel kicked the protruding Rampuri handle, driving it farther into the fleshy cavern between the man's legs where it was already embedded.

J. Christopher's eyes widened. His gaping mouth let loose a sharp squeal, and then filled with a torrent of thick, red blood before turning again to a smile. "Koschei."

"Is going to join you soon enough." Daniel kicked the man again, this time in the chest, driving him backward and out the shattered window. "Now go to hell."

Twenty-seven stories below, the sidewalk looked as if Jackson Pollock had painted a mural with a multimillionaire.

CHAPTER TWENTY-FIVE

Let You Down Easy

Gerald Feller's contribution to their fight for freedom had been little more than to run into people and fall on the floor, hoping for the best as chaos erupted around him. The strategy might not have been particularly heroic, maybe not even dignified, but it had been successful. He had lived through the shit storm, and survival is its own small victory. Maybe the only victory that really matters.

"We ain't got time for this," Moog snapped as he struggled to open the hotel suite door against the air pressure created by a shattered window at twenty-seven stories. "Just leave his ass here."

"We can't leave him," Daniel yelled above the roar of rushing wind as he knelt on the floor and worked the plastic cuffs that still held Feller's hands behind his back. "He knows too much."

"There's an open window with your solution right there," Moog pointed out.

Daniel shook off the suggestion. "We need what he's got."

"Well, then take it and let's go, because I'm not taking him with us."

"I know," Daniel agreed. (Sort of.) "He's taking us."

The cuffs came free, and Gerald Feller sat up, rubbing his wrists where the ties had cut into them and ringed the swollen flesh with bright red bands. "Don't expect me to thank you."

Daniel got to his feet. "I don't expect you to do anything but take us to Koschei."

"Well, *that* I can do." Feller climbed up off the carpet.

"That we can do ourselves," Moog interjected.

"No." Daniel was certain. "Koschei is like a shadow of smoke in the middle of the night. The only sure way to get to him is to have him think we were brought to him."

"Well, whatever your plan is, Cochise." Moog started out the door. "We've gotta get out of this place."

Daniel moved toward the door. "Something we can all agree on."

The Hyatt Regency in New Orleans has twenty-one floors of guest rooms. Each room opens out onto a hallway that circles an open-air atrium. While standing in the hallway, it's possible to see the entire interior of the hotel, from the elevator banks at the floor level, every hotel room door, and the skylight above.

From that lofty perch, it was easy for the trio to observe the response to the alarms they had set off. Hotel security and the New Orleans PD were filling the lobby like soldier ants responding to a queen's alarm pheromone.

More immediately distressing, there were a number of men in black polo shirts down on the lobby level pointing up at the trio on the twenty-seventh floor. A number of others were running toward the elevator bank.

Moog was the first to evaluate the situation. "This some bad shit."

"They've got the elevators," Feller exclaimed, stating the obvious. "They're on their way up. They'll have the stairs covered too. We're trapped here."

"Like I said," Moog insisted. "This some bad shit."

Daniel knew they were in dire straits, but was less pessimistic. He'd come to believe that salvation was at his fingertips if he could only recognize the opportunity for redemption. "There's got to be a way. I know there is."

Daniel had the faith, but it was Moog who saw the way.

Down the hall, a maid had abandoned her cleaning cart stacked high with fresh linens. The big man looked to it, out into the vast chasm of the hotel's interior, and then back to the cart. "Follow me."

Without a word of explanation, Moog took two king-size sheets from the cart, unfurled them, and seized an end of each. "Take the other end," he instructed the two other men.

Daniel and Feller looked back at him blankly.

Moog made a quick check on the progress the elevators were making in their climb, and then returned his attention to the sheets. "Go ahead, fools. Grab the ends of the sheets. We ain't got all goddamn day."

Each man did as he was told even though he had no idea why.

Moog approached the railing and looked down to the lobby floor twenty-seven lethal floors below. "Now, hang on tight and jump."

Both Daniel and Feller had the same reaction. "What?"

"You heard me. Climb over and jump. I'll swing you down to the floor below us."

Feller looked over the edge and judged the distance. "Are you kidding me?"

"Right now, you got three choices," Moog assessed. "You can get your fat ass over the edge and trust me."

"And the other two?" Feller wanted to know.

"You can wait for the polo shirts to whisk you off to another one of their facilities—and they strike me like the sort that hold a grudge."

Feller looked over the edge again. "You said there was a third."

"You can hope the cops get you first." Moog looked the ex-FBI agent up and down. "But you don't strike me as the type that's going to have a good time on Saturday nights in Angola."

Feller considered all three options. "Don't let go."

"Just get over. We're running out of time."

"You sure about this?" Daniel asked his friend.

"Have I ever let you down?"

That was all Daniel needed to hear. A second later, he was swinging twenty-seven stories in the air from a bed sheet. He managed to kick himself over the railing of the twenty-sixth floor and land safely. A second later Feller clumsily did the same.

"Now what?" Daniel shouted up.

"Just don't you let go."

Daniel looked at Feller, but there was no explanation to be found in his puzzled face.

A second later, there was a high-pitched "Fuck meeeeeee!" Something very big went sailing by, and the sheets the two men held snapped taut with a terrible weight. Caught off guard, both men struggled to maintain their grip.

"Don't let go," Daniel warned through gritted teeth.

The sheets went slack when Moog was safely on the twenty-fifth floor. "Now it's your turn."

Feller looked over at Daniel, who'd already moved to the railing and begun to climb over. Then both men were sailing through the air down to the twenty-fourth floor and immediately bracing themselves as Moog took a leap of faith to the twenty-third floor.

The three men worked their way down, floor by floor, until they reached the chaos of the lobby. The blown-out window on the top floor had triggered alarms throughout the hotel, and people jostled against one another as they tried to evacuate in response to the sirens. No one in the crowd seemed to notice the trio that suddenly appeared in its midst.

Daniel looked up and saw a number of men in black polo shirts pointing down at them, but by then it was too late. The trio drifted into the crowd and disappeared into the Louisiana morning.

CHAPTER TWENTY-SIX

Rumours

"Lindsey Buckingham and Stevie Nicks."

"Excuse me." Vicki wasn't quite sure what the kid meant by his reference.

"Pat Benatar and Neil Giraldo," he continued. Then added, "Debbie Harry and Chris Stein."

"All right," she said with more than a little frustration. "If you've got something to say to me, try explanations instead of riddles."

"You know," he coaxed. "Female singers and their guitar players."

The kid had a winning smile, even if the grin was a little boyish. He was tall and lanky and not so raw that she couldn't see the man he might one day grow into. She, however, had too many other things occupying her mind than to give in to thoughts of tutoring her young guitar player into manhood.

"I'm flattered," she smiled. "I am. But I don't think—"

"It's all right," he assured her.

She was glad that he understood, grateful that their time in the recording studio wouldn't be plagued with personal dramas.

"You're a hell of a guitar player. And you seem like a really nice guy, but I really don't think—"

"I totally understand." He flashed that winning smile again.

On second thought, maybe it was even more winning because it *was* so damn boyish.

"I understand that you're self-conscious about it, but the age difference really doesn't matter to me." He was painfully sincere.

Vicki was just pained. "Excuse me?"

"The difference in our ages," he explained, as if he had to.

"What differences—"

"Don't get mad." He was too young to realize that there is almost nothing more dangerous than telling a woman not to get mad. "I just meant that I don't care that you're older."

The tide was turning on him.

"Older?"

"You know, by a few years. I think it's cool. You know, that you're a mature woman. I'm not one of those guys hung up on young chicks or anything. I think it's hot."

Vicki was too taken aback to be enraged, but just barely. "You think what's hot?"

"You know, that you've been around. Seen things."

His earnestness didn't do anything to offset his oafishness, even if it was largely a matter of youth. "Listen—" She was set to dress him down, but was forced to stop when she realized she didn't know his name. She continued her pause to give him the opportunity to tell her.

"Zack," he said.

She preferred the days when there weren't any more than twenty names for men, and anything other than Steve, Joe, and Tom was exotic. Today there were just too many damn Zacks and

Noahs and Liams. "Listen, Zack. Let me give you some pointers with us older ladies."

He looked at her eagerly, like a puppy waiting for a tennis ball to be chucked.

"First, as far as a woman is concerned, God didn't give you a mouth so you could talk. So, whenever you feel the urge to say something to a mature woman such as myself, you should really resist the temptation and just shut the hell up."

His smile fell to a frown. No tennis ball chucking today.

"Second," she continued, "no woman likes to hear herself referred to as older, I don't care whether she's barely legal or Betty fucking White."

"Got it," he said sullenly.

"Mature is worse."

"OK."

"And last, but not least, while I'm not the used car with a busted odometer you make me out to be, you are absolutely right in assuming that I have had more than my fair share of lovers. And if I had any interest in schooling the chronically immature"—she leaned in and whispered in his ear as she rubbed his crotch, just once but firmly enough to get his attention—"I could rock your motherfucking world."

She left him standing there, his eyes wide and his mouth agape.

Without another word she just walked away, more than a little proud of herself. *Older. Mature.* She scoffed at the idea, knowing she was still hotter than a Harley manifold after a daylong ride to Joshua Tree.

Her guitar player's face (and jeans) was exhibit A. She hadn't lost a step.

"What do you think of him?" Koschei's voice—like the man himself—seemed to come out of nowhere and took her by surprise.

"Who?"

"The guitar player I selected for you?"

She looked over her shoulder, satisfied to see him still standing there with the same toaster-in-the-bathtub look on his face.

"He's a little green." She grinned. "But he's learning."

"I'm sure he is." Koschei looked back at the kid and smiled too. "I'm sure he is."

One of the engineers stepped out into the hallway. "Excuse me, Mr. Koschei."

"Quite all right, Leddy. What is it that you need?"

"We're ready to get the redub on the guitar line."

Koschei pointed toward the still-stunned young man. "Well, there he is."

"Hey, Erickson," the engineer yelled. "Get back in the booth."

The kid shook off his shock and trotted off to the recording booth.

"Erickson?" Vicki asked.

"Excuse me?" Koschei seemed amused at pretending that he didn't understand why she was so alarmed.

"Zack?" The disturbing pieces of the Freudian puzzle came together for her. "You hired Zack Erickson for my band? *That's* Zack Erickson?"

"I believe that's the young man's name," the old man said coyly. "There's not a problem with that, is there? I thought since you got along so well with the father you might enjoy the same chemistry with the son." He sneered at her and made the creepies she already felt crawling under her skin a thousand times worse. "Was I wrong?"

She wanted to slap the smug off his face, but knew better. She wanted to cry, but knew better than to do that too. In the end, she felt the only secure course of action was to turn and walk away as quickly as she could.

She walked straight to the women's room, where she punched the first stall door and made it slam against the partition. It felt good, but it didn't make her *feel* better.

So she sat down on the seat and cried. For a long, long time.

CHAPTER TWENTY-SEVEN

Bump in the Night

The night air was a cool contrast to the bright-light stuffiness of the Hi-Lo Truck Stop somewhere in West Texas. Daniel and Moog stepped outside, and each of them took a breath that was just a little bit deeper than the one before it.

"Nice night," Daniel said.

The big man took another deep breath. "Any night you're free and alive is a nice night."

Daniel found it to be a painful truth. "I wasted a lot of years not understanding that."

"Most people do."

Daniel took an extra-deep breath and followed his friend across the parking lot to where Feller was waiting for them in the Lincoln they'd boosted from a pay-to-park lot two blocks from the Superdome.

"He's gonna be a problem," Moog said grimly, gesturing toward the stolen car and the man behind the wheel.

Daniel kept walking. "I know."

"Like any problem, the best time to solve it is *now*."

"Except that we've got bigger problems than a bloated henchman. Let's get done what we need to get done, and then you can *solve* him however you want." Daniel couldn't help but add, "Besides, there's something about the guy's middle-aged fury that I can't help but relate to."

Moog understood. "Doesn't make me wanna kill him less."

"I know."

"What the hell is he doin'?" Moog gestured toward the idling sedan.

Daniel didn't have to look. "I'm guessing that he's reporting in to Koschei on the pay-and-go mobile phone he thinks I didn't see him buy when we stopped at that truck stop in Arkansas."

The big man stopped dead. "What? He's been telling Koschei we're coming? Telling him where we were? And you knew about it?"

Daniel just kept walking. "We're not going to surprise Koschei. At least, not by showing up. I think I may spoil his day once we get there, but if Feller isn't checking in now, then he won't trust us when we finally get there."

"If we show up there." Moog trotted after him to catch up. "We'll be lucky if that snake don't bite us both out here in the middle of the desert."

Daniel shook off the suggestion. "Koschei wants us alive."

"No. Koschei wants you alive. That ain't no kind of insurance for me."

"Then I guess you better stay on your toes."

"Stay on my toes," the big man grumbled as he climbed into the backseat behind a driver he didn't trust at all.

The stolen Lincoln pulled out of its parking spot and rolled cautiously toward the exit. It slowed as it approached the chasm of asphalt and macadam where the Hi-Lo Truck Stop's parking lot merged, without any official line or designation, with the edge of the state route. The car crossed the suspension-rattling divide, and then sped off toward the highway entrance ramp.

"Where'd you get the doughnuts?" Daniel looked across the backseat at the dozen glazed beauties Moog was beginning to work his way through.

"What do you mean where'd I get 'em?" Moog knew what was coming next, and he tucked the bag between himself and the passenger side door as a preemptive defensive maneuver.

"I didn't see them." There was more than a little whine in Daniel's words.

"Well, maybe you shoulda been a little more *on your toes*. Or whatever."

"You know," Feller interrupted, "one of you can sit up front with me. The two of you sitting back there leaves me feeling like a limo driver."

Moog didn't acknowledge him. "First off, there was a big-ass glass case of doughnuts right there. Ain't my fault you jackin' around with those damn protein bars or tofu sticks like some granola-eating tree licker."

Daniel looked down regretfully at the snack he knew wouldn't satisfy him. Not really.

Moog popped the last of the first doughnut into his mouth just to prove a point. "And don't get to thinking I'm some kinda doughnut socialist gonna share my big bag of glazed goodness with y'all just 'cause you're a dumbass and missed out. This the United States of Moog, motherfucker. These outta-the-fryer hot and fresh, and they all mine."

The big man turned his attention to the front seat. "And no one wanna ride up next to your sing-along-with-every-god-damn-song-whether-you-know-the-lyrics-or-not ass, specially not when you're chewing on some nasty two-dollar cigar. So you can just call me Miss motherfuckin' Daisy and keep on drivin', 'cause if I'm gonna be sittin' up front, you gonna be ridin' in the trunk."

Feller didn't say a word as he flipped on the turn signal and slowed to make the left turn onto the highway entrance ramp.

"Someone's tired," Daniel teased, without turning from the window he was staring out of.

"I ain't tired," Moog snapped.

"And cranky," Feller joined in.

"*You* all tired and cranky," Moog retorted before he even had a chance to consider what he was saying. "And what grown-ass man says 'cranky' anyway?"

"A tired and cranky doughnut hoarder." Daniel grinned. "That's what you are."

"You know," Moog said, without exaggerating the restraint he was exercising, "there's more than enough room for *both* of y'all back in that trunk."

The lights came out of nowhere.

One minute they were hotly discussing middle-of-the-night breakfast pastries and who rode where. A second later, the Lincoln's interior was lit up brighter than a tanning booth in Wisconsin in the middle of winter.

Time distorted. An eternity elapsed in a single heartbeat.

Maybe one of the three had time to utter a startled, "What the—" But there wasn't enough time to shout out the "fuck!"

The impact was sudden and sharp.

The lights that had appeared out of nowhere collided with the Lincoln's right rear quarter panel and sent the stolen sedan into a spin.

Feller had taken the defensive driving course at the Tactical and Emergency Vehicle Operations Center while he'd been an agent candidate at the FBI Academy in Quantico. Many years had passed since then, and none of those lessons (he hadn't been a very good student) came back to him in the split second when he might have been able to steer out of the spin and save their asses.

Instead, the two tons of Detroit steel made three full rotations before hitting the rumble strips and skidding off the ramp. The car careened over an embankment, hit a swale, and then nose-dived into a ditch overgrown with long grass.

Moog was too big and Daniel too fatalistic for seatbelts, so both men bounced around the back cabin like a pair of dice in a backgammon cup. When the car came to its final resting place, Daniel found himself pressed against Moog, who'd been slammed against the door. The crushed doughnuts were no longer an issue.

"What the hell happened?"

Moog dabbed at a thin line of blood running down his forehead. "I think fucking Morgan Freeman up there drove off the goddamn road."

Still belted into the driver's seat, Feller's only response was a weak groan.

Daniel wasn't sure about the who, what, how, or why, but he knew one thing for certain. "We gotta haul ass out of here."

Moog's door wouldn't budge at first, but it couldn't withstand a series of desperate kicks from the big man. It creaked open, and he crawled out onto the unmown grass, with Daniel following close behind.

The first slug hit the Lincoln a second later, followed by a volley of six or seven more. Muzzle flashes and sparks danced in the night like lethal lightning bugs.

"Don't shoot! Don't shoot!" The furious order was almost as loud as the shots. "Eee wants heem alive! You kill heem, and I kill you!" The accent was strong.

Moog turned to Daniel, "What is it with you and our south-of-the-border friends?"

Daniel racked his brain. "I haven't killed anyone connected with a cartel since . . ." He couldn't recall an exact time and place.

"Less than a year ago," Moog filled in for him. "LA. Remember?"

"Talk about holding a grudge," Daniel whispered, careful to stay within the cover of the tall grass.

With their heads down, Daniel and Moog instinctively moved through the tall grass as fast as they could to get away from the wreck.

"Who wants who?" Moog whispered in the dark when he thought they were far enough away that the question would go unheard by the shooters.

"Someone wants us," Daniel whispered over his shoulder without ever stopping his belly-crawl until he was at the top of the far rise and looking back down at the scene on the entrance ramp.

There were three cars down there. The Lincoln in the ditch. An SUV, its engine dead and smoking under the hood, at the side of the ramp. And another idling behind it.

Two men pulled Feller out of the wreck and dragged him to the idling SUV. He seemed unable to put up any resistance.

Another pair of men waded through the waist-high grass. When they came across a swath of trampled grass, they stopped and pointed up at the embankment that Moog and Daniel had just climbed. One set off in pursuit, but the other man turned back down the hill toward the idling SUV and called out something that was indiscernible from Moog and Daniel's position on the top of the rise.

"Uh-oh," Moog whispered. "Here comes trouble."

Daniel knew that was true. "For them."

"Them? We're on our belly in the grass with nothing in our hands but sweat, and we got a pair of hopped-up, well-armed Mexicans doing their best Usain Bolt after our asses."

Daniel didn't seem to share those concerns. "I like to think of us as the Keith and Ronnie of ass kicking."

Moog didn't catch the reference. "How's that?"

"Rolling Stones?" The reference didn't spark a reaction. "You know how Keith and Ronnie have their ancient art of weaving? Each guitar just instinctively knows where the other is going, and in turn creates its own path until the music takes on a life independent of its players."

Moog stared at him blankly.

"I like to think that after all this time, we've formed that kind of relationship. You've learned to hit someone, while I know just when to shoot someone else."

"You talk too much. Two solid years I been saving your ass, 'cause I ain't never met no one that more people wanted to kill than you. Two solid years, and I don't think there's been a minute of it when you wasn't talkin' sumpthin' didn't need to be said."

Daniel raised his eyebrows to communicate a wordless *Fine!* And then he sprang to his feet and ran down the back end of the slope, toward the state route.

"Goddamn it," Moog puffed as he followed.

They were halfway down when Daniel came to a stop so sudden that Moog, lumbering behind like a grizzly bear, couldn't avoid a collision.

"What's wrong?" Moog asked as he pushed himself away.

Daniel put his ear to the night. "Hear that?"

"What?" The big man couldn't hear anything but a dog barking in the near distance. "All I hear is a dog."

"Exactly." Daniel turned and began running across the slope and toward the agitated mutt.

Moog stayed put. "Where you going?"

"A dog," Daniel called over his shoulder. "It's a sign from Atibon." He ran all the harder toward it.

"A sign?" The big man exhaled with a labored breath. "Barking dog ain't a sign of nuthin' but a pissed-off pooch."

Daniel didn't slow or turn to make a response. He'd almost disappeared into the darkness before Moog huffed one last puff and resentfully began to trot off after him.

A shot from the crest of the hill behind him turned Moog's trot into a sprint. It wasn't long before he'd closed the distance on Daniel, who stood breathing heavily outside a boarded-up gas station that had lost the fight for survival with the truck stop down the road.

"Where that dog at?" Moog asked, still panting.

Daniel looked up curiously. "What dog?"

"The barking dog you was following."

"Oh." Daniel seemed to have almost forgotten. "I don't think there was ever a real dog."

Moog was more confused than winded, and he could barely breathe. "But you said there was a dog."

"I never said it was a dog," Daniel clarified. "I said it was a sign from Atibon."

The big man knew better than to argue the point. He looked the abandoned gas station up and down. "Well, where the hell did that sign of yours lead us?"

Daniel straightened his back and smiled. "Exactly where we're supposed to be."

From out of the dark distance, a burst of gun shots bit into the garage's weathered exterior and sent a cascade of wood chips into the air, where each of them hit the siding.

Moog was less than convinced, "*This* is where we're supposed to be?"

"Absolutely," Daniel said excitedly.

And then he went inside.

CHAPTER TWENTY-EIGHT

Joe's Garage

The bay of Joe's Garage was bigger than anyone would've guessed from looking at the exterior of the building. Whoever Joe had been, he'd spent his work days beneath two hydraulic lifts. And on the very last day, when he abandoned his namesake garage for good, he left both completely raised. Maybe it was simply an oversight on his part, but Daniel wanted to believe it was a last gesture of resistance and defiance—two raised middle fingers—to whatever bankers or fates had driven him from his place of work.

"We gotta keep moving," Moog insisted in a whisper, though he was crouched down with Daniel behind a stack of old fifty-five gallon drums, three barrels high. "We get caught in here and we're gonna be screwed. They can just wait us out until daytime." He looked around the ancient structure. Worse yet, they could just toss a match. Whoosh!"

"Not that easy." Daniel was certain of that. "They need us alive. Or me, at least. And if Atibon led us here—"

"The old man ain't here."

"No. Not the man. But there's more to him than the face he shows you." Daniel was certain of that too. "If a dog led us here, then here is where we're supposed to be."

"Doin' what?"

Daniel shook his head, and the moonlight filtering through the dusty windows was like a whispered response. "But we'll know when it happens."

As if on cue, the front door creaked open.

From their hiding spots, Daniel and Moog could just make out the silhouette of a man slipping into the garage. Then another.

The two newcomers seemed instantly overwhelmed by the environment. They stood still and stared at the features and fixtures that were clearly foreign to them: the walls were lined with enough antique tools and spare parts to make for a "very special episode" of any reality shows that offer rummaged-through, abandoned storage units and long-sealed boxes as a solid entertainment value.

Together they moved toward the front office and one of them made the other take a look inside. Nothing.

They moved in tandem to another door that might have led to a washroom or another storeroom. Again, the larger of the shadows pointed a silent instruction, and the skinny one checked inside. Again nothing.

Moog wanted to take the opportunity to bolt from their hiding spot, but Daniel put out a hand to keep him there and hold their position. It was against every instinct screaming in his head, but the big man did as instructed, and together they watched their pursuers work their way closer and closer.

Over by the garage bay, there were a dozen stacks of used tires and five or six more stacks of ones that had never met the pavement. There were plenty of options where a desperate man could hide, and it was becoming increasingly obvious that the two hired guns were too lazy or too scared to check all of them.

And that gave Daniel an idea. He found what he was looking for in a four-inch bolt lying discarded on the garage floor. With a flick of his wrist, he flung it out into the darkness and it landed exactly where he'd aimed: down in the depths of the first lift bay.

"They're een there," the larger of the two shadowy figures whispered, though he shouldn't have said anything at all. He moved warily toward what he thought was the source of the sound, pushing his skinny partner in front of him.

Together, they reached the lift bay, and the leader of the duo gestured that his partner should look down into its depths.

"Are you crazy?" the skinny shadow responded.

The other man made a gesture to his companion, conveying that it was only a question of whether he looks into the pit or gets left there for good.

Daniel watched the skinny one move toward the lift, reluctant step by reluctant step, until the kid was right on top of the mechanic's pit. He looked into the depths, adjusted his grip on his pistol, and then slowly sank to his knees, thrusting the pistol down before him into the impenetrable darkness.

Daniel recognized the opportunity and motioned to Moog that it was finally time for them to move.

The larger of the shadows never heard the soft footsteps behind him. His attention was focused on his partner, who had pulled a Zippo lighter from his pocket and was searching the dark depths of the bay by its flickering light.

A sound.

It was nothing more than the skittering of feet across the cement floor, but the larger of the shadows was startled and spun toward what he thought was the point of origin. He fired his pistol once. Nothing.

Another sound.

The same shadow wheeled back just in time to see something darker and denser than a shadow move toward the lift. He raised his pistol to take aim, but everything was happening too quickly.

Before he could fire, something struck him from behind.

And then, as he fell to his knees, the lift came slamming down with a single, terrible crash.

The metal lip of the lift met the concrete edge of the bay and snipped through the skinnier shadow as if he were the unwanted tip of a cigar. His top half and the lighter it still held tumbled into the bay, where the open flame met a mixture of oil and gas that had been fermenting for years, just waiting for a flame. The explosion was worth the wait.

In the instant when flames burst out of the dark pit like tongues of fire shouting apocalyptic prophecies, the survivor simply fell to the ground and curled into a ball as if that might protect him from what was coming for him.

There were flames and shadows. He shot at them all without hitting anything.

An instant later, the room spun wildly like a rigged roulette wheel, and when it stopped, everything went completely black.

* * *

Returning to consciousness was a mixed blessing for the man.

"I've got some good news," Daniel announced. "And some bad news."

The man tried to get to his feet, but something bigger (and meaner) than him knocked him back down.

Daniel gestured to Moog that there was no need to hit the man again, and continued. "The good news is that you're alive. The bad news is that it's extremely unlikely that you're going to stay that way."

"I'm not afraid to die," the man said.

Moog tested his resolve by stepping from the shadows and thumbing back the hammer of the pistol he held.

Although he'd never seen it from that particular angle, the man recognized that it was his pistol the big man had aimed at the center of his chest. "Go ahead. Shoot. I'm not afraid of death."

"Not being afraid of death doesn't make you brave," Daniel said. "It just means you've failed in making a life that's worth holding onto. It's not courage, just an admission of a fundamental failure."

"Do you think I will talk?" the man asked. "El Tigre has a liger."

Moog had never heard of one of those. "A what?"

"Liger," the man repeated. "Half lion, half tiger. Nine hundred kilos. Trained it to eat *el jefe*'s enemies. Or those who fail him," the man added, aware that he now fit into that category. "You can do whatever you want," the man insisted. "There is nothing that frightens me as much as that liger."

"You'd be surprised," Daniel grinned. "I can be pretty fucking frightening sometimes."

"Do your worst." The man gulped. He was aware that they were in an old garage and he knew full well what one man can do to another with an assortment of automotive tools. "I'm not afraid of anything you could do to me."

"Well, the I'm-about-to-shit-myself look in your eyes suggests you're just as scared as you should be," Daniel said. "Because I'm going to kill you." His smile grew truly sinister. "With kindness."

"What are you doing?" Real fear grew in the man's eyes.

Daniel simply stepped away from him. "There's the door," he said, and pointed the way out.

The man didn't understand. "What?"

"You're free to go," Daniel explained.

"I'm keeping the piece though." Moog thumbed the pistol's hammer safely down, and then slid the weapon into the waist of his pants.

The man got to his feet and looked suspiciously at his captors. "What?"

"There's the door. Feel free to walk right through it."

"It's a trap?" The man knew his freedom had to carry some kind of price.

"Well, the door's not a trap," Daniel said. "But I suppose you walking out of here is."

"And the fact that you're still alive," Moog added.

Daniel nodded. "That's probably the worst."

The man couldn't express his confusion about how being alive could be a bad thing.

So Daniel explained it to him. "It's a small world, amigo. This is not the first time your boss, El Pussy, has sent someone like you—better than you—to bring him my head. And I know for a fact that he'll be expecting me to send you back to him in pieces. So, when you return with all your parts where they oughta be, do you know what he's gonna think?"

The man wasn't as quick on the uptake as he should've been, so Moog connected the dots for him. "He's going to think that you pussied out on him. He's going to think you sold him out. And just to cover his ass, he's going to assume you gave up everything."

A cold chill ran through the man.

"And I'm sure you know what that means," Daniel prompted.

Moog was quick to fill in the blank for the poor man. "It means you're one hundred eighty pounds of walkin', talkin' Meow Mix, motherfucker."

"Of course," Daniel interjected, "I bet a fearless badass like you doesn't give a shit about being turned into cat shit." He paused. "But we all know it won't end with you."

Moog shook his head with mock sorrow. "No, sir, it will not."

"It's going to be your papi and brothers," Daniel assured the man. "Your cousins and friends. No, you won't meet that liger alone."

"Gonna be one fat fucking cat," Moog chuckled. "But it ain't gonna end there. Just think what will go down with your sisters. Your mother. You got a wife?"

Daniel smiled, content that his point had been made. "So, I'm not going to bother with trying to persuade you with this assortment of shop tools, because right now you—and everyone you've ever known or loved—only have one thin chance at seeing another sunset."

"Naomi-fucking-Campbell thin," Moog interjected.

"Right now, El Tigre just took away a man we need. And you're going to help us get him back."

"Not El Tigre," the man corrected.

"What?"

"It wasn't him. El Tigre never leaves Mexico. Almost never. He sent Poco to get you."

"Well, Poco then." Daniel was appreciative of the clarification. "Whatever and whoever he is, the fact remains that I want to kill this guy—and now you *need* me to."

Moog folded his arms across his chest. "Time to partner up, son."

"So." Daniel knew it was time to close the deal. "You can walk right through that open door or you can stay here with us and tell us how to kill Poco."

Moog grinned. "Meow, meow, meow, motherfucker."

CHAPTER TWENTY-NINE

Father of Mine

Malaika had spent more than half an hour walking through the studio trying to find Vicki, when she stepped into the ladies room, not as part of her search, but to use the facilities.

No sooner had she sat down on the seat, than she heard a slight rustle in the stall beside hers. Ordinarily, the occurrence wouldn't have struck her as strange, and restroom etiquette would've dictated that she confine her interests to her own stall. But Malaika was aware that the studio had been locked some hours earlier, at midnight, and that she and Vicki were the only females in the building.

"Vick?" she asked tentatively.

Nothing but another sniffle.

"Listen." Malaika focused on making her voice sound bigger and badder to conceal the vulnerability she felt in such a compromising situation. "If you ain't my friend, then you don't belong in here. So I'm pullin' my pants back up from around my ankles, and if you was just playing peep with me, I'm gonna come next door right now and drop-kick your ass."

Malaika was preparing to do just that when a soft voice called out, "It's just me, Meeka."

The toilet stall opened slowly, and there was Vicki.

"Girl, what you doin' in here?" Malaika asked. "They want you back in the studio for some harmony overdubs. I've been looking for you for—" She stopped midsentence when she realized her friend didn't seem to comprehend—or care about—what she was saying. "You been cryin', girl?"

"No." Vicki wiped at her eyes and managed to make her mascara's bleeding, black stains even worse. "I'm not going to do it."

"Not going to do what?"

"The overdubs."

"I don't blame you, sister," Malaika said with conviction. "I think they drowning all our vocals with all those overdubs and shit, but Mr. Koschei is the Man." Her voice trailed off, looking for some positive response from her friend. "You know what I'm sayin'?"

"No. I'm not going to record anything. Not anymore." There was conviction in her words, but not in her voice.

"Girl . . ." Malaika let the word linger as a means of expressing her incredulity. "You gone cray cray sittin' on that ass gasket. Whatchu mean you're not gonna record no more?"

"The guitar player—" Vicki started.

"It's that guitar player, ain't it?" Malaika said enthusiastically, as if everything suddenly made sense. "I could tell from the minute I met him. He's got those hungry eyes just eat a girl up like she were a big slice of strawberry pie. He was looking me up and down—"

"No," Vicki stopped her before she could make it worse. "He's Daniel's son."

"He's whose what?"

"The guitar player Koschei brought in for the sessions," Vicki explained. "He's Daniel's son. *My* Daniel."

Malaika wasn't sure she had the right player on her scorecard. "The dead guy?"

"He's not dead," Vicki said with a roll of her eyes.

It was a small point that Malaika was willing to concede. "The guy who told you he was dead."

"He never actually *told* me he was dead." Vicki didn't want to make any admission that might be exculpatory. "But, yes, the dead guy. Koschei hired his son to be the session guitarist."

"Mm hmm." The girl shook her head. "Now how is that for a coincidence?"

"It's not any coincidence, Meeka." Vicki was certain of that.

"What are you saying?"

"Did you ever wonder why us?"

"I've wondered why *you*, but never *us*." Malaika was nothing if not honest. "But I never wondered why they want someone like me, 'cause I'm the best there is—"

"I think there's something more."

Malaika puffed herself up. "Oh, you best better believe there's something more." She put her hand on her hip and bounced it all two times just to give the world a teaser.

"No," Vicki said adamantly. "I think there's something more going on here. With Koschei."

Malaika didn't understand what was at issue there. "Koschei's the Man."

"He's the biggest player in the music industry," Vicki concurred. "And he called me out of the blue. He said he heard an EP I put out, but I don't think he ever did. How could he? Why would he?" Her voice expressed all the disbelief she'd felt since she'd gotten that call, all of the doubt she'd always harbored (and worked so hard to suppress) in the preposterous chain of events that had delivered her dream and brought her to LA.

"OK . . . ?" Malaika wasn't sure where their conversation was headed. And she wasn't entirely sure she wanted to be a part of it any longer.

"How did he happen to find you?"

The switch in focus convinced the girl that it was definitely a train of thought she wanted to get off of. "He heard me singing at a mall," she answered hesitantly. "Our choir was—"

Vicki was suddenly filled with a certainty that she knew better. "The biggest man in music heard you singing with a church choir in a mall in Kansas City?"

That's exactly what had happened, but hearing her friend say it aloud like that made it sound improbable at best, and the girl's response conveyed her newfound doubt. "Yes?"

Vicki had a thought. A horrible, horrifying thought. "I've got to ask you a question."

There was something in her friend's eyes that convinced Malaika she'd be better off without the inquiry, but she didn't know how to refuse. "All right."

"A personal question."

"All right."

"Your father . . ."

Malaika's posture immediately straightened, and her arms crossed in front of her chest as an unintended display that Vicki was trespassing onto personal territory. Malaika didn't like to talk about him, but couldn't see a way out of it. "What about him?" Her question was guarded.

"His name's not Moog is it?"

Malaika screwed up her face to express the ridiculousness of the question. "No, his name's not Moog. Who's going to name their kid Moog?"

Vicki was just about to concede her mistake, when she realized why she'd made it. "Is it Vernon?"

Malaika stared back. "What?"

"Is your father's name Vernon? Vernon Turner?"

The fear in the girl's eyes suddenly made her seem her age, and her voice was hushed and crushed. "How did you . . . ?"

"Because I know your father. I know him very well."

"How could you?"

There wasn't time to explain everything. Vicki got to her feet and took Malaika's hand. "We're not here for this goddamn album."

That wasn't what the girl wanted to hear, and she tried to pull away. "Seriously, you fifty shades of cray cray."

"I'm not cray cray," Vicki insisted. "We're not here as musicians. None of this is about the music."

"Then what are we—"

"We're here as bait." Vicki had already arrived at the inescapable conclusion, but speaking it aloud made her stomach turn and her knees shake. "We are bait in a trap, and if we don't do something right now, then my Daniel and your father are dead men." She played out the rest of the scenario in her head. "I think we're dead too."

Malaika looked into her friend's eyes and found a plea for faith that she couldn't deny. "What do we do?"

Vicki led her by the hand to the ladies' room door. "We've got to get out of this place."

CHAPTER THIRTY

Tick. Tick. Tick. Boom.

Moog was not nearly as confident as Daniel was pretending to be. "You are like the Yeezus of stupid plans, but even for you this is like the Michael Jackson comeback tour of stupid plans. This plan is so freaking stupid that it's . . ."

"It's genius," Daniel finished for him.

Genius wasn't the word Moog had been looking for, and he shook his head in dismay. "I still think we should just let them keep Pudge. I mean, it was probably his calls to Koschei that led those fuckers to us in the first place."

"I'm sure it was." Daniel didn't seem surprised or disturbed by the assumption. Nor did it stop him from tinkering with the iPad in his hands. "But that means that Koschei knows that someone has Feller, which means he knows that Feller doesn't have us. And that means that we can't get to Koschei. Feller's our line-crashing, no-wait, E ticket to Koschei. We just can't go to the park without him."

"This is my ticket to ride." Moog showed the pistol he'd confiscated. "We should just go in there and BOOM! take him out."

Daniel shook off the impulsive suggestion. "There's no way we're going to go in there and outgun them. We go in with guns blazing, and we're not going to end up anywhere but knee-deep in bodies."

"I'm OK with that."

"Until one of them is your daughter's." The silence suggested that Daniel had overstepped a line. "Or Vicki's." Saying the name out loud felt as bad as his friend's hurt silence.

Daniel pushed the sickening fear to the back of his mind and focused instead on his plan. He checked his watch. "This should be plenty of time. They should've gotten it by now," he said, mainly to himself. Then he pushed the button on the iPad, and five seconds later a cruel and confused face appeared on the screen.

"I know, I know," Daniel said to the individual he'd reached with FaceTime. "You already have an iPad, but I didn't know what else to get you."

"Who is this?" The man on the other side of the connection didn't appreciate the attempt at levity.

"Stop with the bullshit, Poco," Daniel responded, every bit as sternly and seriously. "You know who I am and I know who you are."

"What do you want then?"

"I'll start with stopping the stupid questions. I didn't drop the cash on two iPads just so we can be pals and play Candy Crush. You know what I want."

"And you know what I want," Poco spat right back.

"You're going to let him go."

"And what can you offer me? Would you trade your life for his?"

"Something even better," Daniel said.

Poco grinned as if he had the upper hand. "And what could be better than that?"

"Your life."

Even the suave cartel captain couldn't contain his shock. "My life? I'm surrounded by men who would die for me, but would much rather kill for me. You think you have my life in your hands to bargain with." He laughed at the ridiculous suggestion.

Daniel was undeterred. "That's right, I'll trade you your life in return for—" He stopped in his tracks. For all the planning that had gone into their scheme, he hadn't considered how best to refer to Feller. *Friend?* Absolutely not. *Partner?* Hell, no. "The pudgy white guy."

"That's not much of a bargain." Poco snorted at the offer. "You see, I already have both my life and your pudgy white friend."

"Yeah," Daniel admitted. "But I'll let you keep the first, if you give me the second."

"Is that right? Well, then you should come for me, my friend."

"There's no way I would live through a house call on your sugar shack. But you're not going to know what to do with this." Daniel tilted his iPad so that the image projected back to Poco switched from Daniel's face to a rusted and wrecked red SUV. It was Daniel's ta-da moment.

The intended effect was lost on Poco. "What the hell is that?"

"It's a 2007 Ford Escape." Daniel was uncertain about the nature of Poco's confusion.

"What does your shit car have to do with me? Do you intend to run me over? Is that it?" Poco laughed at his own little joke.

"Oh, I don't think this thing could get going fast enough to run over someone like you."

"I think you're right." The man laughed as if it were a joke he now shared with Daniel.

"Yeah. It wasn't much of a truck to begin with, and now its ass-end is weighted down with about half a ton of meth."

Poco struck a cautious silence, but one he couldn't maintain. "What does that have to do with me?"

"We took it from the Asesinos last night," Daniel said, making a casual reference to the cartel that was El Tigre's chief competitor.

"Good." Poco bluffed. "I am glad to see them lose so much. It means more profits for me, for El Tigre. But I have no interest in getting involved in that."

"Poco, my friend"—Daniel shook his head with mock regret—"we are *long* past that particular off-ramp because I'm going to put out the word that *you* were the one who ordered the hijacking. And that's not just going to piss off the Asesinos, but I'm guessing that's going to put El Tigre in a pretty shitty mood too."

The man tried to pretend he was unaffected, but the 1024 x 768 resolution on the screen in Daniel's hand showed the crystal clear image of a man beginning to sweat. "No one will believe—"

"They will, Poco," Daniel interrupted. "And it gets worse for you, buddy. See, this SUV is parked in front of the friendly neighborhood DEA satellite station, and up on the dashboard is a handwritten note that says it's a good faith offering from you, seeking an opportunity for amnesty from the United States in return for giving up everything that you know about El Tigre, the Asesinos, the Mexican government, *and* the DEA. I believe the phrase is, 'the whole fucking enchilada.'"

"You're crazy! I never—" Poco protested in vain.

"Of course 'you never,' Poco. We both know you're a good little soldier, but I'm going to make sure word gets out just the same. And when the Asesinos hear you boosted their product . . . and El Tigre thinks you made the move without him . . . and the bad apples in the DEA think you're about to give them up . . . Well, maybe they'll all believe you when you cry 'I never.'"

Poco tried to act as if he weren't shocked or scared, like he had options that both men knew he didn't have. "Let's say for a minute that I would fall for your silly story here—and I won't—but what then could you offer me?"

"This." Daniel held up the small, black box.

"What is that?"

"It's the remote to the arrangement of C-4 attached to the undercarriage of the Escape. You give me the pudgy guy. I give you the remote. You press the button, and BOOM! All of your problems go up in smoke."

Poco needed time to think. "How do I know—"

Daniel wasn't willing to wait. "You don't. You don't have time or guarantees. You don't have anything but a pudgy white guy who I'd like to get back—but don't really need. You tell me no, and I throw this iPad away, and you're left alone in a sea of shit holding a brick. I really don't care what happens next. To you or Pudge. But you've got real needs, my friend. You need this remote."

"I need more than that remote," Poco said.

"You're going back to your boss without me either way," Daniel said simply, so it would be easier for the man to accept. "The only question is whether you live to chase me another day or whether you make the top of his kitty's menu for dinner tonight. You call it."

There was no response.

"But call it now, or I'm gone . . . and you're a day and a half from getting scraped out of an oversize litter box."

And that's when Poco broke. "How?"

"It's simple. You send the pudgy guy out and I'll give you the remote. That easy. End of story."

"How do I know I can trust you?"

"You absolutely don't. But you don't have anything to bargain with. And if this isn't going to happen, then I'm just getting on the road. See ya. Bye!"

Silence.

"So what's it gonna be."

"All right."

* * *

Twenty minutes later, Feller was climbing into the backseat of a white Lexus, the latest vehicle to roll off the lot of Moog's U-Boost-It Auto.

He was battered and bruised, but still breathing. "How the hell did you pull that off?"

"Hang on. There's one last thing I've got to tell Poco." Daniel pressed FaceTime again, and Poco's grim frown appeared on the screen. "You ready. Here's the video of the SUV. You just press the button and watch it go BOOM!"

"All right." The cartel captain sounded nervous.

"Ready. Go!"

Poco held up the remote he'd retrieved from the remote control car that Moog had piloted to the gates of his compound. He pushed the button. "Nothing happened!" he snarled.

"Of course nothing happened," Daniel said with a smile. "That's why I wouldn't give you the time to find out on your own that no one ripped off the Asesinos for a load of meth last night. And how would I know how to rig a remote to a bomb? You cartel boys know all about that stuff, but I can barely work this iPad. Hell, this is just some old bastard's SUV parked here on the street."

"So this was all just a trick?" Poco's realization left him more broken than furious. "And this remote?"

"Is as worthless as you."

Poco drew closer to the iPad Daniel had delivered, as if his proximity to the screen would make him seem more intimidating. "I'm going to find you and kill you. I'm going to go straight back to Koschei and kill your bitch."

"Is that right?" Daniel didn't seem worried.

"That's right."

"Well, there's one more thing I have to set you wise to. *I* might not know how to rig a bomb and a remote, but the guy you sent after me last night seems to have had a lot of practice at it."

Poco made no response, but his face twitched with an odd combination of bewilderment and acceptance.

"While I'm the one who rigged your phony remote"—Daniel held up another black box that was identical to the dummy still in Poco's hand—"your boy did me a solid and rigged this to the charge of C-4 he set in your iPad there."

Poco's eyes widened as he looked down at the tablet of death in his hands.

"Oh, and he told me to tell you, 'Adios, *pendejo!*' You want to go see Koschei? Let me send you straight there."

Daniel pushed the button.

The blast could be heard for miles, and a spiral of smoke began snaking its way toward the sky.

CHAPTER THIRTY-ONE

Taxi

The yellow Checker cab looked like it had rolled off of the Warner Brothers back lot during the Eisenhower administration, and the hack behind the wheel seemed equally antiquated. "Where we headed?"

"We're not going anywhere," Zack Erickson said, beginning to realize that the invitation to "get out of here" from the two women had nothing to do with the sordid scenario that had been described to him in their hushed whispers. "I've left my guitar—"

"You can get another guitar," Vicki pointed out.

"It's a Gibson 335."

She understood the clarification. "You can get another *great* guitar."

"My father gave it to me."

"Trust me," she assured him, "your father would want you to leave the guitar and get the hell out of here."

"Yeah?" He was more confused than usual. "What do you know about my father?"

"Oh, she *knows* your father," Malaika was quick to add before a cross look from her friend stopped her from elaborating.

"This is all very entertaining, folks," the cabbie said to the trio stuffed into the backseat. "But this is a taxi, not a coffee house. If you want to have an interesting conversation, go find a Starbucks. But if you want to keep sitting back there, you gotta give me a destination."

A chill ran down Vicki's spine, and she turned to find there was some activity at the studio's front doors. There was nothing about the scene that was particularly menacing: two men walking purposefully toward the idling cab. Still, Vicki had a feeling that if she was ever going to be free again, she needed to get going. "Drive!"

The cabbie seemed confused by the shouted command. "Sure. Where to?"

Vicki looked over her shoulder and saw the men getting closer. "Just. Fucking. Drive."

The cabbie jumped in his seat. And then stepped on the gas.

Vicki watched as the two figures silhouetted by the lights that lined the studio driveway got smaller and smaller, and then faded entirely in the distance as the cab sped away.

"Nobody uses that kinda language in my cab," the driver scolded Vicki while looking sternly in the rearview.

"I'll make it up to you," Vicki said, but it didn't sound like an apology.

The unspoken promise that the tip would make up for the offense seemed to be enough for the wheel jockey—*almost* enough. "I still need a destination."

A destination, however, was something Vicki didn't have to give. She couldn't go back to her apartment. Ever. She didn't know how or where (or if she even wanted) to find Daniel. She didn't know where to go, and that left her with only one destination. "Anywhere."

The driver grumbled something, but then looked at the rolling meter and seemed content enough to take them there.

"What the hell is going on?" Zack asked, seated between the two women but not enjoying it nearly as much as he'd thought he would.

"I don't know," Vicki admitted. "But we had to get out of there." She looked back and was relieved that there didn't appear to be anyone following them, but the mounting miles of separation were cold comfort.

"Listen," Zack said as calmly as he could, "I understand. You get into the studio, and you look for a little *inspiration*, and then next thing you know, you've gotten a little too much inspiration and you start goin' a little . . ."

He paused for the word, but Malaika had it all along. "Cray cray?"

Zack smiled at her appreciatively. "Yeah. Cray cray."

"I'm not cray cray," Vicki insisted, then shot Malaika a look that accused her of mutiny. "That man—"

"Mr. Koschei?" Zack asked.

"He hired you because—"

"Because he liked my guitar playing," Zack said almost defensively in the face of an obvious but unspoken insinuation that there was more to his first big break than just talent.

"No. Because he knows that if he has you—"

"*Has* me?"

The interruption didn't slow or divert Vicki. "He knows if he has you, then your father will come for you."

"You keep talking like you know my father."

Malaika interrupted, "Oooooh, she *knows* your father."

"None of that matters now," Vicki insisted. "What matters is that we get as far away as we can from Koschei before he—"

"Before he *what*?" the cab driver asked, as if he were somehow a participant in the conversation too.

All three of his startled passengers looked up to the front of the taxi. It was odd that a cab driver would inject himself into their conversation.

The cabbie turned to look at them. His face had changed completely. Now it seemed as if the driver really were a remnant of the Eisenhower administration, with gray flesh and wild, yellow eyes that anyone would expect to see on a zombified fossil.

The two women shrieked in horror. Zack screamed just as loud, but a half octave higher.

"You think there's anywhere you can escape from Koschei?" The voice sounded like the scraping of a crypt's stone lid being slowly slid open. And the laugh that followed was a far worse sound, like a jackal laughing with a baby in its mouth. "There's no place to run, bitch. No place where you're safe from Koschei."

As if to prove his point, the driver slowed the taxi to a stop. The back door opened. And there stood Haden Koschei, not looking angry or threatening, but merely amused, like he'd just performed a magical illusion for a theater full of tourists in one of Vegas's lesser casinos.

"There's no direction home." He smiled as he held the door open. "All roads lead right back to me. They always have. And they always will."

Vicki got out of the cab. Zack followed. Malaika slid out last and stood on legs that wouldn't stop shaking.

Zack started to say something that he hoped might eventually develop into an excuse or an explanation. "We were just—"

Koschei grinned. "I know exactly what you were 'just.' And it's all right." He looked straight at Vicki. "I know how difficult our arrangement can be. But trust me, our days together are coming to an end."

Koschei turned without saying another word and walked back into the studio.

"You hear that?" Zack asked, relieved and enthusiastic. "He didn't seem mad at all. He said—"

"I heard what he said." Vicki wasn't relieved or enthusiastic. She knew what the seemingly harmless words really meant. "We just have to find a way out of here."

"You heard him," Malaika said. "There is no way out."

Vicki nodded. "Then we better hope that they find a way in."

Malaika nodded, though her fear wouldn't let her say anything at all.

"Wait. *They* who?" Zack asked.

Neither of the women wanted to take the time to fill him in. With nowhere else to go, Vicki accepted her fate and headed back inside the studio.

Zack and Malaika followed.

And as the studio door shut closed behind them, all three could hear peals of laughter coming from the idling cab.

CHAPTER THIRTY-TWO

Lights of LA County

Whether it was from the auto accident or his time in the custody of Poco and company, Feller had been returned to Daniel in fairly rough shape. Black and blue, he spent most of the evening drive through the desert stretched out on the backseat of Moog's stolen Lexus. Lost in the delirium of a fitful sleep, he twisted and turned, contorted and groaned, called out in woeful mumbles for someone to come back to him.

Moog was unable to make sense of any of it. "If I thought the boy could take a beating, I'd give him one just to shut him up."

From the passenger seat, Daniel looked over his shoulder. "He's taken so many beatings I don't think another would have any effect on him." He turned back around.

"Hard life he's chosen," Moog observed, making mileage conversation. "Over time, killing a man gets easier and easier, but livin' with what you've done never does. You can bluff your way through waking hours, but the truth will always call you on it in your sleep." He tossed a concerned look to the backseat, and then fixed a cold stare at the endless road ahead. "That why I never sleep."

Daniel understood but disagreed. "It's not the killing that's killing him." He cast a look at their restless passenger. "It's that wife he keeps talking about."

"Wife?" Moog couldn't recall him saying a word about a wife.

"Maybe it's just something that I notice," Daniel said, and he thought about the wife that had left him. And the woman that he loved even more. "The killing's hard, but you can lie to yourself that it was all somehow necessary. But losing your love . . ." His voice trailed off, fading momentarily into highway noise. "That's the hardest thing of all to live with. *That's* what twists a man like that." He made an over-the-shoulder nod toward Feller, who was still groaning and twitching in the imagined wreckage of his abandonment. "And that's why *I* don't sleep."

Moog would have continued the debate if he'd felt he had road to run, but there was a squandered love in his own life, and the thought of her kept him silent.

They drove on like that for a long while, three men and the ghosts of the women who haunted them. No one spoke or paid particular attention to the others or to anything at all. They endured the passing hours and miles, listening to the melodic hiss of the tires against the road and an endless stream of songs from others who seemed to understand that sense of loss.

"It's funny," Daniel said, when the scrub-covered mountains parted and revealed the Los Angeles skyline on the distant horizon.

"What's that?"

"I lived here for the better part of twenty-five years. Even before Gerald clued us in, I knew we were headed back here, and I never once thought of it as going home."

"Los Angeles?"

"Yeah." Daniel wondered whether the realization was a statement about him or the city. "You never hear anyone get off a plane in LAX and say, 'Thank God, I'm home.'"

"I suppose not."

"I'm just saying, people who live in New York won't shut up about it. People from Chicago have to convince everyone they love their city more than Manhattanites love theirs. Bostonians need to tell you your city sucks. But I don't know that I've ever heard anyone refer to Los Angeles as home. A necessity maybe, but never home."

"That's because *home* is the realest real thing there is, and none of *this* shit is real."

"How's that?"

"It's the main product, right? Pittsburgh is the steel city. Omaha is the steak city. Vegas is Sin City, and New Orleans is all about the party that don't stop. But LA is just about lies. That's the industry here. Lies. Can't build no home on lies, man."

Daniel looked out at the looming skyline and agreed. "No, can't build no home on lies."

Moog turned to the backseat and gave Feller a less than gentle poke in the ribs. "Wake your ass up!"

Feller responded, but only with a groan and an effort to turn away from the assault.

"Wake your ass up," the big man insisted. "I woulda left your ass by the side of the road a couple thousand miles ago, if it'd been up to me. But we dragged your battered ass all this way so you could get us to Koschei. So sit up and get all GPS on us here, or I'm going to trade you for a sack of oranges at the next overpass."

Feller rubbed his head, but it did absolutely nothing to lessen the crushing pain. "Century City."

"The CEO of Darkness is centered in Century City," Daniel said, pausing to take stock of the situation. "That seems appropriate."

CHAPTER THIRTY-THREE

Century City

The smog-shrouded skyscrapers and office towers of Century City rise from the surrounding landscape of California's commercial sprawl like the CGI spires of a medieval castle that's been ripped from the latest fantasy bestseller and turned into the summer's predestined box office epic.

The most foreboding of the towers was sixty stories of reflective paneled windows and black steel that made it look like a multilensed spyglass, an all-seeing eye staring out at the world without blinking or shedding a single tear.

Feller pointed up to the top. "His offices are up there."

"You sure?" Moog peered up at the very top and was unnerved by something more than just the height.

Feller nodded. "As sure as death and a cold, stone marker."

"Look." The big man may still have harbored doubts, but the high-rise lair was exactly what Daniel had been expecting. "It's Mount Doom for the lunch-at-Spago crowd. Where else would a guy like Koschei be?"

"There's a parking garage right over there," Feller pointed out.

"Yeah," Moog acknowledged as he pulled to the curb across the street, right next to a "No Parking" sign. "I don't think we want to descend into the bowels of evil just to find a parking spot. This'll do."

"They'll tow you," Feller said.

Moog defiantly turned off the engine. "No they won't."

"Yes. They will." Feller asserted.

Daniel chimed in. "They might send a truck, but they won't tow us."

Moog wasn't interested in the car. He could steal another. What he wanted to know was, "What's the plan?"

"Haven't you been paying attention?" Daniel asked good-naturedly. "You're making sure they don't tow the car."

"What?"

"If they send some reality show wannabe looking to hook up the car, you stuff the poser in the trunk."

"Car don't matter," Moog answered. "We gotta—"

"There's no *we* on this one." Daniel's voice was soft but strong.

"What do you mean there ain't no *we*? There's always been a *we*."

Daniel shook his head. "Not this time."

"But—"

"You said it yourself," Daniel reminded him. "For whatever reason, Koschei wants me alive. He doesn't seem to have the same concern for you."

Moog puffed out his already formidable chest. "I'm not afraid—"

"But I am." Daniel looked into his friend's eyes. "I'm afraid of losing you. And I'm afraid of what happens to Malaika and Vicki if they lose both of us. I'm not leaving you behind because I can't use you. I'm doing it because I need you."

Moog wanted to have one last say. "But—"

Daniel's mind was made up. "I'm sorry. The only way to play this is to let Feller take me in. That's it."

Moog wasn't happy with the plan, but he understood the pointlessness of continuing to argue. "And then what?"

There wasn't any more. "That's it," Daniel admitted. "Feller takes me up, and I talk to Koschei."

"Talk to him?" Moog's voice made the lack of a plan sound more like a betrayal. "That motherfucker got my baby girl, and you want to *talk* to him?" Moog reached for the door. "I got a plan of my own, and it don't involve me saying anything but, 'Tell me where my daughter's at, or I'm gonna keep shooting you till you do.'"

Daniel reached out to stop his friend. "While you know I love and appreciate your particular kind of crazy, we just don't have time for that right now."

Moog looked down at the hand restraining him, and then up to Daniel.

"And I don't have time to explain all of it." He took his hand from the big man's arm. "We know Koschei has an office here, but that's it. Do you know where your daughter is?"

Moog hated making the admission. "No."

"Or Vicki?"

Silence. Moog had hated the first admission so much, he wasn't willing to make any more.

"We can go in guns blazing, but that's not going to get us what we want," Daniel explained. "What we need."

"And *talking* going to get us that?"

"You brought me back for a reason."

Moog folded his arms across his chest. "Yeah. Because the old man—"

An explanation wasn't going to divert Daniel's point. "Well, then *he* brought me back for a reason. Let me go do what I'm supposed to do."

"But ain't nobody know what that is."

"Maybe." Daniel shrugged. "But Koschei's gone to a lot of trouble to bring me to him alive. We know it's not because he loves me, so I must have something he wants."

"Who care what the hell he wants?" Moog clearly didn't.

"We do. Or at least you should. Whatever he wants, I must have it."

"How that help us any?"

"Whether it's a homeless guy living out on Century Park East or Koschei living up on top of it all, if you've got something they want, then you've got control . . . If you're only smart enough to use it on them."

Moog had his doubts about that too. "And you're smart enough?"

"I haven't been in the past," Daniel cheerfully admitted as he got out of the car. "But who knows, even a loser gets lucky sometimes."

"And me? I just wait in the car?"

"No. You wait for steroid cases that come along wanting to throw our car up on a hook, and then stuff them in the trunk. Remember?"

"And then?"

"If I'm not out by the time the sun goes down . . ."

"Yeah?"

Daniel's plan B was simple enough. "Then I'm not coming out. So you'll be doing me the biggest favor if you just go in and kill everyone."

"Can do."

"I know you can."

Daniel turned to Feller. "Let's go see a man about a dog."

CHAPTER THIRTY-FIVE

Smack My Bitch Up

Daniel and Feller crossed the street in perfect rhythm with one another, but they did not exchange a word.

By the time they'd reached the oversize glass doors at the building's entrance, Feller had slowed to a hesitant shuffle. "I have to do this," he said as he reached for, but didn't open, one of the doors. "But you don't have to do this."

"Do what?" Daniel reached for the other door and pulled it open himself.

"Go through with this," Feller explained. "I can tell him I lost you. Or that you escaped. Or whatever. I don't really care what I tell him. Or what he says." His voice sounded every bit as battered as his face looked. "Not any more. I owe you that much."

"You don't owe me anything."

"No?"

"Not even close." Daniel stepped into the building's lobby, a vast empty space dominated by an oversize sculpture that demonstrated just how many sharp edges and threatening points a sculptor could incorporate into a single piece of work. "I'm using you, and you're using me. That's just how life works."

"Is that right?"

"Mostly. That's the lesson I've learned, no matter how hard I've tried to wish it wasn't so." It didn't seem sad to Daniel until he'd said it out loud. "Any way, that's what's happening now. No friendship. No honor. Just a mammalian thing going down."

"All right." Feller's response was meant to convey a cynical nonchalance, but the personal disappointment was evident in his words.

The main foyer featured a glass reception desk in front of the main elevator banks. The station was manned by an impossibly beautiful blond woman who seemed to have been born and bred for no other reason but to greet visitors and direct them to the proper elevator. A Los Angeles career.

Daniel walked toward her with a sense of purpose, but Feller stopped him.

"He's got his own elevator."

"Of course he does."

Feller ushered Daniel around to the back of the lobby, where a large black desk had been built to incorporate a metal detector, through which it was necessary for every visitor to pass. Beyond that private point of entry was an elevator with a single button—and a single destination.

Feller led Daniel to the desk, which was manned by an enormous example of just what excesses can be reached with too much free time in a gym and too much money for all the latest pills and balms and mad scientist formulas. The Goliath was concentrating on a Samsung tablet he held in front of him. As he read, his lips moved ever so slightly.

When the pair went unnoticed at the desk, Feller cleared his throat. "Two for the penthouse."

The guy at the desk never looked up. "Name?"

"Feller. Gerald Feller."

If nothing else had come from his career change, he no longer said his name as if it were a shameful admission. Instead, he announced it now with the expectation that it would mean something that had to be respected and would open doors—or knock them down.

The gargantu-goon behind the desk finally glanced up from the tablet and looked Feller up and down. "All right."

The man pointed at Daniel. "And he is . . . ?"

Daniel answered before Feller could. "Koschei's expecting me."

"I'm sure *Mister* Koschei is expecting you." The sentry popped his pectorals and tossed his head back and forth to crack his neck. "So, if you'll tell me your name, I'll check you in and send you up, and we won't keep him waiting." His yellowed eyes narrowed, and he whispered like it was a secret that should scare them both. "Mr. Koschei doesn't like to be kept waiting."

Daniel was unimpressed with the man behind the desk. And his boss. "Listen, Elroid—"

It was impossible to tell how big the guard was while he was stuffed in behind his desk, but the joke about his name prompted him to get to his feet and reveal that he was well over six feet tall, maybe halfway to seven. "The name's Gunter."

Daniel smirked. "Oh, I get it. Because of your big guns."

"Because my father's name was Gunter." The man gritted his porcelain-fused capped teeth. "And his father's name was Gunter."

"That's a whole lotta Gunter," Daniel quipped. "I'm glad you're so free with your name. And your daddy's and your granddaddy's and all, but all I'm going to tell you is that I'm going to get on that elevator and go up and see Koschei."

The chemically enhanced henchman started around his desk. "Is that right?"

"It's not a game," a nervous Feller insisted. "Just tell him your name."

"That's not how it works," Daniel advised, unconcerned with the advancing mountain of a man. "Your name is you. You give it away to something like Koschei, and you give your power away too. He knows who I am, and we all know he's expecting me."

The bouncer-turned-receptionist stood in front of Daniel, his bloated arms crossed against his impossibly large chest. "You're not going anywhere without giving me a name."

"We'll just come back then," Feller said nervously.

Gunter didn't see that as an option. "I said you're not going anywhere. You're not running away. And you're sure as hell not going to see *Mister* Koschei."

Feller turned again to Daniel, looking for the easy fix to the situation. "Just tell him."

"I don't have time for this." Daniel took one step around the recepti-bouncer, then another two toward the metal detector archway. The alarm sounded, but that didn't stop Daniel.

Gunter did. He grabbed Daniel's arm. Hard. "No one goes up without giving a name."

"That's a mistake." Daniel looked down at his arm, and then up at the man who was holding it. "And now I'm going to have to hurt you."

"You're going to hurt me? What are you, *fifty*?"

It hurt a little. "Forty-nine."

"You're sure about this, Gramps?"

"Absolutely." Daniel tried to struggle free, but he only succeeded in getting pushed into the desk. A collection of pens and a stapler fell to the ground.

A fist with all the impact of a cannonball struck Daniel in the gut and shut him right up.

"You think I don't know who you are?" Another shot to the gut. "Mr. Erickson?"

All Daniel could do was gasp for air as he lay on the ground.

"You think I don't know all about you?" Gunter shouted down at him. "I know all about you. You're the reason that Mr. Koschei's been keeping that quiff around." He grinned. "She's a real piece of ass. And I think when he's done with her, I'm going to take a turn on her just because you've pissed me off so much today. I think I'm going to hit that hard. This hard."

Gunter's next kick was supposed to be his coup de grâce, but Daniel wrapped himself around the man's leg and absorbed the force without taking any more damage. He clutched Gunter's black leather Brunori zipper boot and reached for one of the pens that had spilled to the floor.

With a fist formed around the writing instrument, Daniel shot up to his knees, and with a single savage motion, buried the pen just behind Gunter's right kneecap.

Daniel got up, and then launched his right foot into Gunter's crotch. "Why don't you fuck *that*," he screamed.

Like a beast fueled by fury, Gunter charged forward, wrapped his arms around Daniel, and drove them both back into the far wall. They collided with an impact that hurt both men, but Gunter wouldn't give up his constrictor grip around Daniel's ribs. He squeezed until Daniel could barely breathe, and then squeezed even tighter.

Daniel took a breath, but didn't waste time taking another before he lashed out with the side of his hand like a knife blade and struck Gunter's windpipe. There was an audible pop, and shrieks of pain changed at once to a hollow gasping sound, and then a disturbing whistle. Gunter's eyes bulged as he struggled to breathe. It was a losing battle, and he fell to the floor in a heap of hurt.

Daniel bent down to grab the recepti-bouncer's right arm, and easily twisted it back until a sharp yelp escaped from between low moans. Without letting go of the now useless limb, Daniel advanced to the pinkie and slowly bent it back until the nail of the digit touched the wrist. "Now, why don't you dial up that security code for the elevator? Then, if you're still breathing, you can tell Koschei there's a supernaturally psychotic bad man on his way up to see him. He'll know just who you're talking about."

CHAPTER THIRTY-SIX

Bargain

The inside of the elevator doors were mirrored. When they closed, they left Daniel with little choice but to look at the beast caught in the cage. Wild eyes stared back cruelly from a face stained by blood. He wasn't sure whose it was, and he didn't particularly care.

If there had been any possibility of escape, Daniel would've taken it and run. But a box is a box and there was no way out. The slow ascent was an unwanted opportunity to contemplate the reflection of what he'd become. Killer. Casualty. Walking dead man.

And if there was an indictment in all the blood he'd spilled, Daniel was willing to reserve judgment until he'd finished the business he'd come for.

When the elevator doors opened, Daniel wasn't surprised that Haden Koschei was right there waiting, his arms spread wide. "Welcome, Mr. Erickson. You have quite a talent for surprising me in the most expected ways."

"You mean surviving." Daniel took a wary step out of the elevator and out into the office suite. Feller followed him in. "You make it sound like you're sorry to see me."

"Oh, quite the opposite. I just hadn't anticipated your arrival would be this"—he paused for the word, but couldn't find one he liked better than "entertaining." The old man gestured to a video monitor by the elevator, which showed the recepti-bouncer spread across the floor, crying in pain. "Poor Gunter. He's no good to me now. I suppose I'll have to find some other use for him."

Daniel just nodded and continued to look around the penthouse.

"And you, Mr. Feller," Koschei called out. "Congratulations to you." It was impossible to tell if the old man was being sincere or sarcastic. "I expected Mr. Erickson would follow you back to me, but I never thought you'd actually escort him through the door. *Bravissimo!* Perhaps the only obstacle that ever stood between you and success was simply the matter of your moral orientation."

Feller seemed uncertain whether to receive the critique as an insult or compliment. "I did what you told me to do."

"You did indeed." Koschei flashed his crocodilian smile and then an open hand at the still-open elevator. "But a henchman's work is never done, and now I need you to go attend to our poor Gunter. I'm afraid he's of absolutely no use to me in the shape that Mr. Erickson's left him."

Feller's face screwed up in the habitual look of confusion that had etched itself in deep lines across his jowly face.

"Oh, come now." Koschei's voice was light and dismissive. "You've been in law enforcement. You're aware of what's done with some wretched dog that's been struck by a car and left whining in a ditch." He sneered, "I believe it's known as 'roadside mercy.'"

Feller was unprepared for the assignment and could only respond with startled silence.

The old man repeated the instruction like he'd already grown bored with the lesson. "Well, I'm telling you now to go back down and show poor Gunter some *mercy*."

Feller didn't move.

"Oh, Mr. Feller, there's no sense in you rediscovering your conscience now. We both know what you've done, and you're too far past redemption to ever get back there now."

Feller's doughy body seemed to buckle under the weight of the assignment. But still he went; his shoulders slumped forward, and he shuffled back into the elevator as if he were stepping out onto a gallows floor.

Just before the elevator doors closed, Feller looked out at Daniel with an unspoken plea for forgiveness. Or maybe assistance. Perhaps it was just an expression of appreciation for the only bit of friendship he'd ever really known.

Daniel was left alone with the old man.

"Come in. Come in," Koschei invited. "Can I get you something to drink or eat?"

"It's not really a social visit."

"Another appetite, perhaps?" A prurient grin.

Daniel was too tired to play. "I find I have fewer and fewer appetites these days."

"I understand completely." The thin, old man gestured at a couch. "Here, have a seat, and let's talk for a minute before"—he hesitated, but merely for effect—"*whatever* it is you have planned here."

Daniel took the offered seat, and Koschei positioned himself opposite him.

With a vague gesture to his own face, Koschei indicated his interest in Daniel's. "That's quite a workout you've gotten over the past few days. Cold Water?"

Daniel touched the bruises he'd more or less forgotten about. "Is that who they were? Black polo shirts? Former military?"

"I'm not sure how *former* they are." Koschei crossed his legs, careful not to wrinkle his suit pants. The deliberate motion reminded Daniel of folding origami. "The lines between government and private interests are like atmospheric oxygen, they get thinner and thinner the higher you go."

"And how high are you?"

Koschei looked around his penthouse suite to indicate the answer was all around them. "I'm the pinnacle."

Daniel was unimpressed. "You're a regular Yertle the Turtle. Got it."

"I, of course, had nothing to do with any of that." Koschei gestured directly at the wounds on Daniel's face. "Even among the elite, there are factions. Your unfortunate encounter was with an organization that calls itself the Legacy Group. I'd advised one of their board that I had your situation well in hand, but the very nature of being elite is that you resist direction."

"Dissension," Daniel observed. "That's dangerous for a turtle perched as high as you."

Koschei shrugged. "The matter's been taken care of." He smiled. "I believe you threw one of their representatives out of a twenty-seventh floor window."

Daniel looked around pointedly. "Just like this place."

"Don't get ahead of yourself, Mr. Erickson. Before you go fantasizing about my plummeting demise, you should wonder why I've gone to such lengths to bring you here."

"I do wonder."

"It's not so much what I want from you as what I want *for* you."

Daniel thought it over. "I've pretty much got everything that I need."

"Except one thing." The old man's eyes narrowed with predatory focus. "A future."

"Thanks, but I've already got one of my own."

"I'm afraid you're about to find that it's a bit on the short side," Koschei clucked.

"Maybe," Daniel said. "But it's mine all the same."

"That's tragically shortsighted."

"Seeing clearly isn't shortsighted."

"Oh, but it is," Koschei corrected. "When there are so many other fates intertwined with your own."

"There's no one else involved in this except me." Daniel had meant it when he said it, but once the words were spoken, he recognized they were just a reaction to the old man's jab at what they both knew was his weak spot.

"We'd come along so far in our conversation without you trying to lie to me." Koschei grinned triumphantly like he was the combatant who'd drawn first blood. "Why start now?"

"I'm not . . ." Daniel struggled.

"You can't even get the words out. We both know your Mr. Turner is waiting out there with the mistaken impression that he's bulletproof and that I haven't anticipated his intrusion."

"Moog can handle himself."

"Handle himself?" Koschei stretched his arms out along the back of the couch. "He wouldn't make the lobby. A fit end for such a cold-blooded killer, if you ask me."

"I wasn't asking."

"Then perhaps you'd rather talk about the real reason that you're here?"

"I'm here because you had Feller—"

"Oh, please." Koschei smiled sourly, both insulted and amused. "We both know that flour sack of a man couldn't take you across the street, much less across country. The plan was never to have him bring you to me, but always to have his incompetence lead you right here."

"Well, then put on your flight suit and wave to the crowd. Mission incompetent: accomplished."

The old man wasn't put off or slowed by the mockery. "The straw man led the way, but what brought you here was love."

"I don't know what you're talking about." Daniel folded his arms across his chest, and then realized too late he'd given away a tell. It was a stupid thing to do, and it pissed him off. And caused him to do something even dumber. "I came here to kill you."

"And yet here I sit," the old man challenged.

Daniel shifted in his seat uncomfortably. "I'm getting around to it."

"No, you won't. You won't kill me, because I have something you want. Or should I say, someone you love?"

"And I must have something that you want," Daniel bluffed. "Or you wouldn't have gone to so much trouble to bring me here in one piece."

"That may be true, but if you think that having something I want gives you control over me, Mr. Erickson, then what does my having someone you love give me?" He grinned like a fat Texan raking in a fatter poker pot.

Daniel tried to be gracious in defeat. "I suppose that depends on what you want."

"You're quite right that it should be obvious after everything I've done to get you here in one piece."

"Bottom line me."

The thin man seemed genuinely surprised by Daniel's failure to grasp the obvious. "Why, Mr. Erickson, all I want is . . . *you*."

"You went through all of this just so you could kill me?" Daniel scoffed. "You have some sort of Goldfinger laser set up? Or a jigsaw game of Would You Rather?"

"You underestimate yourself, Daniel." He leaned forward. "May I call you Daniel?"

"You just did."

"You've always underestimated yourself." Koschei leaned back again, casually making his reveal. "Even if I wanted you dead, I have to admit that the task would be harder to accomplish than you'd think. Even for me."

Daniel couldn't contain the admission. "I don't understand."

"Clearly." Koschei paused, wondering where to begin and debating what to divulge. "They like to pretend that all men are created equal, but that's simply not the case. Sometimes Fate steps in and disturbs Life's delicate balance by making a few of us a little more equal."

"If you were driving toward an explanation, I think you missed my exit."

"Most people are born, live their little lives, and die. But some few of us do it the other way round."

"Excuse me?"

"We are born. Die. And *then* live."

It was a lot for Daniel to take in, but the one, small detail that resonated most strongly with him was: "We?"

Koschei knew the revelation had landed a solid punch, and he was quick to follow up. "You never noticed, Daniel? Before this? Not once?"

"I don't . . ." Daniel stammered.

"More lies." Koschei's voice was harsh and dismissive. "You were born, and then *really did* die as an infant. What kind of a mother would make up a story like that?"

Daniel didn't have an answer.

"All your life, people have always reacted to you like you're something to be wary of, something to be feared or hated on sight. Why do you think that is?"

Daniel didn't have a ready response for that one either.

"And all of the times you should've been dead. And yet here you sit. No explanation?"

If Daniel suspected he might have a clue, he couldn't bring himself to speak it aloud.

Koschei had no such difficulty. "Because you're already dead. You're soulless. You're a walking dead man."

"And you're crazy."

"Then go seek sanity somewhere else." Koschei chuckled. "Because what I have to offer is truth." His eyes weren't exactly kind, just uncharacteristically flat.

"And what is the truth?" The words weren't out of Daniel's mouth before he regretted speaking them and wished he could swallow them back down.

"The truth?" Koschei sat back and pondered the question. "The truth is that 'there are more things in heaven and earth, than are dreamt of in your philosophy.'"

"Shakespeare." Daniel was unimpressed. "I suppose you're going to tell me that you knew him."

"Knew him?" Koschei seemed to scoff at the suggestion. "I killed him."

"You killed Shakespeare? William Shakespeare?" Daniel made no attempt to contain his disbelief—or ridicule.

Koschei shrugged them both off. "It's what I do."

"You kill Elizabethan laureates?"

"Elizabethan. Renaissance. Bronze Age. Atomic Age. Time is a concept of interest only to those who know they are always running out of it," Koschei said, with almost a touch of melancholy. "Time is a broad plain, and I've killed across all of it."

"You're an immortal killing machine?" If Daniel had learned anything from Atibon it was that anything was possible. But *this* seemed to be way outside of those boundaries.

"Killing makes it seem so barbaric. It's not like I eat them whole." He thought on that one. "Mostly. What I do is consume energy, personal and unique energy." He could tell that Daniel was having a hard time following along. "What you—and other less imaginative people—would call the soul."

"You eat souls?"

Koschei shrugged. "You and yours eat pigs' asses. The universe is all about energy and the infinite and endless transfer of it from one state, from one body, to another. You do it your way and I do it—"

"You're Feodor Pushkin," Daniel blurted out in a *eureka!* moment.

Not even the old man could hide the glint of recognition in his eyes at hearing something old, but so familiar. "I've been known by many names."

"You're the man—the *one*—who killed Jimi Hendrix."

"Hendrix," he admitted. "I was the last one to see Belushi at the Marmont. Poor Dr. Murray went to prison rather than admit I was there at Michael's bedside that night. I drew Whitney her bath and poured Amy her last drink. And they were all"—his eyes sparkled—"exquisite!"

Daniel couldn't believe what he was hearing. "You're a monster."

"Perhaps," Koschei admitted. "But one of discerning tastes."

He looked hard and long at Daniel. "And I'm not the only one who has worn many names over many lifetimes."

"What are you talking about?"

"I've told you. You're no more Daniel Erickson than I am Haden Koschei. I suppose the names fit, serve their purpose as well as any other, but we've both known many others."

"What names?"

"William Truelove," Koschei said simply.

Daniel tried to conceal the fact that the name caused a sensation of suddenly dropping off of a height. "I've never heard—"

"Was a young man of noble birth and impossible moral standards. Normandy. 1060."

"What does this have to do with anything?"

"If you'll let me finish, I'll show you that it has to do with everything." He stopped to collect his thoughts. "I was enjoying myself as Abu Ben-Adam, a merchant from Constantinople. It provided me with the necessary cover to travel the world. And live as I need."

He flashed a contemptuous look at Daniel. "And then along came William Truelove. He was too bright for his own good and discovered my secret." The memory seemed to disturb him. "And swore to destroy me."

"Obviously he failed," Daniel said, without bothering to offer a spoiler alert.

"You did."

"Me?" The words scared Daniel more than anything.

Koschei nodded his head sadly, not triumphantly. "William knew my secret weakness, but I knew his."

"And?"

243

"His wife was the love of his life," the old man said as he remembered. "I seduced her. Repeatedly."

"And William?" Daniel asked, though he was terrified that he might already know.

"Was unable to live with the realization that love was . . . something else." Koschei's voice softened. "He took his own life. Threw himself from a cliff and into the Channel."

"And what does that have to do with me?"

"Because every action has a consequence, even if we almost never understand the who or why or what of it. And William found himself trapped between worlds, shall we say. Found himself caught between his oath of honor to end me and the shame of his ignoble and faithless death. And so, for more than a thousand years now, he has appeared in my life, again and again, wrapped in the flesh and bones of some poor, soulless body he's managed to hijack."

Daniel didn't want to follow where the story was leading. "I repeat, what does that have to do with—"

"You, Daniel?" Koschei smiled patiently. "This time around it's you."

"You're joking."

The old man looked at him blankly. "Have I ever struck you as the humorous type?"

"Then why tell me all of this?" Daniel's mind was racing. "If everything you're telling me is true—and I know that it can't be—then why tell me that my life mission, my eternal life mission, is to kill you?"

"Has telling you changed anything?" Koschei asked simply enough. "You came to kill me anyway. You can't, but you've come anyway. And unless I persuade you otherwise, you'll just keep coming. I've only chosen to tell you on this particular go-round because I've tired of the cycle. I've tired of having to sort through every generation's possibilities in search of that one individual which Truelove has found and inhabited. I'm simply tired of the annoyance."

"So, what is it that you want from me?" Daniel asked suspiciously.

"I've told you, I want you."

"Me?"

"I want you to join me."

"I'm not going to—"

"Oh, don't be so hasty, my friend. I'm prepared to give you exactly what you want."

"I'm not interested," Daniel said, his arms folded across his chest.

"Maybe not," Koschei conceded. "But you're curious, so go ahead and ask."

Daniel pretended for a moment that he didn't have any idea what the old man was suggesting, but could only keep the unconvinced act up for so long. "What do I want?"

Koschei grinned triumphantly. "What we all want: everything."

"I'm pretty satisfied right now," Daniel insisted.

"I'm disappointed with all of the lies you tell yourself, Daniel." Koschei shook his head to demonstrate just how deeply. "Even now, you're worried about Moog. His daughter, Malaika. Your son, Zack." A pregnant pause. "And then, of course, there's the very lovely Vicki Bean."

Daniel set his jaw, and his eyes narrowed.

"I told you there were more lives than yours in play. And with all of them on the great gaming table of life, I think that leaves you with quite a bit that you want."

"And in return?"

"In return, I get exactly what I told you I wanted: you."

"I don't understand."

"What I have here is not exactly an Internet start-up in my mom's garage off in the Valley." He gestured around the luxurious penthouse as just one example of his holdings. "This isn't an enterprise that allows one to work from home. No, holding the position requires getting into the pool with both feet and sinking straight to the bottom."

"And you want me—"

"As an apprentice."

"Apprentice?"

"You've already shown you have the aptitude for it. Look at poor Gunter downstairs." His lips smacked with mock pity.

"I warned him," Daniel started out in his defense. "And he—"

"Was someone you could've brought down easily enough." Koschei was quick to cut him off. "But you beat him half to death . . ." He paused to consider the order he'd given Feller. "Given what's happening to him now, I suppose you beat him all the way to death."

"I didn't—"

"You *did*," Koschei insisted. "Because inside your dead man's heart is a rage you can barely contain. And all your life you've just been waiting."

"And just what is it exactly that you think I've been waiting for?"

Koschei smiled because he knew the answer. "For the opportunity to let it all go."

Daniel felt like someone had stolen something from him.

"You may want to be a good man," Koschei continued, "but you enjoy everything else so much more."

"You don't know anything about me." Daniel's words couldn't conceal the fear he felt in knowing he was wrong.

"I know more about you than anyone else." There was one exception. "Or almost anyone else . . ." Koschei's voice trailed off like he was an animal close on the trail, dampening its own chuffing to better hear its prey. "Your old friend, Atibon, hasn't told you anything about this, has he?"

"There's nothing to tell."

"More lies. Or you're too foolish to realize." An intriguing third option popped into his head. "Or all of the above!" He smiled knowingly. "Atibon must have his own reasons for keeping you so clueless."

Koschei had trouble reading Daniel's expression. "Are you surprised that I know about that black bastard, or are you actually surprised that he's played you like a fool?"

Daniel's head was spinning in overload, and the only response he could gather together was a weak "He's not playing me."

"Oh, I see," Koschei sneered. "All this time, you've been searching for a daddy to love you because your real daddy didn't, and you thought you'd finally found it in Atibon. It'd be laughable if it weren't so damn pathetic." The old man laughed. "I want to use you too, but at least I'm willing to be up front about it. All the more reason to consider my offer."

"You haven't given me your offer."

"I shouldn't have to spell it out. But if you're making me, here it is: you come and learn the business. Twenty some years in the music industry, and the amount of blood you've spilled in the past couple of years, you're practically an initiate already. You pitch in and help run things so that I don't have to any longer."

"And in return?"

"Exactly what I've promised: whatever you want. Vicki? She's yours. You want Moog to have his daughter back? Done. Zack? Done. Whatever you want . . . Yours." His nod was almost kindly. "It's a win-win."

"Thanks for trying to tempt me, but I'm kinda affiliated with the other team."

"Then what a delicious victory to have my rival's chosen replacement become my own."

"Replacement?" The prospect frightened Daniel.

"Your Mr. Atibon is nothing more than a cloak worn by something far darker. Something darker even than myself. And though it will never end, that physical form gets worn with age, like any suit of clothes, and needs to be changed every so often. And in Atibon's case that means right now."

"Atibon never said anything about—"

"No, he wouldn't. That's not his style. He'd just keep playing the daddy card with you and getting you deeper and deeper into his debt until there was nothing else you could do but take his place."

"I'm not interested in anything you have to offer." The words implied a greater conviction than Daniel felt in his heart. "I'm satisfied with the position I have right now."

"And what exactly is that?"

"I'm an agent of music. Real music. The sound of the soul," Daniel announced. "I'm going to find out who's been working so hard to keep the people from hearing it. And then I'm going to stop them. I'm going to free music."

"You're wasting your time."

"Well, according to you there's not much left to waste."

"What can I tell you," Koschei said. "Music is powerful. And there will always be people—powerful people—who will find ways to control power to get more power. You can't stop them."

"I can slow them down," Daniel declared.

"And what would you do? Save a singer here. A guitar god there. You wouldn't change anything. Not really. There will always be power in controlling the music that people hear. And always be money in controlling the people who make that music."

"Including killing them?"

"When it becomes advantageous we kill a pop star or two. Mea culpa."

Daniel thought he understood. "Because nothing sells like a dead pop star's catalogue. Is that it?"

"Of course, there are financial advantages," Koschei admitted. "Michael. Whitney. Everybody sells better after they're dead.

"But their deaths also help to make clear to Joe Lunchbox and Sally Cubicle that their lives are just as pointless. I mean, if the King ain't happy then who could be? With Kurt Cobain, we stole hope from a whole generation. I'm sure Amy Winehouse inspired a few people to get clean, but I guarantee you that we've inspired far more people to give up and surrender to the same demons that consumed their hero."

"Where's the profit in that?"

"You still don't understand, do you? Didn't you once wax on and on about music being the soundtrack to our lives?"

Daniel silently wondered how he could've known that, but it was not the most alarming thing the old man had said.

"Well, guess what. You give all the people the same soundtrack, and they live the same lives. They think the same things. They buy the same crap, and put up with the same shit. You control the message and you control the masses. And surprise, surprise"—he paused for effect—"that's all the sheeple want. They just want someone to spare them the difficulty of living their own lives. You starve their souls and break their hearts, and they pay you for the privilege."

"Not everyone."

Koschei seemed annoyed that someone could be so naive. "All those chain restaurants with their disgusting happy hour hors d'oeuvres. You think someone comes up with a dish that just happens to be a heart attack on a plate. No, sir. They've got scientists who analyze the human metabolism and deconstruct the insatiable need for poisons like sugar, salt, and fat. The guys with the test tubes and the beakers devise some diabolically addictive chemical formula, and *then* the chefs create the so-called food to hide the poison.

"Music's no different. They break down the human mind. They run spreadsheets and conduct focus groups. They make music to hide the poison they create. Hell, it's not even music anymore."

"There are still people making music," Daniel insisted.

"In bars and on street corners," Koschei scoffed. "I'm talking about people who understand the psychology of music, the effects of music. There are diabolical formulas for that too, and then all that needs to be done is slap it over the Auto-Tuned pawn of the hour. It doesn't matter if someone really sings like an angel; if they don't look like a porn star, they don't stand a chance of making it."

Daniel wanted to disagree.

"But it's bigger than that," Koschei continued. "In the last thirty years, the most successful album of political subversion was what? *American Idiot*? Which is now a Broadway musical. Is there any greater sellout than a Broadway musical? Are you kidding me? America's in the longest war of its history, you've got economic meltdowns, global disasters . . . and take a listen, and tell me what you hear. Any protest songs being sung? Any anthems? Not a one. Justin's bringing sexy back, and Miley's grinding her ass into everything she can."

"Springsteen—" Daniel began to offer.

"Springsteen is writing songs about bankers fucking the little man, but who do you think is in the front rows at his shows: bankers, because they're the ones with the cash to buy the three-figure tickets. It's all bullshit. It's not meant to liberate, it's meant to control. And you think you can stop that?"

"I think I can try."

"And what do you think that will get you? There was a dream for civil rights, but what's happened to that dream? You know how to make people content with their limitations? Make their limitations cool. It doesn't matter what civil rights you throw to the people like a sop if you send a third of all black men to prison. And they'll do it themselves if you just make prison cool. Make being a thug cool. And, guess what, private prisons are a booming business.

"And now do you hear a voice like Marvin Gaye's 'What's Going On'? You do not. You have Jay-Z marrying a model, pretending to be a pop singer, and owning a basketball team, rapping about how he used to sell drugs. What's your message there? Sell drugs and you might get your own model and basketball team. What's the reality? The country's prisons are overflowing, and so are the coffers of the corporations that own them.

"You can try all you want, but they will never let you stop them."

"And just who exactly is *they*?" Daniel asked.

"You think I'm referring to the people who make the music? Or to those who control the music? Or even the elite who control those people? Oh no. I'm referring to the sheeple. We steal their tomorrows by trading them a lie today, and they're desperate for that bargain. We've turned *party* into a verb, and they don't give a shit about outsourced jobs—all they want to do is party. And if there's a party tonight, they don't give a goddamn what happens to them today. Or tomorrow. And that makes life easier for them. And if you try to stop that, they will hate you."

"I think you underestimate the people."

"I've been among people for thousands of years. They've grown bigger, and some of them smell better, but other than that, they really haven't changed over the millennia. They cause a ruckus every now and again, but they've always hated those who've tried to set them free."

"Well, then it's a good thing I'm used to being hated."

"It is a very good thing. One way or another, you're going to hell, Mr. Erickson."

"No more 'Daniel'?"

Koschei was past niceties. "You're going to hell. You can help me run the place, or the place will own you. That's your decision for the time being. But don't fool yourself into thinking there's any other fate for you. There's no way out."

"You must be really scared, Koschei."

"Scared? I've never been scared a day in my—"

"Now who's lying? If my fate was certain, you wouldn't be offering me a choice."

It was the old man's turn to be uncharacteristically silent.

"So what is it? What are you so afraid of? We both know that you're only interested in one thing: yourself. And I scare you." Daniel thought on it for a minute. "I can end you, can't I? That's it.

I can end you. And the only thing you can think of to save yourself is to offer me half of this kingdom of dirt."

"You're not as clever as you think."

"No. But I'm working at it. And I'm getting close. I can see it in your beady eyes and the sweat on your wax-figure face. I'm getting close to the secret of how to end you once and for all."

"You're making a huge mistake, Mr. Erickson."

"We both know my whole life is just a long chain of them."

"There are all sorts of ways to drag a man to hell."

"And just as many ways to rise above it." Daniel got to his feet. "Which makes me wonder why you haven't killed me yet. Here I am. Why not just have it over with right here and now?"

Daniel thought on it. He could only come up with one reason. "Because you can't, right? You can't kill me. That's the flip side of all of this, isn't it? I'm the one person who can end you, and I'm the only person you can't kill."

"Even if that were true, I have no problem with killing the others." It was a weak bluff on the old man's part. "Have you forgotten what brought you here? Have you forgotten about the love of your life?"

"I haven't forgotten about anything," Daniel said defiantly. "But I know the way to get it isn't here any longer."

Koschei got to his feet. "Don't push me, Mr. Erickson."

"Push you? You've been pushing me a long time. I thought you would've heard by now," —Daniel smiled—"I'm a push-back man."

"You're making a serious mistake, Erickson."

"And so are you. You had yourself convinced that you knew me and what I wanted, but you're worried now that maybe you misjudged me. Maybe there's something that I want even more. Because whatever you think about the human race, there are a whole lot of people who have sacrificed themselves *and* the ones they loved just to stand up to the likes of you." Daniel took a deep breath. "And you know in your heart that if I'm one of those people, then you are altogether screwed. And that's what's making you sweat right now."

"I'm not someone to play games with, Mr. Erickson."

Daniel looked him straight in the eyes. "Apparently, neither am I. I've got no big rescue raid planned," Daniel said as he headed toward the elevator as casually as his trembling legs would take him. "Because it seems to me that everybody's where they want to be. But if something happens to Vicki or Zack or Malaika, then you should know that there's not a steroid-swollen doorman in heaven, hell, or earth that can keep me from you." The elevator doors opened, and Daniel gratefully got inside.

"You're making the mistake of your life, Erickson."

"I've lived a life of mistakes. But for the first time in my life, I'm absolutely certain that I'm doing exactly what I'm supposed to do." The elevator doors began to close. "I'll see you soon."

"Sooner than you think."

"I'm looking forward to it."

The elevator doors closed, but Daniel could hear something scream back in the penthouse, something wild and dangerous, untamed and furious. It made him smile.

For a while.

Before he reached the lobby, his smile had disappeared and a more concerned look had appeared on his face.

Everything he wanted.

The words kept running over and over in his head until he couldn't help wondering if maybe he'd made a mistake after all.

CHAPTER THIRTY-SEVEN

The Waiting

"'Bout time." Moog was leaning against the car, his arms folded across his chest. "I was just getting ready to go bust up the place."

"Yeah." Daniel slid into the passenger seat. "Wouldn't have done any good."

"No?" the big man asked as he climbed back into the driver's seat. "You ain't never seen me when I'm mad."

"What are you talking about? I don't know that I've ever seen you when you *weren't* mad."

"I mean really mad." He stretched the seatbelt as far as it would go and clicked it around his massive chest. "Like fire-pissing, people-eating, skull-fucking mad. I'm three hundred pounds of hate when I get *that* mad."

"You lose some weight in the car while I was up there?" Daniel smiled.

"I'll lose some weight. I'll lose 'bout two hundred pounds of dead weight when I throw your ass outta the car. Now what happened up there?"

"I'm not really sure. I'm still trying to figure it out."

"Did you see my girl?"

"Nobody but Koschei."

"Vicki?"

"Nope. And not Zack, before you ask."

"Then how come you so goddamn happy?"

"Because I got a sense of hope. And purpose."

"I don't have any idea what you mean."

"I went in there more or less convinced that there wasn't any way of getting out of there alive. Much less getting our folks out of there. Or keeping them alive even if we did."

"So why'd you go in?"

Daniel shrugged. "Because we had to do something, and being convinced you're going to fuck it all up is no excuse for not trying."

"And now?"

Daniel nodded as he considered a plan he wasn't quite ready to share. "I think I've got something. It won't be easy. And Vegas won't be taking any bets on us."

Moog was quick to remind his friend: "Last time they put money against us, they lost their fucking shirts."

"I gotta tell you, I'm fairly certain that we can't get out without getting bloody on this."

"I ain't fragile," the big man reminded him.

"I mean, I think there's every chance that we get ourselves killed."

"It gonna get my little girl back? Vicki and Zack?"

"I think it's their only chance."

"Then what choice you think I got?"

"Zero to none."

"Just like our odds." Moog smiled and started the car.

As the Lexus pulled away from the curb, Daniel took a quick, last look up at the top of the building across the street. He couldn't be sure, but he thought he might've just been able to make out a man's silhouette staring down at him from his perch sixty stories above the street.

CHAPTER THIRTY-EIGHT

Do Me a Solid

"What happened to . . . ?" Feller took a look around the penthouse for some trace evidence that might answer his question before he finished asking it. There wasn't. "Erickson."

"What indeed, Mr. Feller?" Koschei stood at the window glaring down at the speck of a man getting into a car parked across the street. "He seemed awfully resilient for a man who'd been dragged across the country."

Feller could tell there was an implication hidden in the words somewhere, but he wasn't quick enough to find it.

"One might even wonder whether you brought him to me, as I'd asked. Or whether he brought you back as a two-hundred-forty-pound 'Fuck you' delivered to my doorstep."

"You said you wanted him brought back alive."

"That did not mean imbued with life, Mr. Feller. That meant breathing. Barely, would've been fine. In a car trunk would've been understandable. I would think that after chasing him for as long as you have, you might have figured out he turns every opportunity into one of his goddamn road trips."

If Feller had had a tail, it would've been between his legs. "You're right."

"Of course I'm right." Koschei turned back from the window. "Now, if you're finished with Gunter . . ."

"I didn't feel right about that," he confessed.

"You're not supposed to feel right, Mr. Feller. You're not supposed to feel anything at all. You're merely supposed to do what I tell you to do. And right now, I have something to tell you to do."

During the course of his road trip, Feller had begun to think about his career, and the thoughts had left him wondering. "I've been thinking—"

"Thinking is worse than feeling, Mr. Feller. Right now, there's something that needs to be done." Koschei just then thought of the idea, and his diabolical mind had already worked out the specifics. "We're going to kill Daniel Erickson."

Feller, however, had come to understand his limitations as a man. "I don't think I can."

"Of course you can't." Koschei thought on it a minute. "If I can't kill him, then you certainly can't. But I know one man who can."

"Who?"

"Daniel Erickson."

"But—"

"If you try to kill him and fail, Mr. Feller, a wound to your enemy only enrages him, only makes him stronger and more determined to kill you. So, if you cannot kill your enemy, you do the next best thing."

"What's that?"

"You kill everything he loves. You strip him of everything and take and take and take, until he has nothing left in all the world except the words to beg for death."

"But how?"

"I've arranged for those bitches and his punk-ass son to be part of the Black Rock Festival."

Feller wasn't sure where this was leading. "All right."

"There will be a fleet of helicopters taking talent to and from the venue. After the show, I want everyone that Daniel Erickson loves to be on a copter headed back to the city."

Feller knew he could manage that. "OK."

Koschei smiled. "And then, I want that helicopter to drop into the desert and burn. Do you understand me?"

Feller did, but his eyes were wide with shock. "You want me to crash the helicopter."

Koschei just laughed. "Yes, Mr. Feller. I want you to give us another example of why rock stars should never fly."

CHAPTER THIRTY-NINE

Should I Stay or Should I Go

A dog ran across the beach, chasing the waves back to the sea, pawing at the foam, and then racing across the sand, back behind the dune where Daniel was sitting. He was amused enough by the show, and watched the pup at play for a while before he called out to nothing more than the coming night, "I know you're here."

"Course I'm here." The gruff voice behind Daniel was not unexpected, and it didn't startle him at all. "I ain't sneakin' nowhere."

The dog was gone now, of course, but Daniel kept his gaze on the surf where he'd been playing. He watched silently, without offering any invitation or other pleasantry, and so the old man grumbled as he settled himself down onto the sand beside him.

"So, what brings you all the way out here to the edge of the world?" Atibon asked.

"That where we at?" Daniel asked, fixing his eyes on the far horizon.

"Feels like it sometimes. Don't it?"

"Yeah. It does." Or, at least, Daniel liked the idea.

"So?"

Daniel shook off the inquiry. "I'm just thinking."

"Well, I can see you ain't surf fishin'," the old man snapped. "What you come all this way to think 'bout? What was it you couldn't think about where you was?"

"Koschei made me an offer today."

"Course he did."

"A good offer."

"You sure about that?"

"Everything I want," Daniel said brightly. "How could it get any better?"

"Could be everything you *need*," the old man offered, and the distinction he made was not subtle. "Or maybe it'd be an offer that wouldn't cost you everything you got—like his will."

Daniel nodded his head, but still searched the sky. "I'm tired. Been a long time, you know?"

"Look who you sittin' here talkin' to 'bout a long time." Atibon let out a sigh, uncharacteristically sad and distinctly human. "I close my eyes, I can still smell the sweetness of the grass where I was a boy."

The notion intrigued Daniel. "You were a boy?"

"I ain't wearin' panties 'neath my pants. Course I was a boy." He smiled. "You call it Mali now, but back then it was just home." He closed his eyes like he wanted to go back, and then opened them suddenly, like he was afraid he just might. "And I can remember the cold steel of chains on me and the stink of death, so strong it seemed like a livin' thing. I can remember the soft, warm touch of a woman's love and the cruel force of a coward's hand. Beat me half to death, he did. And I remember thinkin' that him not beatin' me all the way there was the cruelest act of all."

Daniel felt tempted to say something to fill the silence, even though it was clear no words would fit. But he had learned to resist those moments, and kept silent.

He knew Atibon was grateful for it.

"But it wasn't his failing. I can't count the number of men over the years who've tried to finish what that bastard started." He chuckled. "A lady or two as well, I don't mind tellin' you."

"So you can't die?" Daniel's question was more self-interest than curiosity.

"Haven't yet."

"How's that possible?"

The old man shook his head. "You tell me."

Daniel fumbled with the question. "I don't . . . Why would I know?"

Atibon grinned. "I was an orderly in that hospital when you came down with that fever. I was a visiting physician six years later when your lungs gave out on you like that. When you was eighteen, I was just a passerby who helped you outta the wreckage when that tractor trailer damn near took the back half off of that ol' Buick of yours. And I was the EMT kept you talkin' when you went and swallowed that fistful of pills. I been with you since the start, my boy. And I lost count of the times they should've called your game on account of darkness. But here you is, sittin' and thinkin', tellin' me all about how it's been a long time."

"Koschei called me a walking dead man. Is that what I am?"

"You don't look dead to me, son." The old man got to his feet awkwardly and made no secret of his annoyance as he brushed the sand from his pants. "Lots of folks gonna call you lots of things. When it come right down to it, you're Daniel Erickson, and you're the only one who can decide just what that means."

"He said you're just using me."

"That what it feel like to you?"

Daniel thought about it and nodded. "Sometimes."

"And sometimes you wouldn't be wrong." The old man shifted his feet in the sand. "But I'd like to think those other times more than make up for it."

Daniel didn't bother to look up at Atibon. "I should take his offer."

"Nothin' stoppin' you. Least not me."

"It would make things easier."

"No doubt." The old man nodded. "If easier's what you want, then you'd be a fool not to take it, 'cause the road ahead of you is long and hard and paved with pain, some of it yours, some of it you'll just wish was yours."

"When you paint it like that . . ."

"I ain't never painted nothin' with you, son. I told you the honest truth every time I spoke to you, and this ain't no different. If you want easy—if you want everything you think you want— then you'd be a fool not to go give that sonbitch everything he askin' from you." He stopped, but he wasn't done. "But it won't be you no more. And to my way of thinking, that would make you some walking dead man. Givin' yourself up just to get what you want the easy way, and then havin' to live with it. That, to me, would be hell."

Daniel watched the last of the sun sink into the Pacific and wondered just where it was that the bottom half of the sun was appearing as the first light of a brand new day. "Paved with pain, huh?"

"A highway of hurt, my son."

Daniel nodded. "I'm done."

"You ain't paid up yet, son," Atibon objected. "Ain't no 'done.'"

"The hell with that," Daniel said. "You asked me to find out who killed Jimi Hendrix. And I did. Haden Koschei killed him. There you go. I'm out."

"You ain't out. And it ain't over." There was a snarl in his voice. "Sonofabitch got what's mine, and you're gonna get them back."

"You mean the souls?" Daniel asked.

"I mean a whole lot more than souls," Atibon said. "Everyone got a soul." He looked down at Daniel. "Well, not everyone, but damn near it. And what I can give a man is a whole lot more than just a soul."

"Just what is that?"

"It's mine, that's what it is. And you gonna get it back for me."

"That wasn't part of the bargain," Daniel pointed out.

"Don't you go tellin' me what our bargain was or wasn't. I coulda left your ass high and dry a thousand times, and I didn't worry 'bout no bargain."

"That 'cause you love me or 'cause you needed me?"

"Love," Atibon scoffed. "Goddamn it, boy. You always goin' on and on 'bout love. Love made you soft in the head. Ain't nothin' 'bout love."

Daniel looked off at the far horizon. "I'm all about it."

Atibon made a grumpy, gruff sound in the back of his throat.

"And I'll tell you what. I've got a bargain for you."

"What's that?" Atibon concealed his interest, but not very well.

"Über-soul-retrieval was not part of our deal, and you know it." Another guttural grunt.

"But I'll get them back for you. Every last one," Daniel offered. "But in return—"

"Lemme guess, you want your Vicki come back?"

265

"I do," Daniel admitted. "But that's not the deal. I get your supersouls back from Koschei, and in return, you make certain that Vicki finds her true love."

"You sure 'bout that, boy?" Atibon loved nothing more than the twisty, razor-sharp edge of an ambiguous bargain. "Maybe her true love ain't you."

"I don't care about that. I'm not looking for my true love, I just want Vicki to find hers."

"Done." Atibon spit in his hand and offered it to Daniel.

Daniel shook on the bargain, then turned back to the ocean. "And then I'm done with you for good."

"We'll see when it's over." Atibon's voice was soothing, as if he were talking a child out of a tantrum.

"No. I'm giving you my notice now. This is it for me. One more, and then I'm done."

"You just worry about your end of the deal. We'll worry about saying good-bye when it's all over." The old man's voice was well behind Daniel, but he did not turn to see Atibon walk off into the night.

Somewhere in the darkness a dog barked.

CHAPTER FORTY

Such a Lovely Place

Like many wealthy men in Los Angeles, Haden Koschei owned a number of houses in the area, but never lived in any of them. Instead, he migrated from hotel to hotel, like if he stayed in one place too long something bad (or good) might catch up to him. Often he would make more than one reservation for the night, and then choose the one he'd actually stay at on a whim.

That night the hotel he chose was on North Crescent Drive just off of Sunset Boulevard. He'd had the presidential bungalow booked for the week, though he doubted he would stay there for more than a night.

Angelina emerged from the bathroom in a haze of smoke. The warm smell of colitas followed her to his bed as she stripped off her robe and stood there in her negligee for him to admire.

He didn't. His eyes never left the iPad propped on his lap.

With a frustrated huff, she pulled back the sheets and slid between them. The silk against her skin stoked the fires of her desire, and she moved toward him with determination. Her hand displaced the tablet for a moment, but he only pushed her aside. "Stop it. I've got to work."

Undeterred, she kissed his neck, and then his chest, trying again to gain the high ground the iPad had reclaimed. There was no lack of effort on her part, but the renewed assault was rebuffed just as quickly. "I told you. I've got work to do."

She turned to the side of the bed and reached for the silver bucket she'd had placed there. "I had the captain send up a bottle." With a little work, she freed the magnum from the crushed ice it had been buried in and presented the bottle to him like a trophy. "Rosé."

He was not tempted by her offer.

"Dom Perignon." She searched the label. "Nineteen sixty-nine."

"I thought they were out of that vintage." It wasn't that he'd become interested in the wine she was offering, just curious about why he'd been denied it earlier.

"I told them it was a special occasion."

"Work is my special occasion."

"Work," she spat, her frustration eclipsing her lust. "All you ever do is work."

"Nothing just happens, my love. Work is what makes all of this possible." He gestured around the opulent accommodations. "Work brings in money, and money makes the magic happen."

"But I need a man in my bed." Her protest was something between a moan and a purr.

"I thought that was why you had all of those friends." He said it as a casual aside, to stress the fact that he was utterly disinterested in anything that didn't directly involve him.

"They're just boys," she exclaimed, never offering an explanation or apology. "Pretty boys. But just boys."

"Well, I'm afraid they'll have to do until I've figured out the solution to my problem."

She wasn't impressed. "Seriously, I don't even know why you want me with you."

"I have my reasons."

"Reasons that don't include my *panocha*," she purred.

"It's on my list." His eyes were still focused on the items on his iPad. "But not nearly as high as some others."

"It's to torture my poor husband?" The question betrayed a certain hopefulness that he might admit her suspicion was true.

"Your husband's discomfort with our situation is not a motivator, but certainly an unintended benefit."

"Then why? My powers?" she asked suspiciously. "You like that I can channel Santa Muerte, don't you? You can't have her power, and you want everything you can't have."

"Your abilities certainly intrigue me." That he was willing to admit freely. "I've often wondered what it might be like if we could *merge* our powers." The thought of it was suddenly compelling enough to pull his eyes from the screen and turn them to her.

"Is that what you'd like? A little merger?" she wondered out loud.

He ran a withered hand through her raven-black hair. "Yes."

She kissed his lips, his chest. "I've often wondered about merging our powers as well." Her hand snaked its way toward his crotch and found that the third time was the charm. "I think that your powers would please Lady Muerte."

"Or she would please me."

She giggled evilly. "What did you have in mind?"

"Here. Let me show you."

He rolled her onto her back, and whatever aspirations she'd held for the evening were matched and surpassed. It was not love. Not even lust. They were two bodies thrashing at one another in fits of fury that seemed more like combat than sex.

"I have a surprise for you," she whispered in his ear between gasps of pleasure and cries of pain.

"What's that?" he panted.

She was beneath him, and she took his head in her hands and looked him in the eyes so that she could watch the look on his face. "I'm no one's *puta*," she hissed. "You're mine."

Still looking hard into his eyes, she didn't see the surprise or fear she'd expected. Instead, she saw something far more frightening than she could have imagined. "Santo! Santo!" she cried out in a panic, not at all in the way they'd planned it but out of genuine fear. "I'm in here! Hurry, hurry!"

A second later, the door splintered loudly, and Angelina's husband stormed into the bedroom.

Koschei pulled himself away from her and turned to face the intruder, but it was an awkward maneuver, as he was twisted in the sweat-soaked sheets.

In a matter of seconds, the enraged husband had Koschei pinned to the bed.

"Do you have the *tecpatlixquahuas*?" Angelina asked frantically.

"Right here," Santo answered, holding the old man down with one hand as he reached for the bundle of knives with the other.

There were five ceremonial blades in the red velvet bundle, and Angelina took the first one in both her hands and raised it high above her head. "*Mate a mi enemigo*. Kill my enemy." She plunged the blade into Koschei's abdomen.

The old man squealed in pain and thrashed harder under Santo's restraint.

She took the second knife. "*Róbele el poder*. Steal his power." She put the blade into his right lung.

A third knife. "*Róbele el alma*. Steal his soul." His left lung.

A fourth. "*Le ofrezco su vida a usted, Santa Muerte.* I offer his life to you." Just beneath his Adam's apple.

The fifth. "*¡Déme su poder!* Give his power to me!" She brought the last blade down into the middle of Koschei's chest.

"Get off him!" she ordered her husband, and she quickly climbed astride Koschei's thrashing body. She raised her hands up to the ceiling and began to chant a prayer, repeating the same spell over and over as she waited for her sacrifice to be rewarded with a transfer of power.

And then . . . absolutely nothing.

"What's happening?" her husband asked.

"Shut up," she spat in his direction.

Still astride Koschei's body, she looked down at what she'd done, befuddled and confused as to why the expected transformation hadn't taken effect.

Koschei's eyes opened. "What did you expect, bitch?"

Angelina jumped back in horror as Koschei calmly sat up in bed with five knives protruding from his neck, chest, and abdomen. "You can stab it with your knives." He grabbed hold of the knife that had pierced his left lung and pulled it free. "But you can't kill this beast."

Without looking at his target, Koschei drove the blade into Santo's chest.

Angelina screamed in horror as her husband dropped to the bed beside her. She crab walked backward, away from Koschei, but there was nowhere for her to hide.

"Relax," he told her, as he pulled another blade from his chest. "I don't know where you think you're going." He grabbed a handful of her raven hair and pulled her to her feet. "Because you can never leave." He drove the blade into her belly.

And then another. "You can never leave."

He held her body in his arms and felt the life begin to drift out. He cupped the back of her head so that he could put his mouth to hers. She tasted warm and wet with blood.

He pulled her close and put his mouth near hers. He was trembling with anticipation, assuming her soul would be reward enough for the evening. But there was more. Angelina had the power of Santa Muerte within her, and Koschei was eager to have it as his own.

He inhaled the pale blue light that had once provided the spark of life to Angelina Silvano, and with it, he felt his entire body tingle with a charge of universal energy.

But there was still more. There was Santa Muerte.

It came to him not as a ball of light, but as a long, serpentlike wisp of smoke. He inhaled it greedily, and it filled his lungs. There was a moment of ecstasy unlike anything he'd ever experienced in the whole of his existence, but it was all too short-lived.

He coughed and coughed until he had to drop Angelina's corpse just to steady himself. His stomach turned, and he retched, but nothing would leave him. On all fours like a beast, he barked and hacked and howled like he'd been poisoned.

For the first time ever, he was conscious of limitations to his physical form. And that realization introduced him to something else he'd never known before: fear.

CHAPTER FORTY-ONE

Same as the Old Boss

In his nineteen years with the FBI, Gerald Feller had seen more corpses sprawled across blood-splattered crime scenes than he could remember. Hell, in the year he'd spent inflicting Koschei's wrath on the world, he'd been responsible for more than his fair share of them.

In all his experiences on both sides of the badge, however, he'd never seen a crime scene quite as surreal as the one he found smeared across the presidential suite that night. "What the hell happened here?"

"Yes, exactly," Haden Koschei said, freshly showered and wrapped in a fluffy, white robe. His coloring, however, looked pale and chalky—even for him.

"You all right?" Feller asked, so surprised by the old man's pallor that he forgot the formality of their relationship.

"I'm fine," Koschei snapped, although the tone of his reply made clear that he was not.

Spread-eagle across rumpled sheets that were saturated with something sticky and brown was the body of the cartel king-pin the world had come to fear as El Tigre. His belly had been ripped open as if one of his pets had come to daddy for a midnight snack—and then made him into one. The back of his head was missing, and it looked like someone had packed the shattered skull with a heaping helping of grandma's Deep South pink Jell-O salad.

An abstract painting that had been chosen to match the colors of the room's décor, but might have been intended by some starving artist to be the flames of an autumn campfire or maybe the sun reflecting off the Pacific, had been taken down from the far wall and thrown in a corner. Hanging in the place of the artwork was the naked body of a woman, which Feller recognized immediately as having once been the lovely Angelina.

She was hung upside down, a single knife driven through her abdomen and pinning her to the wall. Her four limbs were pulled away from her body and fastened to the wall with four more knives. The wall that held her was stained with a single stream of blood that had pooled and soaked into the rug beneath her.

Feller looked down at the horror-twisted face he'd admired from afar as the most beautiful he'd ever seen (with maybe the single exception of his wife . . . *ex*-wife). He jumped back in shock as he realized the wide open eyes were watching him and the twisted mouth was struggling to let one last word out into the world. "*Vengarme.*"

Feller shook his head in disbelief. "What?"

"I believe she's asking you to avenge her," Koschei explained, coming up behind Feller and scaring him as badly as anything else in the room.

The old man then picked up a lamp from a nearby end table and struck Angelina's head, hard and sharp. "Bad bitch." A wound opened across her forehead and whatever last breath of life she'd held onto spilled out into the night.

"Are you going to, Mr. Feller?"

The voice shook him from his own little personal nightmare. "What's that?"

"Avenge her?" the old man said simply. "I knew you fancied her."

"No. I didn't."

"No sense lying in a room full of corpses," Koschei said. "Speaking of which . . ." He paused until he had Feller's full attention.

"Yes?"

"Just that," he said simply enough. "The room is full of corpses, and I suppose it shouldn't be when we check out at the end of the week."

"Yes, sir."

"I'm going to need you to take care of this, Mr. Feller." He casually gestured at the bodies.

Feller's response was lost in his regard for Angelina. Even now, in such a grotesque condition, she seemed nothing but lovely to him. And still impossibly far out of reach.

"Mr. Feller," Koschei said, snapping her fingers impatiently. "I need you to focus."

Feller mumbled something that neither of them understood. Then he realized his lapse and offered a very distinct, "I'll take care of everything."

Feller looked the bodies over and still couldn't put any of the puzzle pieces together in his badly rattled brain. "What happened here?"

"Haven't I warned you about thinking, Mr. Feller," he scolded. "What happened is unimportant. The truth is never as important as the presentation of your version of the truth. So what matters is what we're going to tell the world happened."

"I can't." Feller tried to shake all the temptations from his head. "Mr. Koschei"—he pointed to Angelina's corpse—"I can't just . . ."

"I'm not offering you an opportunity, Mr. Feller. I'm giving you a command. Take care of things."

"But how?"

"That's why you get the big bucks, Mr. Feller. Step up and earn them."

In the swirling sea of madness, there was one thing only that Feller knew for certain. "It's impossible."

"Far from it, Mr. Feller. I have a little bit of experience with scenes like this," the old man admitted. "I suggest you create a narrative around a murderous cult. Sprinkle in some bits of pop culture like we did with all of those Beatles references," he explained with a smile. "Stupidest song in the world and it still scares people today."

"Excuse me?" Feller wasn't sure he understood the reference.

"Never mind." Koschei swept the past behind him with a casual wave of his hand. "Just handle this however you see fit."

Feller hadn't realized that Koschei had been getting dressed the entire time they were speaking, but when he finally pulled his attention from the carnage and turned to face his boss, the man was neatly attired in a suit and tie.

"I will," Feller promised.

"I'm sure you will." Koschei patted his minion on the arm.

Feller turned back to assess the task at hand and heard a gulp and groan behind him.

He wheeled around to see Haden Koschei leaning against the doorway for support.

"Are you all right?"

"I'm fine," Koschei responded weakly. Not because he was, but because he had never not been fine before. "I don't know what . . ." he muttered to himself, and then walked out of the room without looking back.

Feller watched him go, closing the door on the scene. Even though he knew he was alone, he was *almost* certain that he heard a faint voice behind him. "*Vengarme*. Avenge me."

CHAPTER FORTY-TWO

If You Love Somebody

Vicki Bean picked at the salad, but she didn't much feel like eating anything on the chilled plate.

"You don't like the truffles?" Koschei asked before filling his mouth with some.

She smiled politely, uncomfortable that her unease had been discovered and now revealed. "They're wonderful," she lied, still not sure what a truffle was exactly. "I suppose I'm still shocked about Angelina."

"Yes," he said, casually stabbing something on his plate. "Terrible news, that." He chewed whatever he'd put in his mouth, swallowed, and then put down his fork. "Who would've thought there'd be murderous cults in Los Angeles again. It's like the Manson killings all over again."

"I still can't believe it," she said.

"What's not to believe?"

She thought his question, or rather the way he voiced it, was odd, and she didn't make any response. He was similarly silent for a moment, then leaned forward and began to rub his temples.

"Are you all right?" she asked from the other end of the table he'd had set for their lunch.

"I'm fine," he answered. Although it concerned him that he should suddenly be experiencing his first headache after millennia without pain of any kind. His worsening infirmities were a growing source of concern. "It's nothing."

"Are you sure?" The question was born out of the sort of concern that comes more from societal mandates than any genuine caring, so his response was that much more stinging.

"I told you, I'm fine." He slapped the table emphatically and with such force that his fork shattered the porcelain plate, spilling its contents all over the linen tablecloth.

"Damn it!" He shot to his feet, as if the scattered salad fixings posed some danger.

Vicki observed the scene wide-eyed.

It took a moment before he realized he'd made a spectacle of himself. "Excuse me," he said through a smile that was tight lipped around clenched teeth. He took his seat and placed his napkin on the table, like a fighter throwing in the towel. "There's been much to do with the Black Rock Festival," he explained. "Even for a man of my means, that show represents a significant investment. I suppose nerves can take a toll on even the best of us." His headache was worsening. This troubled him too much to let on.

"I understand." She busied herself with her salad.

"It is a big stage." He crossed his legs and set about making himself as comfortable as anyone can be in a dining room chair.

"The biggest." She knew that was true.

"I'd like to give it to you," he announced, absentmindedly folding and refolding the napkin he'd tossed off to the side.

She tilted her head as if she were confused.

"Angelina was scheduled to be a headliner." He washed away whatever bitterness he found in the statement with a sip of Chateau d'Yquem. "I want you to take that spot."

"Really?" The excitement made her put down her fork. "But I don't even have my album out yet."

"What better way to build buzz?" he asked.

A crowd of one hundred thousand. The possibilities were as impossible for her to comprehend as her excitement was to contain. "Oh my God!"

He gave her an isn't-that-nice smile before adding, "There is a slight catch."

She wondered what more she could possibly give him. "Catch?"

"He's coming for you, you know."

"Who's coming?" she asked cautiously.

"Don't be coy, my dear. It doesn't suit you. You can feel his presence," he told her. "I know that you can."

Her look wasn't a denial but a careful examination of his cold eyes for some tell as to how he could've known what she hadn't shared with anyone.

"For God's sake, stop the games." He slapped the table again. "You're searching my eyes like you'll find something there, but all the time yours are screaming to me. We both know he's coming for you."

She looked down at her plate, wishing she'd just eaten the damn truffles.

"He thinks he's going to rescue you."

She secretly rejoiced at what he'd said, but still felt the need to be defiant. "If I need rescuing, I can do it myself."

"Oh, I don't think so." He pushed himself back from the table. "I'm not sure anyone can save you, my dear. Except maybe me."

"I don't understand."

"Of course you do. Your Daniel—"

"He's not my Daniel," she said defensively.

"No, no he's not. He left you alone. Let you think he was dead."

There was no need to remind her of the pain Daniel had caused her.

"But the fact is that he's made a lot of enemies. When Daniel comes for you in his misguided Sir Lancelot fantasy, these people are going to follow him to you. They may even use you to get to him."

She took a sip of wine. "What are you saying?"

"I'm saying that you are at a crossroads, my dear. One path will take you to superstardom, to wealth and success and pleasures beyond your imaginings." He cleared his throat and tried to pretend the throbbing in his head wasn't worsening. "The other road will take you straight to hell."

"What do you want?"

"I want you to help me help you take the right path."

She was rightfully guarded. "And how would I do that."

"Daniel has no future." He said it like it was fact. "The question is whether you do. When he comes to you—and we both know he will—then you can go with him and suffer his fate. Or worse. And I can think of circumstances that would be much worse for you, my dear, than any scenario involving him."

"Or?"

"Or you can simply do nothing. Send him away. Tell him that you'd rather stay and flourish with me than run and die with him."

"He's not mine. And I don't love him. Not anymore," she lied.

"And you're telling me this because you're worried about me?"

"Of course not."

He knew no one would believe such a lie about him. "I have a hard time caring about people. I'm guessing you've picked up on that by now." He didn't wait for her reply. "But I have an intense interest in my investments. And right now, you represent a significant one, which I don't want to see squandered over something so trite as a love gone tragically wrong."

"There's nothing trite about love."

"Love is a momentary lapse of reason. That's why it never lasts. Never. Fame can last. Fortune can last. But love never stands a chance. Everyone thinks they've held it at one time or another, but day after day, it fades away to nothing."

"You're wrong." She hated what he'd said, but she wasn't sure in her heart that he was wrong.

"Am I? Then prove it. When he comes for you, prove to me that you love him and want to protect him by sending him away. *That's* the only chance he has." Koschei was done with the conversation and rose to his feet. "It's also the only chance that you've got."

CHAPTER FORTY-THREE

Good News/Bad News

"Where the hell you been?" Moog asked.

"I told you not to stay up, Mom." Daniel stepped through the door that connected their adjoining hotel rooms. "I brought you cheeseburgers," he coaxed, and set a grease-marked paper bag down on the desk.

Moog wasn't laughing. "This some serious shit, man. Makes me nervous when you disappear for the night. I don't give a damn about any—" The big man reconsidered his hasty remarks. "They In-N-Out burgers?"

"I think you know they are."

"That don't fix nothing," Moog insisted. "But bring 'em here."

Daniel delivered the bag of burgers, and Moog pulled out the first one. "So, where were you," he asked again, with a mouthful of meat and cheese.

"I went to the beach."

"The beach? What the hell you going to the beach for?"

"I had some thinking to do."

"You had to drive all the way out there just to think?"

"I do my best thinking while driving, you know that."

Moog balled up the wrapper of the first downed burger. "I ain't yet to see no best thinking outta you."

"Well, then I won't disappoint you now," Daniel said with a smile.

"What you got planned for us?"

"How'd you like to walk into a trap?" Daniel asked brightly.

Moog took a bite of cheeseburger number two. "Not much at all."

"What if I told you that your little girl was the bait."

Moog put down the burger. "I'd say I'm about to bust up somebody's trap."

"Don't get too excited all at once," Daniel cautioned. "It's a helluva trap."

"Ain't no concern, if they got my daughter. What are we talking here? How many men Koschei got?"

"I don't know," Daniel admitted.

"Ten? Twenty?"

"I'm guessing hundreds," Daniel answered.

"Hundreds?" Moog hadn't been anticipating that kind of opposition. "How'd Koschei get that kinda manpower?"

"I'm guessing it won't just be Koschei's people."

"You think those black shirts will be back?"

"I'm fairly certain."

Moog could tell it got worse. "And the Mexicans?"

"I wouldn't be surprised."

"Give me some good news." Moog picked his burger back up. "How the two of us gonna go up against all of that."

"We're gonna slip in undercover."

"Undercover of what?"

"About a hundred thousand people."

"What the hell are you talking about?"

"There's a big music festival this weekend. Out in the desert. And they just added Vicki and Malaika to the lineup."

"Seems awful convenient."

"It's awful trappish, is what it is," Daniel said. "But Koschei's putting them out there for a reason, and I don't think we're going to get another chance."

Moog wondered if he'd gotten the plan right. "So, you expect us to walk through the gates with a hundred thousand people, find our girls, and get them out, while being hunted down by hundreds of folks who's expecting us to be there?"

Daniel considered every element that his friend had recited, and evaluated them against his actual plan. "Yes. Well, not exactly."

"Not exactly?"

"Yeah. We won't be walking in there."

"See," Moog said, taking a resentful bite of burger. "There ain't no best thinkin' with you."

"Then it's decided," Daniel said cheerfully. "We're going to Black Rock."

CHAPTER FORTY-FOUR

Black Rock

There once was a boy who had a dream that one day he would be a pop star—not just a pop star, but the biggest pop star of all time. As the years passed, he grew up clinging tightly to that dream, refusing to let bullies rob him of it or jaded teachers cheat him of it. He ignored his parents' well-intentioned admonitions and the wizened advice of more realistic unbelievers. He nurtured his dream, protected it from the intrusions of everyday life—like his complete lack of musical talent. He clung to that dream and, one fine day, he made it real.

Of course, it wasn't music that made the dream come true. One day that boy, Jonathon Hesher, invented a software writing program that revolutionized computing, and that was what made his rock-and-roll dream a reality. The software made Hesher a K2 of cash, and currency can make any dream come true. In this case, he set up some tents on a tract of land he owned adjacent to the Anza-Borrego Desert State Park, and signed the checks to bring all of the biggest bands together over the course of a single weekend.

He was an instant rock star.

And that was how the Black Rock Music Festival got its start.

"They have a festival for black rock?" Moog asked as they passed the checkpoint.

"No." Daniel lifted his hand from the limousine's steering wheel and pointed out across the line of limos and town cars, out toward a barren horizon that was broken only by a grouping of boulders that seemed to appear out of nowhere. "There's a big, black rock over there that they named the festival after. The music is decidedly white."

It made Moog wonder. "Is there even such a thing as black rock?"

"Yeah, but they call it blues."

"Confusing shit, man."

"Sweeping shit under the rug always makes more of a mess."

Daniel hit the brakes as the line of traffic slowed to pass through the first security checkpoint. On the driver's side door, there was a panel, straight out of a Bond film, with too many buttons and switches. It took him a minute before he could find the one that rolled down the window.

"Wasn't there an easier way to get into the place?" Moog asked as they inched closer to the check-in station at the head of the long line.

"Yeah," Daniel admitted. "I guess we could've just bought a ticket like everyone else."

"That's what I was thinking."

Daniel nodded in acknowledgment of the point. "But I'm guessing all of those nice men and women in the black polo shirts that are working security at the gates might have noticed the two of us walking straight in through the front door."

"This don't seem no better," Moog countered.

"What are you complaining about?" Daniel asked. "I didn't make you drive."

Moog didn't find that funny. "I would've rathered."

"Well, you'll get your chance," Daniel assured him. "Because the bitch of it is going to be getting out of here, if everything goes as planned—"

Moog had to laugh. "And you know goddamn well it won't."

Daniel did, but that didn't alter his plan. He rolled the limo forward to where a black-polo-shirted guy, holding a clipboard, stood waiting.

"You don't have a pass," the guard said, pointing at the vehicle's rearview mirror, which had a new-car-scented pine tree hanging from it but no access pass. "And without a pass you're not going anywhere near the artist tent."

"No problem to me. I'd love to beat the traffic getting out of here," Daniel said good-naturedly. "But you should probably take it up with the boss." He made a casual motion with his thumb toward the back of the limo.

"I don't care who you've got in the back. If the vehicle doesn't have a pass, it doesn't get through."

"Hey, Paul Blart, mall cop!" a voice called out from the limo's backseat.

The guy with the clipboard turned angrily, looking for who'd called him out. He immediately took a step back when he saw the young girl's face clearly. "Miss Wannaman," he said eagerly, recognizing the face he'd seen all over the Internet and on those magazine covers everyone can't help but read while waiting in the supermarket checkout line.

M. F. Wannaman was still just a teenager, but she'd *lived* more than most octogenarians. Her father had been Mark Wannaman, better known as Marco Pharaoh, the lead singer and driving force behind the megaband Taco Shot. He'd been beaten to death by killers hired by the girl's mother, who had briefly enjoyed a musical career of her own until an on-stage breakdown had led her to put a pistol to her head.

Rock-and-roll folklore had embraced the rumors that the gun at the mother's head had been held in the daughter's hand. Those whisperings significantly increased her cool rating. And there was certainly a darkness in her twinkling eyes that seemed to joyously confess to having capped the bitch.

Those with a heart had infinite compassion for a girl who'd lost both of her parents in extraordinarily tragic ways. Others, who viewed life more darkly, admired a little girl with the brass fixtures necessary to put a slug in her mommy's head. However she was seen, M. F. Wannaman was viewed as rock-and-roll royalty.

"I didn't know it was you," the clipboard guy said apologetically.

"And I thought you didn't care who was back here," M. F. called him out.

He chuckled self-consciously and made a just-look-at-him gesture at Daniel behind the wheel. "I thought it was like some gynecologist from Glendale or, you know, the used-car king of Sacramento, you know?"

If she did, she didn't care. "Do I look like either?"

"N-n-no," he stammered. "I just—" He looked back at Daniel. "This is your driver?"

"The guy behind the steering wheel of my car?" Her words cut him like a box cutter. "Yeah. He's my driver."

The clipboard guy looked further into the front seat, past Daniel. "And who's this guy?"

"Do you think I would come someplace like this without a body guard?"

The clipboard guy understood, but made a point of being unimpressed. "He's your security?"

Before M. F. could form a response, Moog offered his own. "Why don't you smack wise to the lady and see where that clipboard ends up."

The clipboard guy took a step back.

"And you are?" M. F. asked him.

"I'm Roger—"

"Got it." M. F. wasn't interested in his whole name. "You're Roger the clipboard guy," she announced. "So now that everybody knows each other, why don't you wave us through, and we'll be on our way."

"I can't do that," he nervously explained. "You don't have a badge for your car, and none of you have passes."

"I thought it was passes for the car and badges for us." She caught him.

"Right, but—"

"Listen, Roger the clipboard guy. This whole scene is my idea of hell. So, I don't want to be here, and I'd have no problem turning around and getting out of this madness. But Todd Golding—you do know who Todd Golding is?"

Everyone knew the rock-and-roll hall of famer. "Sure, I—"

"Fine. Then I'll just go back home and I'll call *Uncle Todd*"—she made air quotes and everything—"and tell him that I would've been his special guest, but Randy—"

"Roger."

"Whatevs." She didn't care about little things like names. "I'll tell him that the clipboard guy wouldn't let me through because I didn't have a piece of laminated cardboard. And then he can tell the promoters that they're going to be minus one headliner because some guy named Roger wouldn't give his friend a laminated badge. Is that what you want?"

"No, no."

"Then give with the badge." She held out her hand.

"Oh no." He looked down at his own credentials. "I don't have any badges here to pass out."

"Isn't that one around your neck?"

"But I only have this one," he said almost plaintively.

M. F. didn't take her hand back. "Give with the badge, Roger."

Reluctantly, he took it from around his neck and handed it to her.

"I still can't let the car through without a pass on it." He smiled like he'd just outsmarted her.

"Roger," M. F. told him sternly, "there's no one allowed on the festival grounds without a badge," she pointed out. "And you don't have one."

He looked down at his chest as if he needed to verify that.

"So why don't you just call security and explain to them why someone without a badge is giving shit to someone who has one." She held up her prize.

Roger cast his eyes down in defeat.

And then waved them through.

CHAPTER FORTY-FIVE

Even Now

"Are we even now?" M. F. asked Daniel, whose eyes were focused forward as he drove slowly toward the VIP parking lot.

"You never owed me anything," he answered.

"That's not how the old man tells it."

"Atibon?"

"He tells me I'm free." She paused to make her point. "Because of you."

"I'd hock my soul for you anytime." Daniel casually dismissed the matter, but everything he'd done during the months he was in England had been to pay back a debt that M. F. owed to Atibon. Daniel had taken it upon himself to spare the girl from having to satisfy her own indebtedness to the mysterious man.

"Well, I appreciate it." When she wanted to, she could sound like the sweetest girl in the world. And she was.

"Nothing to it."

"Whatever you're doing must be important." Her face was set with a matter-of-factness beyond her age.

"I have no idea what you're talking about," Daniel lied.

"Yeah, well, Atibon told me he'd owe me one if I helped you."
She smiled proudly. "And I'm guessing he doesn't do that a lot."

Daniel looked out at the crowd on the festival grounds. "Is
he here?"

"He's the ghost of a shadow of a wisp of smoke, so who
knows?" She was also wise beyond her years.

They were waved into VIP parking just behind the artists'
tent without further interference from the hordes of black polos
patrolling the grounds. One of them waved Daniel into a parking
spot. He set the limo in park, killed the engine, and turned back
to M. F. "You sure you're going to be all right?"

"Absolutely," she assured him, and her eyes confirmed it. "I'll
go find Todd and—"

"I'd stay close to him." Daniel tried not to convey the depths
of his concern, but he came up short.

In turn, his apprehension fed hers. "It's going to be that bad?"

"Maybe." He tried to smile reassuringly and failed at that too.
"But if you're close to Todd then you'll just be one less person to
worry about when it all goes off."

"I can take care of myself," she reminded him. "And Atibon
owes me."

Daniel smiled. "What can go wrong?"

"I guess that's up to you, huh?"

He shrugged. "It always seems that way."

"Here." She handed him Roger the clipboard guy's badge,
then turned to Moog. "I'm sorry. I only have the one."

The big man looked at Daniel. "Where's mine at?"

"You're eight feet tall and four hundred pounds," Daniel
explained. "If you need a badge to get through the door, then
we're in a world of hurt before all this even begins."

"I ain't no eight feet," Moog objected, although he was secretly pleased he'd been described in such gigantic proportions. "And I ain't no four hundred pounds neither."

"Here." Daniel offered him the badge. "You can have the badge. You can be—" He looked for the exact name. "Roger Wojohowitz."

Moog snatched the card from his hand.

Daniel hadn't been expecting the big man to actually take him up on the offer, but he couldn't let on. "Better?"

"I'm better." Moog said, then corrected himself. "I ain't good, but I'm better. Good would be some actual goddamn credentials here, so we could move around the place and find what we looking for."

"Well, listen," M. F. interrupted. "So you two don't have to fight in front of the kids, I'm going to take on out of here." She opened her door, but Daniel jumped out to get it for her.

"You'd blow our cover if I was just sitting there," he explained, although that wasn't all of it. And they both knew it.

"All right," she said, not exactly sure why she felt so emotional about telling him good-bye.

"Wish me luck."

She threw her arms around him and did just that.

She sniffled and wiped a single tear from her cheek. "I'll see you around."

He smiled. "Count on it."

"I am." She waved, and then turned and disappeared into the crowd.

CHAPTER FORTY-SIX

Hamsters

The entrance to the artists' tent was manned by two guys in XXL black polos. They looked like half of the defensive line of a community college football team.

"Where's your wristbands?" One of them asked when Daniel and Moog approached them.

"Our what?" Daniel looked down self-consciously at his wrist, and found himself wishing he'd stood his ground and kept the badge.

"Wristband," chimed in the other guy at the door, pointing to the joint between his own forearm and hand in case there was any confusion. "You gotta have a green wristband to get in the artist tent."

Daniel was trying to think up a lie when Moog stepped forward. "Mr. Phil Collins don't need no motherfuckin' wristband to get into no motherfuckin' artists' tent."

Neither of the guys was preparing a doctoral thesis in their spare time, but they were both smart enough to realize that they risked a high probability of chronic pain should they tangle with Moog. And they were both smart enough to regard Daniel with suspicion. One of them squinted his eyes and slowly asked, "You're Phil Collins?"

"I thought you were dead," the other added.

"This is Phil 'In the Motherfucking Air Tonight' Collins, bitch," Moog said excitedly. "He ain't dead. He's hungry and thirsty and tired of waiting out here talking to you two fools 'stead of going inside and getting some food and beverages."

The two plus-size polos stood their ground.

"So you best both step aside," the big man continued with snarling menace. "'Cause you best better believe we going inside, and if I have to have anything around my wrist it's gonna be one of your assholes." He balled up his hand and let them both take a good, long look. "And I got a big, fucking fist."

The pair stood like monoliths at the entrance, but it was clear they were both thinking over their situation: job responsibilities versus angry guy with big fist.

"Sorry to keep you waiting, Mr. Collins," one of them said with an ingratiating smile.

The other unlatched the velvet rope and ushered them inside with a sweep of his arm. "Right this way, Mr. Collins."

Daniel smiled appreciatively at the duo and followed Moog into the tent. They walked a dozen steps or so before he couldn't contain the question any longer, "Phil Collins?"

"What was I supposed to say?" Moog was more concerned with scanning the crowd. "They wasn't gonna believe you was Fiddy Cent, was they? And it's not like I know a lot of over-the-hill white guys in rock bands."

"And still, you know Phil Collins?"

"Everyone know Phil Collins, man. That 'In the Air' shit is some badass shit, man. Fuckin' Mike Tyson sings that shit."

Daniel shook his head, mourning the days when he might have been passed off as someone with a full head of hair. "Phil Collins?"

Moog was done with the back-and-forth. "Let's just find what we're looking for and get out of here."

The tent was maybe forty feet by a hundred, with a long buffet, a bar, and a number of tables arranged at the far end. There were upwards of three hundred people crammed into the space.

"Quite a herd of hamsters." A man in a silk shirt-and-short set remarked casually as he sipped a gin and tonic.

"Excuse me?" Daniel asked, not sure if, or why, the comment had been directed at him.

The man took a half step closer and used his sweating glass of gin to indicate some of the young women in the crowd. "Hamsters, mate." The man's English accent was distinctive, Surrey maybe.

Daniel shook his head. "I don't—"

"Hamsters," the main repeated, pointing around more emphatically. "You know: hookers, actresses, models, strippers, trainers, entertainers, runaways." The man smiled, clearly pleased with himself. "Hamsters: the lifeblood of rock and roll!"

Not unexpectedly, there were a lot of beautiful women scattered throughout the crowd, but Daniel's only response was a half-hearted smile meant to acknowledge the comment but not encourage the conversation.

Moog might have offered his thoughts on the subject, but he suddenly spied something in the crowd that made his whole body go rigid, as if someone had plugged him into a 220 outlet. "There she is."

"Who?" Daniel asked.

"Malaika." The big man said the name as if it were a magic word. "My girl." Excited, he began to point across the crowded tent, but Daniel stopped him.

"Just be easy," Daniel cautioned as he purposely looked past the point his friend had indicated, searching for signs that someone might be watching them. "Let's ease into this."

Moog wasn't listening. Or slowing. "Who the hell is that?"

Daniel searched the crowd for someone who seemed out of place. "Who?"

"Fool with his arm all over my little girl's shoulders. I tell you what I'm going to ease into, gonna ease into kickin' his ass all the way down the road back to Leave My Little Girl Alone City. Population: your sorry ass."

"Zack."

The name was only a momentary distraction for Moog. "You see your boy too?"

"Zack," Daniel repeated. "The kid you want to boot stomp. That's my son."

"What? Don't be—" The big man took another look to be sure. "When the hell he grow a beard?"

"Puberty. What can I tell you?"

"Tell me? You need to tell your son to keep his hands off my little girl."

"Nobody's hurting anybody."

"Not yet."

"We'll worry about chaperoning the kids in a minute." Daniel looked over the crowd. "Right now we've got two of them together in one spot. That's a better beginning to all of this than we had any right to hope for. You keep an eye on them." He caught himself and quickly added, "From a distance." He went back to scanning the crowd. "I'll see if I can't find Vicki."

"What?"

"You've got to play this cool. We can't do anything that would attract any unwanted attention before—"

The words weren't even out of his mouth before everything fell completely apart.

"What the hell are *you* doing here?" Vicki screamed. Just before she slapped him.

CHAPTER FORTY-SEVEN

The End of the Line

Daniel's sole motivation for walking into the lion's den that was the Black Rock Music Festival was to spring Vicki Bean from the trap in which she'd been ensnared. If he hadn't necessarily envisioned a happy ending to the rescue effort (and he hadn't), he'd at least convinced himself that she would be overwhelmed with emotion at seeing him again.

And while she was clearly overwhelmed by his presence, it wasn't the sort of emotion he'd been counting on.

"Maybe I deserved that." His face stung from the slap. "But there's no time for that now. I came to get you out of here and we've gotta go now."

"I'm not going anywhere." Vicki was adamant. "And I'm sure as hell not going anywhere with you." She seemed pretty certain about that part too.

"You don't understand." Daniel wanted to explain the totality of their dire circumstances, but he'd overlooked the inevitable consequences of telling Vicki she didn't understand something.

"No, *you* don't understand."

Vicki also had a lot she wanted to explain. She wanted to make clear that she was scheduled to take the stage at Black Rock, and that she'd worked too hard and waited too long to just walk away from that opportunity now. She wanted him to understand that she'd been taking care of herself since she was a child, and that she'd managed to survive a whole year without him tilting at windmills for her. And she wanted to share with him everything that she'd been through since the last moment he'd held her. She wanted to do all that, but all that came out was, "You. Left. Me." And she accompanied each bitter word with a sharp poke to his chest.

Daniel was willing to endure her blow-by-blow version of their shared history, but there was little point in resolving those issues if they ended up as guests at Hotel Black Polo. "Vicki, you have to listen to me."

"I haven't seen you in . . ." She didn't want to count the days, so she punched him again instead.

Daniel understood her stress, but he was running out of time to be patient. "We can work this out later," he told her in measured syllables meant to calm her down.

It didn't work. "Work what out? Why are you even here?"

That was the end. He caught her next punch and held her by the wrist. "Because you're in danger. Because if I don't get you out of here—and soon—then none of us are getting out of here. Ever."

She tried to pull away. "I've got a show to play."

"It's all just a trap," Daniel tried to explain.

"Maybe." Her look told him she understood, and that none of it mattered. "But it's all I got."

"There's nothing for you here."

"No. That's not true. Right here, right now, I've got a chance."

"To do what, Vicki?"

"To take the shot I've worked so hard for."

"Will you stop it? This doesn't have anything to do with you. It never did. You're bait. That's all. You're a lure to get me here."

There was a look of betrayal in her eyes, as though he'd trespassed across boundaries he'd silently promised not to cross. "Then I've done what they wanted me to. I might as well get my reward."

Daniel shook his head, exasperated and frustrated with his inability to explain things that he didn't fully understand. "It's not that simple."

"It's exactly that simple," she assured him. "I had a dream. Now I've got a chance to realize that. To make it real. I'm not walking away from that. I can't."

"I'm sorry, but there's no future in music. If you take that stage, if you don't come away with me right now, then you've only one possible future. And it's not superstardom."

"It doesn't matter." Her voice was small and weak.

"We need to go now."

"No," she said, casting her eyes away from his. "I didn't mean my dream didn't matter. I mean the consequences don't matter."

"Look what I got runnin' off to God knows where." Moog emerged holding Malaika's arm with one hand and the scruff of Zack's collar in the other.

"Dad?" Zack asked, surprised to see the father he hadn't seen in years. "What are you doing here?"

"Zack," Daniel said awkwardly.

"And Vicki?" Zack asked. "How do you know my—" The uncomfortable pieces came together. "Oooh."

Moog suddenly realized he was standing in a deep pool of awkwardness. "Hey, Vicki. 'Sup."

Vicki was too distracted by the news of her situation to offer anything more than a halfhearted, "Moog."

"Well, I'd love to stand around here and talk whatever the hell you all talkin' about," the big man said, still holding on to his daughter, "but we gotta haul ass before it's too late."

"And go where?" Malaika demanded.

"They want us to leave," Vicki told her.

"Leave?" The word didn't seem to have any meaning to her. "Leave when? Where?"

"Now!" Moog cleared it up for her.

"Oh hell, no," the girl protested. "I'm not fucking going anywhere but up on that stage."

"You watch your mouth, young lady."

"You ain't my daddy."

"The hell I ain't your daddy." Moog didn't leave any room for doubt. "And your smart ass is coming with me, back to your mother."

The girl looked over to Vicki, who stood silent and broken, unable to answer for a moment, before saying, "They're right." Everyone turned and looked at her. "You should go."

"I'm not going anywhere," Malaika insisted. "I'm not leaving you."

"I know." Vicki nodded with forlorn resignation. "Because I'm coming with you."

"All right then," Moog said, hoping to cut the discussion short. "Now that we got that settled, let's get to gettin' outta here."

"No." Daniel's words took everyone by surprise. "We're not leaving. Not yet."

"What's that, one more time?" Moog asked in confusion.

"We're not going anywhere." He looked around at the crowd, trying to get a sense of the element that surrounded them. "At least not yet."

"What are you talking about? We went through all of this just to get them out."

"Vicki's right. What good would it do?"

"It'd keep our asses outta prison. Or a grave. And I like both those reasons right off the bat."

"We don't let them change a thing that we're doing." Daniel tried to smile. "What's going to happen is going to happen. We've run out of room to run." He turned to Vicki. "So the only thing left to do is sing the song you've got to sing."

Moog wasn't buying it. "Man, we can't just sit here and let them tighten the noose."

"I've got a plan." Daniel turned back to Vicki. "I can buy you time. I can get you that shot, your shot, but . . ."

Her eyes were wide, anticipating what condition he might apply.

"You're only going to get the one shot. You've got to play this show like it was your one and only."

She hugged him. "Thank you." And kissed him. Then kissed him again. "Thank you."

Daniel turned to Zack and shook his hand. "Good luck."

Zack looked at the ground and muttered something.

Without letting go of the young man's hand, Daniel pulled him into an embrace. "I'm proud of you. Of everything you've done and become and accomplished. Everything you are despite me." He tried to look into Zack's eyes. "You take care of your mother. And you take care of everyone you ever love"—he looked across the way—"particularly if they've got an oversize father who's a stone-cold killer."

"Straight up on that," Moog agreed.

"And you remember what I told you."

"What's that?" Zack wondered.

"You keep playing 'today music.'" He knew it was the best advice he could give. "You play every show, love every love, live every day like it was your one and only."

Zack hugged Daniel and took Malaika's hand to go.

Daniel turned to Vicki. "Have a good show."

"I will," she promised. "It's my one and only."

He smiled and watched her turn. "Hey."

She looked back.

"About everything . . ." They both waited for him to find the words. "I went away because I had to. I never left you." He needed her to know. "And I never will."

She smiled. "I know." Then she turned and disappeared up the stairs toward the backstage.

CHAPTER FORTY-EIGHT

You Go Your Way, Maybe I'll Go Mine

Daniel and Moog watched them go.

"That's a fine girl you got," Daniel offered.

The big man nodded proudly. "Too good for your son."

Daniel smiled. "You just see that you take care of them."

Moog didn't say a thing.

"Vicki too."

"What the hell you talkin' about?"

"I'm just saying. You know, if anything . . ." Daniel trailed off.

Moog knew only too well. "She's not going to take to you leaving her again."

"Didn't you hear? I'm never going to leave her."

The big man nodded, but he understood what his friend wasn't saying. "We coulda made it, you know." He looked around just to be sure. "Still enough people coming and going. Enough traffic for cover. If we'd slipped out now, we just might've made it."

Daniel just laughed. "How far?"

"Far enough." Moog was certain of that.

"I've been running my whole life." Daniel shook his head. "There's no such place as far enough."

Whether or not he agreed, Moog understood. "You gonna have to make a hell of a distraction when the time comes."

"That's what I'm thinking."

Moog knew his friend better than that. "But you ain't got no plan, do you?"

"Something will turn up. It always does."

"Your mojo?"

"My mojo."

The big man shook his head and didn't try to resist laughing. "I gotta give it to you, but goddamn if that mojo of yours hasn't damn near got me killed more times than I can count." He laughed again, and then paused a moment to think on it. "I shoulda killed you when I had the chance."

"You gave it a good goddamn try." Daniel smiled broadly. "I remember that first time. You sliding on your ass down that incline out behind my old house in Malibu."

"I remember," the big man assured him. "Ruined my fucking suit. I was pissin' mad."

"You shot that guy's Lotus." Daniel recalled with more glee than anyone else would've understood. "I think he damn near shit himself."

"I gotta give respect. I wouldn't have bet ten dollars that you could've lived through that day." The big man laughed to himself. "Remember when you drove that tractor trailer through the line of cop cars in Chicago?"

"Not really. A lot of that is just a little fuzzy."

"Man, I wish you could. 'Cause that was some funny shit."

"Yeah?"

"Yeah. I wonder why that is. Why is it the most fucked up shit's the funniest when you look back on it?"

Daniel had a theory. "Maybe because there's no fear in the past. Fear is all about worrying about what *might be*. No future, no fear."

"Well, then I hope you got one hell of a plan, because without it I don't think we got much of a future."

Daniel shrugged the comment off. "Don't you forget about me. I've been surprising folks for a long, long time now."

"That's the damned truth."

CHAPTER FORTY-NINE

Stardust, Golden, and Caught in the Bargain

Civilization is the gold gilt on the human condition, but the slightest provocation can scrape all the pretty stuff off and show the real ugliness underneath in a New York minute. Order, propriety, and decency are as delicate as the rarest of orchids, and exist only under the right conditions. When the shit hits the fan, it's every man for himself. And the conditions that day were optimal for maximum splatter.

The concert promoters had planned on an attendance of over two hundred fifty thousand. But with a single day pass starting at three hundred dollars (and headed northward from there) and a less than convenient location, the number of actual attendees was something more along the lines of two hundred twenty thousand. And while the bean counters behind the scenes might have found that a disappointing number, by the time the evening headliners were prepping to take the stage, the crowd had swelled to a gathering roughly equaling the population of Baton Rouge.

Once the well-heeled music fans had dished out the heavy cash just to get onto the festival grounds, and made the three-hour drive out to downtown Armageddon, they discovered that making the scene was no easy thing. The lines to get through the door were crazy long and moved slowly. The promoters claimed that the lack of speed in processing ticket holders was all a matter of the-times-we-live-in security measures, but the guys at the gate were also screening for, and prohibiting, outside food and beverages.

Inside the gate, once they'd gotten to the head of the long lines for the concession stands, concertgoers found post-apocalyptic prices for food and drink. True, it was the middle of the desert, but seven dollars and fifty cents for a bottle of water seemed unreasonable, and fourteen-dollar beers struck many in the crowd as positively anti-American.

Of course, the difficulty in obtaining sustenance might have been all for the best. Last minute "budget adjustments" had significantly impacted the available number of Porta-Potties. The few crap crypts that were available became virtually unusable in a matter of hours.

And while music journalists and hipster music snobs all praised the show's wonderfully diverse lineup of artists, the blend of fans wasn't harmonious from the very start. Kids with their pants around their asses and flat-billed baseball caps, doing the angry alpha-dog thing, mixed uneasily with the guys who wore white wifebeaters to show off their artificial tans and pharmaceutically enhanced muscles. Groups of women passed one another, casually tossing out "skank" and "ho" from under their breath; and it was true that many of them did seem challenged to dance to the music without the assistance of a pole.

The only other thing this unstable social gumbo required was a little heat, and Mother Nature turned the flame all the way up with a scorching day of merciless sun. Undeniably, there was a minimalist beauty to the site's long, forbidding lines, but the promoters had failed to factor into their plans the inescapable fact that the Ansel Adams landscape was desolate for a reason. By lunchtime—a meal many in the crowd could not afford—the mercury had hit 115 degrees, and with the exceptions of the VIP and artists' tents, there wasn't a shady spot to be found for a hundred miles.

By the time the sun had begun to set, the teeming crowd was hot and dehydrated, hungry and exploited, drunk and high. Ripples of discomfort, turned to aggression, ran through the festival grounds—pushes exchanged over insults, punches thrown in response to pushes—and all of it hinted at the bubbling volatility at the crowd's core.

Security for the event had been assigned to the Cold Water Group, which had extensive experience in running nations in turmoil, but had never been tested in rock concert crowd control. While there were certainly many similarities in the two situations, it was the differences that ultimately proved to be disastrous.

CHAPTER FIFTY

The Show Must Go On

Hellena was just one of the factory-made singers who prowled the stage like a panther in heat—if a sexually receptive panther were to wear a leather teddy and thigh-highs. Two dozen dancers behind her matched her, pelvic thrust for pelvic thrust and ass shake for ass shake. Lights and lasers went off in rhythm with the pounding beat. One hundred and thirty booms per minute.

You gotta do me, do me, do me till I scream, "Stop!"
Then you do me, do me, do me some more!
You gotta do me, do me, do me till I scream, "Stop!"
Then you do me, do me, do me some more!
You gotta do me, do me, do me till I scream, "Stop!"
Then you do me, do me, do me some more!
You gotta do me, do me, do me till I scream, "Stop!"
Then you do me, do me, do me some more!

She repeated the line over and over until the entire festival grounds seemed to be chanting along. Musicians behind her seemed to be playing their instruments furiously. And no one appeared to notice that it was impossible for Hellena to be singing her own harmonies. Or, at least no one cared.

The song ended without her needing to count her band down and without anyone missing a beat. The whole production was choreographed perfectly.

Although the dance routine had left her breathing heavily, she managed to scream out, "Hello, Black Rock!"

Two hundred thousand voices roared back.

"Hello, Black Rock!" she screamed even louder.

Two hundred ten thousand voices called back in response.

"Hello, Black Rock!" she screamed again, this time sounding frustrated and pissed that she wasn't getting the response she wanted.

The third time was the charm. Everyone on the festival grounds seemed to join in with one rousing cheer.

"You know I love you, right?"

More cheering.

"You know I love all you guys." She pranced back and forth like a streetwalker at the end of a long night.

A deep growl of male voices.

"And you know I love the ladies too!"

A squeal of approval.

"But there's nothing I love more than some guys and some girls together!"

The crowd erupted in howls and cheers.

"The more the merrier!" she screamed.

Her audience screamed back.

"I'm going to bring out a special guest. A special *friend*, you know what I mean?"

Apparently everybody did. Or, at least, they all kept screaming.

"And I know she likes the guys and the girls and the groups and the gangs even better than me!"

More screaming.

"Join me in giving a nasty-ass Black Rock welcome to Vicki Bean and the Jimmys, featuring Miss Behavior!"

There was a loud cheer, but not nearly as loud as the ones the audience had just given up.

"We gonna do their new single, 'Love Train'!" Hellena announced. "And believe me when I tell you that she's a nonstop locomotive of love! Line up to take a ride on her, guys!"

The cheers amped up louder this time.

Vicki stepped out of the wings with a sunburst Stratocaster strapped to her shoulder. She waved to the crowd as she strode out across the stage. Zack and Malaika followed close behind her until they all found their spots at the center of the stage.

"Ready?" Hellena asked, though it was clear she was looking past Vicki and at someone just off in the wings.

"Actually," Vicki interrupted, "we're not going to do that awful song tonight. And we're not really Vicki Bean and the Jimmys. We're just the Vicki Bean Band. And this talented lady is Malaika Turner."

The crowd sort of murmured, not sure how to respond to something so unexpected.

"We went through a lot to get this spot up here in front of all of you. A lot of people, a lot of people I love have given up a lot, have given up everything to get us up here tonight. And this is our one chance to play our music. See, we've only got this one opportunity to play one song. You've all got that same opportunity too. So this is for you. This is "If I Never."

Well I'm scared to be loved. More scared to be alone.

I don't want to need someone, but so tired on my own.

I need your arms around me, but I'm so damn mad.
Why does love feel so good, when it hurts so goddamn bad.

Malaika looked to her friend, smiled, and began to rap her part.

Give you my heart. You take it for a joyride.
Drive-by lover, you kill a girl from the inside.
You playin' at stayin', so, boy, go and run and hide.
Stealin' what I gave, but you can never take my pride.

When their song was over, Vicki raised her hand triumphantly, not for the performance or its reception, but simply because she'd done it. But before she could start a second song, she was surrounded by men in black polo shirts, who escorted her and the rest of the band from the stage. Vicki and the others left without protest, waving to the crowd as they were being escorted away.

Not everyone objected, but a small portion of the crowd of two hundred thirty thousand began to boo. "Let them play!" someone screamed, and that was echoed until it became a chant. "Let them play!"

"Sorry about that!" Hellena tried to cover as she rushed back out onto the stage.

"Let them play! Let them play!" The crowd continued to chant.

"If she doesn't wanna pull your love train, then you know, baby, I pull that train myself!" The throbbing bass line started, and Hellena began her dance moves, struggling to keep her composure as she focused on hitting her marks.

Boy, you know I like you. I like your friend too.
I like all your bad boys and I know what we can do.

I want to get filthy. Yeah, I want to get insane.
Get your bros together, and I'll pull the love train.
Love train.
Love train.
I'll pull the love train.

She danced as hard as she could, popping every pelvic thrust and twisting every gyration like she was more than ready to pull a train of two hundred thirty thousand if they'd only follow her down. And the crowd seemed to respond to her prompts. The women in the audience mimicked her gyrations, and the men hooted and howled. Although it was a brand-new song, the minimal words let everyone sing along. It seemed for a minute like she had succeeded in wiping away Vicki's stand from the collective memory and had brought them all right back under her control.

And then, it happened.

CHAPTER FIFTY-ONE

Set You Free

Everyone fears something. For some it's spiders or snakes or heights. For others its failure or success or love or loss. In their depths, everyone harbors a fear of death and a greater fear of what might lie beyond.

Everyone fears something, but for the choreographed pop star, nothing—*NOTHING*—is as scary as the ever-looming prospect that their backing tracks might stop.

That night at Black Rock, in front of two hundred thirty thousand fans, and on countless subsequent YouTube views, Hellena's greatest fear came true. All of the backing tracks stopped dead. The feeds from the musicians playing along on stage went silent. The backup vocals disappeared right along with her lead. Everything went dead in the middle of the song.

Everything except her headset mic, which allowed the assembled audience to hear seven seconds of an out-of-tune, breathless wheezing of:

Love train.
Love train.

I'll pull the love train.

She stopped mid-gyration and looked, with a panicked fury, to the wings off stage right. Her eyes blazed, and it was clear that someone in her crew was about to get the ass-chewing of a lifetime. Then, she suddenly stopped, and those same eyes went wide with fear. From their vantage points, no one in the audience could tell what horrified her so much. But Hellena, who could see what was happening offstage, saw all too well that the man in charge of keeping the tracks synced to the performance was not at his station. No one from her crew was anywhere around.

An AWOL sound crew was disaster enough, but what worried Hellena even more was that there was a stranger at the soundboard. A man she'd never seen before was busily preparing a surprise of his own. In that terrible moment, there was nothing that Hellena could do except stand there in her thigh-high boots, staring out blankly at two hundred thirty thousand judgmental sets of eyes.

A second later, a man's voice boomed over the loudspeakers. It was Haden Koschei's voice.

"You give all the people the same soundtrack, and they live the same lives. They think the same things. They buy the same crap and put up with the same shit. You control the message and you control the masses. And surprise, surprise. That's all the sheeple want. They just want someone to spare them the difficulty of living their own lives. You starve their souls and break their hearts, and they pay you for the privilege."

Daniel pushed another button on the board, and Koschei's voice boomed again.

"You think I'm referring to the people who make the music? Or to those who control the music? Or even the elite who control those people? Oh no. I'm referring to the sheeple. We steal their tomorrows by trading them a lie today, and they're desperate for that bargain. We've turned *party* into a verb, and they don't give a shit about outsourced jobs—all they want to do is party. And if there's a party tonight, they don't give a goddamn what happens to them today. Or tomorrow. And that makes life easier for them. And if you try to stop that, they will hate you."

There were angry boos from the crowd, and more than a few obscenities hurled at Hellena, who exited stage left amid a shower of beer cups, overpriced food wrappers, and sweaty, muddy T-shirts.

Realizing that their party had been brought to a sudden, buzz-killing halt, the crowd began to bubble with frustration and resentment.

"We're not sheeple!" someone yelled. Others liked the sentiment so much that they repeated it, again and again, until it had swelled into a throbbing chant. "We're not sheeple! We're not sheeple!"

The security forces in black polos tried to contain the masses, but they'd never contemplated that the situation could go so wrong. There were plans in place for dealing with problem individuals. Even groups of problems. They had miscalculated the big numbers, however; and as a matter of mere mathematics, there was no way for them to control what was happening on the festival grounds.

"We're not sheeple!"

"We're not sheeple!"

"We're not sheeple!"

The growing unrest would have been problematic in the best of situations. Unfortunately, as so often happens in life, that's exactly when the situation went all to hell.

CHAPTER FIFTY-TWO

We Didn't Start the Fire

There was a time when music was music, theater was theater, and fireworks were for Fourth of July picnics. Pop music put an end to those days and brought them all together in the concert spectacular.

Daniel had surreptitiously recorded his conversation with Koschei on his iPhone in the hopes of catching the old man saying something incriminating. What he'd captured was nothing short of a full-on confession.

So, while Daniel thought he was being clever in killing Hellena's backup tracks and exposing the fraud behind the entire show, he considered it pure genius to replace that overdubbed noise with the old man's diatribe.

What Daniel had overlooked, however, was that the sound was just one piece of a larger, more involved show. So when he tampered with the sound, he knocked every other component of the show into disarray too.

It didn't particularly matter that musical tracks turned on and off as the crowd continued to boo and chant. The misfiring lasers and lights only gave an appropriately eerie cast to what was happening out on the festival grounds. None of that particularly mattered. The pyrotechnics, however, were another matter.

There were supposed to be pyrotechnics throughout Hellena's big finale—a number entitled "Come with Me"—all of it computer controlled to sync with the show. And when Daniel flipped the switches to sabotage the show, all of it went terribly wrong.

A set of sparklers went off first. Then more sparklers, not in any discernible pattern, but igniting chaotically in a hissing spectacle of spitting sparks.

When the crowd realized that the sparklers had ignited without any particular musical cue, there was an energized cry—not quite outright panic, but something more than alarm—and for a minute, it seemed as if everyone in the crowd had frozen in time, silently waiting to see what would happen next.

No one, however, was expecting the entire, planned, twelve-minute fireworks show to go up in a single burst. The night sky split open with an apocalyptic display of colors: reds and greens and blues that cut through the blackness above. Concussions shook the ground below, and a crowd that had spent the day listening to music at permanent hearing-loss levels covered their ears against the terrible sound. For one endless minute, it seemed like the festival grounds, maybe even the entire world, was under attack.

The fireworks subsided as suddenly as they'd ignited, but the damage they left in their wake was substantial. The oversize curtains that flowed at the back of the stage caught fire in the unplanned eruption, and the huge flames, like the devil's backup dancers, seemed fanned by the crowd's screams and grew higher and higher. They spilled out into the night above and ran to left and right, consuming the stage and the tents behind.

Not all the fires were the result of the single man-made accident. Fire is the primal source of life, and its appearance on the scene rekindled ancient urges within many in the crowd. Soon, the overpriced concession stands that had taken advantage of the concertgoers all day long were burning in the night, with the remaining contents and much of their profits consumed by the flames. The Porta-Potties were set ablaze, along with many of the tents and awnings that people had brought with them.

People ran in all directions across the festival grounds, which were now lit only by fires. Some people ran in fear, while others raced toward the mayhem, eager to claim their share. Some fled the human eruption, and others rushed headlong into its depths.

The scene was chaotic. There were many who tripped and fell as they ran; some were helped back up to their feet, but some were trampled beneath the crowd.

Some women stood on overturned tables or boxes and cheered, eager to respond to whatever attention they attracted. Others ran like rabbits who know that the wolves have come for a playdate.

There were fistfights and beat downs. There were gangs of guys taking anything worth stealing, and other howling packs that wanted to break everything that wasn't.

Chaos was the headliner at Black Rock. And that night, there was one hell of an encore.

CHAPTER FIFTY-THREE

Kick-Ass Mojo

"When I said you was gonna have to pull out a helluva distraction to get us outta here, I didn't mean setting the whole fucking place on fire," Moog screamed above the deafening riot.

"Oh sure, *now* you tell me." Daniel didn't let the quip slow him down.

People ran here and there, but everyone was headed to the same place: out.

When Daniel and Moog came upon Vicki and Malaika and Zack, they were standing offstage, surrounded by four guys in black polos. None of them seemed surprised to see the pair arrive on the scene.

"We've got visual," one of the black polos said into his headset mic. "Affirmative."

The other three drew their weapons and held them at the ready.

Moog already held his Desert Eagle at his side, but Daniel just seemed bored by the display. "Listen, guys. This is going to go down one of two ways. The first is that you're going to realize that there's nothing on the table worth dying for here. There's nothing at stake worth turning your wives to widows and your children to fatherless souls."

"Put your hands in the air," the black polo with the headset mic ordered.

"Or that's the other," Daniel said with an exasperated sigh. "We can stand here like guys with guns, and do that whole thing, but where's that going to get us?" He looked at the chaos coming down all around them. "Guys, the roof is on fire! No one is coming to back you up here. You're going to walk away right now, or I'm going to kill you dead away, but make no mistake that my friend and I are walking away with our families."

"Put your hands up!" the head black polo ordered.

"Is that your final decision?" Daniel checked them all. "All of you?"

Two of them didn't look all that certain.

"Get out of here," Daniel told them. They looked at one another and took off.

"Get back here," their leader yelled, but there was no calling them back.

"That leaves you two," Daniel said. His voice had changed noticeably, like something in him had resigned itself to the fact that it was time for the killing.

"We need backup! We need backup!" the leader yelled.

"They're not sending anyone," Daniel assured him. "You're a pawn. They're all worried about saving their asses, and they're going to leave yours hanging. So I'm going to ask you one last time."

The third black polo took advantage of this final offer, turned, and ran, leaving his leader behind.

"Now what?" Daniel wanted to know. "We're all running out of time here."

The leader raised his pistol. "I've got a duty."

"Duty?"

"Duty and honor. Things that you wouldn't know anything about."

"No." Daniel shook his head. "I don't know anything about that. I know about taking care of mine though, and that's what I intend to do."

"I'm not going to tell you again. Put your hands up."

"I don't want to have to kill you in front of my son and friend here. And I don't want him"—he gestured to Moog—"to have to kill you in front of his daughter."

"Then I guess that leaves you plumb out of luck." The young man raised his gun.

"Not entirely," Daniel said.

An instant later, a blazing curtain attached to a flaming rafter fell from above and landed on the black polo leader.

Vicki and Malaika recoiled in horror, but Daniel just looked on, sadly shaking his head. "I've got some kick-ass mojo."

Moog nodded enthusiastically. "Kick-ass mojo."

CHAPTER FIFTY-FOUR

Your Eyes

"Come on," Moog called to Daniel. "We gotta get back to the truck before the fucking roof falls in on *us*." His tree-trunk arms were wrapped protectively around Malaika, Vicki, and Zack, as he began ushering them through the madness so that nothing in the crowd could touch them.

Up ahead, Daniel was torn by competing fears. He knew he had to get Moog and the others off the festival grounds, and he fought off the thought of what might happen if he didn't. At the same time, letting Koschei slip back into the ether put everyone Daniel loved in certain peril.

He decided to face the most immediate fear.

"Come on," he called over his shoulder to Moog. "Follow me."

They worked their way back to VIP parking, but the limo was no longer in the spot where they'd left it. Instead, a two-ton bonfire burned brightly in the night, an assortment of enthusiastic men and women dancing around it.

"What now?" Moog asked.

"I guess we just try to hoof it out. Hope for the best."

"No," Zack interjected. "We need to get to the helipad. They've got a helicopter waiting for us. Reserved just for us."

"Forget it," Daniel said sternly.

Zack wasn't willing to. "Forget it? If we just get to the helipad, we'll be in LA in half an hour, and all of this will be behind us."

"You can't fly out of here," Daniel said firmly.

"Why not?" It was Zack's question, but one he voiced for the others as well.

"Because rock and roll doesn't fly well. That's why." Daniel knew they were running out of time, and he wasn't willing to debate further.

"Then what the hell are we supposed to do?"

"You're supposed to keep calm and—"

"And what?"

"And have faith that something will turn up."

"What? What exactly is going to turn up?"

"Whatever's supposed to."

And that's when the ducklike horn sounded.

CHAPTER FIFTY-FIVE

Magic Bus

The 1964 VW Microbus rolled across the festival grounds and stopped just short of Daniel and the others. Its horn sounded like a duck.

"You need a ride?" the driver asked.

Daniel recognized the man immediately and nodded. "You know we do."

"Well, then don't just stand there lookin', *mi key*," the man behind the wheel said. "Things is bad, and they're only gonna get worse. You best all get aboard, so we can get the hell outta here."

Zack was unimpressed. "That thing doesn't look like it can make it off the grounds."

But Daniel knew better. "Trust me, this man can get you wherever you need to go."

Daniel pulled open the side door and held it open for his son. Before his son climbed on board, Daniel stopped him. "Hey, I'm proud of you."

His son seemed nothing but embarrassed in front of Malaika. "I thought you said we needed to get out of here."

"Just don't ever forget that," Daniel insisted. "No matter what."

"All right, Dad. Maybe we should, you know, hurry up."

Daniel nodded self-consciously and helped them both aboard. Vicki came next. "This is our getaway vehicle? Really?"

"It's the safest place for you," Daniel told her, and he was certain that this was true. "Just hang tight, and before you know it, you'll be out of here and beyond all of this."

He held her hand as she put a foot up and in the cargo bay. Before she climbed in with the others, she stopped and turned. "I'm sorry. For everything."

"There's nothing to be sorry for. Ever."

"I can't help but think that if I didn't—"

He stopped her. "Everything works out the way it's supposed to."

"You think so?"

"I know so."

She climbed uneasily into the van.

Moog was next. He looked up at the driver, then back at Daniel. "Ain't that—"

"I need you to get on board, big man."

But Moog had already wandered over to the driver's side. "Whatchu doin' here?"

"I thought I already done told you," Atibon said. "There ain't nowhere that I'm not."

"Well, all right then," Moog said, his spirits lifted. "Let's all get the hell out of here." He trotted around the van and held the door open for Daniel. "I can't believe we gonna make it out of here."

"I can't go," Daniel said flatly. He turned to Atibon. "That's what you're here to tell me, isn't it?"

"I'm not here to tell you nothin'. Every man's gotta make up his own mind." Atibon looked uncharacteristically choked up. "But this van can't take you where you gotta go."

"What are you two talking about?" Moog asked. "Get on in here, and let's get going."

Daniel ignored him and turned instead to Atibon. "You seen Koschei tonight?"

"I imagine he down by the helipads."

"Why's that?" Daniel asked.

"He mighta worked up one of them copters to crash. Maybe with your lady love and your friends aboard."

Daniel nodded. "Why would he do that?"

Atibon shrugged. "Maybe to drive you to do something that he can't do himself."

"Kill me?" Daniel had a moment of clarity. "That's it, isn't it? I'm the only one who can kill me."

"That's true for most folks. Whether it's something drama-queen drastic like you tried or just a lifetime of numbness, most folks end up killing themselves. One way or another."

Daniel understood. "Down by the helipad?"

"What are you doing?" Moog shouted, now growing increasingly concerned. "Get in the goddamn van."

"I can't, man."

Moog didn't understand. "Can't?"

"Then let me come with you," Moog said.

Daniel shook off the offer. "You can't do that. I need you to get them out of here. I need you to keep them safe. I need you to set them free from all of this."

"Man, don't do this," the big man pleaded.

"I'm doing what I have to, what we both know I have to. I wouldn't have made it this far down the line without you, but I've got to run this last bit of road on my own."

"And what am I supposed to do now?"

"You're supposed to take care of them. You're supposed to climb on that bus and take it straight back to Kansas City. You've been looking all your life for the father you never had, and you've never found him. You've got a family. A *big* family. And they need you now."

"You my family too, man."

"And I'll always be. But I've got something I've got to do, and nothing is going to be right until I get it done."

Moog didn't like it, but he understood. "Then go get it done."

"Thanks."

"For what?"

"For everything."

"This ain't over," Moog insisted.

"No. No, it's not."

"Not by a damn sight." Moog called as he climbed into the van, "I'll see you on the other side, my brother."

Daniel nodded. "You know you will."

Daniel walked up to the driver's side and leaned in until his face was close to Atibon's. "I'm going to go get what's yours."

"I know you are," he said from behind the wheel.

"But you remember your part of the deal."

Atibon was almost hurt. "You ever know me to fail a bargain?"

"Her true love," Daniel reminded him, just in case. "And you make sure you take care of her."

"Aw, son, you know I will." The old man's voice was uncharacteristically sympathetic.

* * *

It had all happened so fast. Vicki was sitting on the sticky bench seat with her arm around Malaika, making sure the girl was all right. The van door slid shut. The gears groaned, and the microbus lurched forward and began to roll.

A moment passed before she realized it. "Where's Daniel?"

She pulled away from Malaika and frantically turned in her seat. Through gaps in the bumper stickers slapped across the dirty rear window, she saw Daniel standing in the midst of the chaos, calmly watching her go.

"Wait!" she screamed. "Daniel's not on yet."

The van kept rolling.

"We have to go back," she pleaded. But looking at the others, she realized that she'd been the only one who hadn't understood the price of their escape. "No!" She reached for the door, but the rusty handle wouldn't budge, and the van wouldn't stop. "I have to go back!"

Moog wrestled her into his arms and didn't try to stop her when she beat on his chest. "You can't go, Vicki. You can't go with him now."

"But I love him," she cried as she tried to pull free.

The big man understood too well. "He's my friend too, baby girl. I love him too."

She turned to him. "Then you'll let me go to him."

Moog shook his head and pretended there wasn't a Moog-size tear running down his cheek.

The van came to a stop.

"Let her go," Atibon said.

Moog looked back at the old man. "What?"

"Let her go," he repeated.

The big man was intent on honoring his friend's last wishes. "But Daniel said—"

"And I promised Daniel something myself."

"What's that?" Moog asked.

"Promised I'd let her find her true love." He looked farther back into the van. "Let her go."

CHAPTER FIFTY-SIX

Free Fallin'

The last helicopter sat on the helipad with its rotors slowly spinning in a state of readiness to get the hell out of Dodge. There were two men in black polos by its bay doors, trying to hold back a crowd of about twenty people who were trying their best to press their way on board.

"Keep back!" one of them ordered, though his voice wavered with doubt that any of them would heed his warning.

The other tried to calm the crowd. "Take it easy. We will get you all out of here. We need to load this bird slowly and one at a time."

That seemed to do the trick.

Several of the men in the crowd stepped back and helped the women begin to climb onboard. It seemed as though in the middle of the surrounding chaos, calm heads and cooperation might save the day. And then, the cart showed up.

During the day, the golf cart had been one of a squadron that had been used to whisk those who were too important to walk all over the festival grounds. But in the crisis of the night, it had been put to use as a getaway car.

Although he was moving feebly, Haden Koschei climbed out of the cart and walked toward the helicopter like he had a reservation for salvation.

"Whoa," one of the black polos said, his hand raised. "We're getting on board one at a time. First come, first—"

"Do you know who I am?" Koschei demanded.

"I think you're the one going to the back of the line and waiting to get on this copter," the black polo said.

Koschei didn't even bother to address the man, but simply looked over his shoulder. "Mister Feller, take care of this, will you?"

"Happy to." Feller pulled a 9mm from a holster beneath his arm and pointed it at the black polo standing in the way.

"Whoa," the man said. "You don't want to do that."

The other black polo seemed more determined to stop the line cutting, and his right hand reached back for something at the small of his back. He reached, but he never got there. A shot from Feller's pistol caught him in the chest before he had the chance.

The other black polo looked back at his partner, and then straight at Feller. "Don't shoot!" He held his hands up high.

"Everyone off of the helicopter," Feller ordered.

"We're not getting . . . ," a woman on board started to shout, but she shut up and changed her mind as soon as she saw that Feller was intent on getting her off the helicopter one way or another. She was the first one off, and one by one the others followed.

When the helicopter was empty, Feller turned to the others. "Nothing for any of you to see now. If I were you, I'd be more worried about finding another way out of here than watching us take off."

One of the men in the group stepped forward to explain that he and the others weren't used to being treated so rudely. "I'll have you know—"

Feller shot him in the left arm.

"If anyone thought I was inviting a discussion on the subject"—Feller swept the gun across the group so that it stopped for a moment on each one—"I wasn't. Now get going, because the last one standing here isn't going to be left standing."

Two of the men reached down and collected their fallen friend. They helped him to his feet, and then the group went off into the night, hoping they'd find kinder people elsewhere.

Koschei was having trouble walking, and Feller had to help him up into the helicopter. Then he climbed aboard himself.

"Take it up," he ordered the pilot.

The helicopter started to shift, and then to gently rise from the pad.

As the helicopter began to lift, a figure ran out of the darkness, jumped into the night, and grabbed hold of the landing post. The helicopter swayed a bit under his weight as the man pulled himself up and into the bay.

"I hope you didn't think you were leaving me behind," Daniel said as he got to his feet.

"You're too late, Erickson." Koschei coughed. "You can't get me off this helicopter now."

"I know," Daniel said sternly. "I'm here to make sure you stay on it."

The response surprised Koschei for a moment, until the realization settled in on him like a buzzard on day-old roadkill. There had been a dozen helicopters waiting to transport this act or those celebrities, but all of them were now in the air and safely away. By process of elimination, that meant that this helicopter—the one that was now climbing into the night sky—was the one that Koschei had ordered Feller to have "fixed" so that Vicki and the others would crash. "Fuck!"

Feller stood face-to-face with Daniel. "You shouldn't have come." He pulled his 9mm free. "I mean it. You shouldn't have come."

"Bring it down!" Koschei screamed at the pilot, "Bring it down! Now!"

For half a second the pilot complied and began a gentle descent, but a shot through the windshield changed his mind. "We're not going down," Feller informed him. "Not just yet."

"Are you crazy," Koschei screamed as he tried to get to the open bay door to see just how much night air separated him from the ground below. "This is *that* helicopter," Koschei screamed. "The helicopter you had rigged to blow up!"

"I know," Feller said calmly and coldly. "I know. She wants me to tell you, '*Vengarme*. Avenge me.'"

Koschei's head had hurt for days, but now it felt like it might literally explode on his shoulders. "God damn you, Angelina."

"Probably." Feller's mouth moved, but it was Angelina's voice that came out. "You think I was a bad bitch? Now let Santa Muerte avenge me."

"You can have the bitch back," Koschei coughed.

"Oh no." The voice coming from Feller declared. "The bitch is back."

"Feller?" Daniel said, shocked by what was happening in front of him.

"I've got this now," Feller said calmly in his own voice. "But I'm guessing you've got other places to be, so best you should probably get out while you can."

Feller grabbed Daniel and moved him back toward the open bay door. Daniel braced himself by grabbing his arms. "What the hell, Feller?"

He just smiled. "You're the walking dead man. A little fall won't hurt you."

A second later, Feller gasped. When he pulled away from Daniel, Koschei was behind him, and there was a blade in the pudgy man's back. Feller fell back in the seats, wheezing as the last breaths of life worked in and out of his lungs.

Koschei turned on Daniel. "I should've killed you when I had the chance."

"You would've, if you could've. But that's the secret, isn't it. You can't kill me." Daniel punched Koschei in the chest and heard a dry crack. The sound sparked an inspiration. He hit it again and again, striking Koschei's chest furiously, like he was a trapped man and it was the wall that kept him from freedom. He hit the breastbone with all his might until, finally, it could not resist his will, and Daniel's hand plunged deep into Koschei's chest.

Daniel screamed in anguish and triumph. But when he retracted his hand, there was no blood. Instead, it was covered in a thick, black, macadam-like substance.

Koschei howled in pain and his eyes widened, but he did not fall. And he did not die. "You should've known that my heart was the least of my vulnerabilities. You on the other hand . . ."

Koschei put his hand on Daniel's chest, and immediately his body arched with pain like he'd never felt before. A thousand memories of his life came to him and rushed through his head like 220 volts of current, cooking his brain and burning his blood.

"And now I'll have what I've always wanted most," Koschei crowed. "The soul you hide from Death."

Daniel could feel it was true. He could feel himself drowning in a thousand painful memories that Koschei was consuming whole. There was no point in resisting. And he didn't. He was going away. Forever. And the end was all right with him. He only wished he could tell Vicki one last time, "I love you."

In his heart, he heard her voice telling him: "Then don't give up. Don't ever give up." And those words were enough. He turned back to Koschei, renewed with resistance.

Soul, Daniel thought. *The eyes are the windows to the soul.* And then Daniel knew. "The eyes," he gasped.

The fear Daniel saw in Koschei's gray eyes confirmed he was right.

Without wasting another second, Daniel struggled to take Koschei's head in his hands and gouge the old man's eyes. Koschei struggled to free himself, to drain Daniel's life from him. But all of his efforts were in vain. Daniel pressed harder and harder. Koschei howled in pain, but his plaintive wailing didn't stop Daniel, who pressed and pressed until the old man's eyes were pushed back into his head.

There was an explosion of light from Koschei's eye sockets. A thousand dots of bright blue light shot out into the night, dancing in a brief expression of joy, and then shooting off one by one into the darkness.

"Nooo!" Koschei screamed as he collapsed into Daniel's arms. A wisp of smoke, blacker than black, escaped from his gaping mouth and shot off into the night. Koschei sank to his knees. "Noooooo!"

With one last surge of energy fueled by hatred, Koschei's body lunged forward. Daniel took a step backward and slipped. He tried to steady himself, but there was no footing to be had. A half step back, and then Daniel disappeared into the night.

The helicopter climbed higher still, but it was a very short flight.

* * *

Daniel Erickson tumbled through the night, a hundred feet, maybe more. The sensation was different from what he'd expected. It wasn't so much that he was falling, as the rest of the world was rushing toward him. When they hit one another, there was nothing but pain. And then nothing at all.

Vicki rushed to where he returned to earth and wrapped her arms around him. "I'm so sorry. I would do anything in the world if I could—"

He stopped her there. "It's all right. All of this was just you trying to get past the pain. I'm just sorry I didn't see it in time. I'm just sorry I couldn't free you sooner."

"I'm not free. I can't be. I don't deserve to be."

"But you are. You're free to do whatever you want. You're free, and it's all right."

She shook her head. "It's not. It never was. How could it ever be right once I—"

He stopped her again. "I love you. That's all."

"I'm—"

"The most amazing person I've ever known. You're not the things that you've done or the things that have been done to you. You're not any of that. I know who you are, even if you've forgotten."

"Who am I?"

"You're the woman I love. And that's who you'll always be."

And then, for the second time in his life, Daniel Erickson died.

CHAPTER FIFTY-SEVEN

There Is a House in New Orleans

A dog barking in the distance woke Daniel from his sleep with a start. "What?"

A hand softly stroked his cheek and ran its fingers through his hair. "Shhhh, it's all right. I gotcha."

Vicki was a breath away, nothing separating them but skin. "Am I dead?" he asked, fearing she was something less than flesh and blood.

"Not anymore." She sighed at the memory of it all.

"What happened?" His throat was dry, his voice nothing but a hoarse whisper.

"It's over," she assured him. "It's all over."

"Koschei?"

"There was a helicopter crash."

He remembered. "But I—"

"You survived," she promised.

What he recalled about it all seemed to suggest that she must be lying about that, but he didn't want to argue the point with her for fear he might be right. "I fell. I fell so far. I felt like I was—"

"No." She wouldn't let him finish.

"How?"

"Because I love you," she answered. "You survived because I love you."

He wasn't sure how that could be, but he didn't want to question it. He wanted it to be the truth, and so he let it be.

"Where are we?"

"New Orleans," she answered.

"How did we—"

"Todd Golding found us. He flew us here on his jet."

Daniel's thoughts were scattered. "Moog?"

"He's fine. He's with Malaika in Kansas City."

"Zack."

She grinned. "He's with her too. Everybody's fine."

Daniel laid back and looked up at the ceiling. "New Orleans, huh?"

"The Crescent City."

"I've been to New Orleans a couple times." He remembered each visit, but they all seemed like they belonged to different people in different lifetimes. "Crazy times."

"It's all over now," she assured him, and pulled herself closer to him.

"I never thought I'd get free." He was so tired, he could barely get the words out, but he felt the need to say them. "All I wanted was to get free. To get back to you, and be free of Atibon once and for all."

"You are," her voice cracked with the whispered response. Not enough that anyone else would have noticed, but enough that he knew she was keeping something from him.

"What's wrong?"

"Nothing." She sealed the promise with a kiss.

"We're free, right?"

"You are one hundred percent free." She gave him another kiss just to convince him. "Now get some sleep."

"Sleep," he murmured. He was grateful for it. Grateful to be in her arms. To be alive. And to be free. "I love you."

"I love you too," she told him, but he was already asleep.

She was grateful for the opportunity to be alone. She pulled his arm around her and forced herself to stay in that moment, knowing there was no peace to be found in letting her mind wander to the events of her past. And painfully aware that there was no peace to be found in her future either.

She closed her eyes and focused on memorizing that perfect moment, knowing it had come at a cost. She held on to Daniel and drifted off to sleep, aware that there was a day coming when a heavy price would have to be paid.

There was always a heavy price to be paid.

CHAPTER FIFTY-EIGHT

The Song Remains the Same

The boy was no more than twelve years old, and it was later than a child of his age should have been out on the streets alone. But there was no one at his home to keep him there or care that he wasn't, so he was out that evening all by himself, with no definite direction in mind but vaguely feeling like there was somewhere he was supposed to be.

"Whatchu doin', kid?"

The voice came out of the darkness and startled the boy, who jumped at the gruff sound and found an old man standing in the shadows behind him. "I ain't doin' nuthin," the kid said defensively.

"Is that right?" The old man removed his porkpie hat with one hand, ran the other through the brambles of gray curls on his head, and then replaced the topper. "Seems to me like you're lookin' for trouble."

"No, sir." The boy wasn't usually so polite, but he was too frightened to be disrespectful. Or to run.

"Gotta name?"

"Charles, sir?"

"Anymore'n that? Or is it just Charles?"

"St. Charles, sir."

"Charles St. Charles?" the man asked, not hiding his skepticism. "Really?"

"Really."

"Well, whoever named you had them a sense of humor." The boy frowned. "But they gave you one hell of a name." The boy smiled. "It's a pleasure to meet you, Charles St. Charles." He offered his weathered hand to the boy, and the boy took it.

"What you doing?" the boy asked, emboldened by their handshake.

"I'm just checkin' in on a friend of mine."

The boy looked up and down the street but didn't see anyone else but the two of them. "Where he at?"

"See that house right there?" The old man pointed to a Victorian across the way.

"Yes, sir."

"He's in there."

"You gonna go visit him?"

The old man shook his head. "Oh, he doesn't wanna see me. Not now at least."

"Why that?" Charles St. Charles wondered.

The old man thought on it. "He used to work for me. And he thinks that maybe I took advantage of him just a little."

"Did you?"

The old man put the tips of his arthritic forefinger and thumb a hair's breadth apart. "Just a little."

"Does he still work for you?"

"He doesn't think that he does." The old man grinned. "But he does. Or he will."

"Why that?"

"Because he loves someone."

The boy was too young to follow the connection.

"You need to understand, son. When you love someone, when you're truly bound to them, then you're bound to everything they're bound to. Understand?"

The boy lied and nodded his head.

"You see, my friend in there was hurt somethin' awful."

"How awful? Dead awful?"

The old man thought on it. "Past dead awful."

"What happened?"

"Well, it just so happened that this man was loved by a woman—loved by her very much. And when she saw how hurt he was, when she saw that he was past dead—"

The boy was intrigued by the story. "Yes?"

"Well, she made a deal with me."

"What kinda deal?"

"She agreed to do me a favor in return for making him . . ." He paused to consider how best to explain to a boy of his age what he'd done. "Well, in exchange for me bringing him back past dead."

"You can do that?" The boy's eyes were wide with wonder.

"Child, you'd be surprised what I can do."

"And the man?"

The old man laughed. "He in there thinkin' he free of me, but what he don't know is that he bound to me still. That woman loves him so much that she made a promise that gonna bind him too. She made a promise, but I got 'em both." He seemed pleased by the bargain he'd gotten.

"And what kinda favor they gotta do for you?"

"I haven't thought that up yet. I tend to let my debts just sit out there till I needs to collect on them." The old man rubbed at the gray stubble on his chin. "But you best better believe I'll have somethin' for them both real soon. Real soon."

The boy nodded, pleased by the story and not caring whether it was true or not. "Well, I gotta go now."

"Hold on a second," the old man said. "What about you?"

"What about me what?"

"You seem like a fine young man. A special boy."

Charles St. Charles had always thought that of himself, even though no one around him had ever given him any reason to feel that way. "I suppose so."

"You have any interest in the guitar, son?"

"I don't know."

"Well, what would you say if I told you that I could make you the greatest guitar player in the whole wide world?"

The boy was excited by the possibilities. "The whole wide world?"

"The best there ever was," the old man confirmed.

Charles St. Charles thought that he'd like that very much. "You could teach me?"

"In a way." The old man hedged. He took a last look at the house across the way and began to walk slowly down the street. "Take a little walk with me son, and we'll see if we can't arrive at a bargain."

The boy followed along. "You mean in exchange for a favor?"

"That's right," the old man said, his footsteps echoing in the night.

Somewhere in the distance a dog barked.

"I could do that," the boy said. "The best in the world?"

The old man smiled. "You gonna be the best there ever was, *mi key*. The best there ever was."

ABOUT THE AUTHOR

Eyre Price is the author of the Crossroads thriller series, including the award-winning *Blues Highway Blues* and *Rock Island Rock.* Born in Syracuse and raised in Scranton, Price has lived in Las Vegas, Minneapolis, Phoenix, Dallas, and Nashville, but the highway is his home and inspiration. Eyre and his wife, Jaime Myers, currently reside in Illinois, where they are raising their son, Dylan, to have a musical heart and a wandering soul.

ACKNOWLEDGMENTS

Writing is easy. Comparatively, at least. Transforming my manuscript into the book you're reading now was a long, arduous process that required the commitment and contributions of many talented people whom I'd like to acknowledge and thank.

My developmental editor, Kevin Smith, has shaped the Crossroads series and given it a dimension that reflects his considerable talents and tireless passion for the creative process.

Jill Marr is my agent, advocate, advisor, and very dear friend. My deepest thanks to her and everyone at Sandra Dijkstra Literary Agency, and to Kevin Cleary at Pooka Entertainment.

Thanks to all of my editors at Thomas & Mercer—Anh Schluep, Alan Turkus, and Andy Bartlett—and to everyone at Amazon Publishing, especially my copy editor, Elisabeth Rinaldi, and the truly amazing Jacque Ben-Zekry.

Much thanks to my great friend Robert Pobi, who has long provided me with literary inspiration and treasured advice. For this project, he also shared his friendship with Mr. Murray Head, a rock-and-roll legend and treasure trove of history and insight. I owe them both immensely.

I'm moved by the support I've received from many wonderful people and want to thank Steve Lewis, Joe Loveless, Rick Robinson, Beth Terrell, Dale Ward, Gerard Nolan, Zachery Petit, Anthony J. Franze, Scott and Beth Gallante, Dave Beardsley, Jeremiah Johnson, Cesar Torres, the one and only Fuzzhead Jones, Chefjimi Petricola of blues411.com, Marty and Nancy Warren, Dietrich Stogner, Josh Mathue, and Clay Stafford and the Killer Nashville community.

Thanks to Mary Price, Kaitie M. F. Robertson, and Michael Robertson.

Most of all, I want to thank my son, Dylan: eleven years old, and he's already a better man than I'll ever be. Best. Man. Ever.

And finally, my thanks to everyone who has come to the Crossroads with me. I appreciate every mile (and page) you've logged and hope you'll stay along for the ride because there's a whole lotta highway left.

Please visit me at www.eyreprice.net.